THE
EMERALD
DRAGON

THE LOST ANCIENTS: BOOK THREE

MARIE ANDREAS

Megan—
Thank you for reading!

Marie Andreas

BOOKS BY MARIE ANDREAS

The Lost Ancients

Book One: The Glass Gargoyle
Book Two: The Obsidian Chimera
Book Three: The Emerald Dragon
Book Four: The Sapphire Manticore

The Asarlaí Wars

Book One: Warrior Wench

DEDICATION

To my family and friends, you have all made me who I am. Although, that does mean the faeries are your fault as well.

ACKNOWLEDGEMENTS

It takes a village to build a book, and I have some amazing fellow villagers. I couldn't have gotten this far without the love and support of all of my family and friends.

I'd like to thank Jessa Slade and Sue Soares for editing magic. For my most awesome team of beta readers: Lisa Andreas, Ashli Elsperman, Patti Huber, Lynne Mayfield, Caroline Self Onstott, Sharon Rivest, and Ilana Schoonover. Without their eagle eyes and talents, the faeries would have run amuck. Any errors remaining are all mine (with help from the faeries and Bunky).

My cover artist, Aleta Rafton, for another wonderful cover.

Thanks to Julie Fine who introduced me to the wonders of movie trailer music—best writing music ever! And to Laurel Porter for the emergency tech support.

CHAPTER ONE

I swore as I folded up the paper tracings of the sarcophagus pieces and put them back in my coat pocket. I'd been studying them for two hours this morning—and almost three months prior to that—and I still wasn't any closer to figuring the damn things out. Alric and I had been finding sections of a huge sarcophagus around town. I had a feeling they were from the one I'd accidentally found in the abandoned aqueducts under the city. Accidentally in that I found it by crashing inside of it and almost drowning when it filled with water.

The pieces we'd been finding in the last few months were made of some oddly strong gold-copper mix, all cut into five-inch-by-five-inch squares. Trying to translate them was starting to eat away at my brain. I didn't know if they tied into our growing collection of tiny archaic weapons of mass destruction, but I knew they tied into something.

Right now they were giving me a massive headache.

Annoying documents secured, I sat back in my chair and watched the less than powerful citizens of Beccia stroll by, wondering when things had gone so wrong. Oh, it was a lovely day, nice and cool with a bit of sun warming the edges. And the Beccian populace was no more annoying than usual. However, instead of being inside my favorite pub, I was relegated to sitting outside of it in a cute little area called The Shimmering Dewdrop Café. Sipping tea and eating dainty little sandwiches just didn't have the same sense of comfort that a nice mug of ale did.

The Shimmering Dewdrop was an established pub—one of the best—it should not have a cute café attached to it. I was sure the existence of this café was a sign of the wrongness that had invaded my life and continued to wreak havoc on a daily basis.

No sooner was that thought in my head, than the center of the havoc, Alric, sauntered into view. He'd taken off again for a few weeks right after our near death experience in the mine, supposedly to do research and meet with his people about the Ancients' final weapon. He'd come back a few days ago and was working on translating scrolls to find the other missing pieces of the weapon. He was also trying to convince a bunch of stubborn rich people here in Beccia that he needed to get back into what was left of the mine.

So far, neither was working for him. And he hadn't found out anything more from his time of roaming the countryside or from checking in with his mysterious clan.

Normally, I'd say Alric wasn't hard to look at. Even when he drove me crazy and I wanted to kill him, I would admit he was good looking. Tall and lean with enough muscle to make things interesting. His black hair caught the sun as if it wasn't naturally the white blond of an elven lord. His magic had come back completely at this point, so he had no problem glamouring away his elven lord tattoos and stunning beauty.

I'd started to fall for him when he first showed up in my life. Not too long before he gave me one of the most passionate kisses I'd ever had and vanished. Literally. After he'd come back, I'd been determined to keep a safe emotional distance. Up until a near death moment had both of us admitting far more than a passing interest in each other. The relationship hadn't gotten very far with his most recent bout of taking off, and I fell back into a wait and see cautious mode. My dating life had been catastrophic to say the least the last few months, and with Alric seeming to be a flight risk, I wasn't sure I was up to taking another chance. I studiously ignored the way my heart beat faster when he came near.

"I think we have finally convinced the High Council that they need to drop the magic shields they have around the mine, and that we need to go into it. Harlan and his committee persuaded at least five of the members that it would bring them a hell of a lot of gold coins down the line." Alric flung himself in the chair across from me, ignoring the swoons from a group of women sitting a few tables down.

We'd been trying to get back into the collapsed mine, where my unlamented, and hopefully very late, ex-boyfriend, Glorinal, was dead and buried. More importantly, where the tiny second potential bauble of destruction, the obsidian chimera, was buried. Part of me wanted to leave both of them where they were and be done with the whole thing.

That nice little dream had lived for about a week before treasure hunters and relic thieves started arriving in town and asking questions. Alric pointed out that the obsidian chimera was assuredly intact and waiting for some idiot to find it. And that it was much better if the idiots who found it were us.

That was the same time the High Council of Ten formed. The rich and powerfuls answer to Harlan's Committee of Concerned Citizens of Beccia. They pulled in one of their heavy magic users to blockade the entire area around the mine with a spell until they could figure out how to best benefit from the situation.

I had no patience for political maneuvering so I let Alric and Harlan do all the heavy lifting on that end. I went back to digging in the ruins with my patroness Qianru.

"Harlan thinks he can get at least two of the others over on his side and with enough pressure those will bully the three hardcore holdouts." Alric snagged and finished off the second to last sandwich and started looking at the last one. I glared at him. They weren't substantial, and my magic training made me eat like a dockworker.

He sighed at the almost empty plate and then waved down the cute little waitress. Out in the café, they had cute little waitresses; in the pub, they had trolls and half-giant barmaids.

I liked the pub better.

"You'd think they'd be at least a little bit grateful to us." I said. "We did stop Jovan and Glorinal. They'd kidnapped some rich people too." Jovan and Glorinal had taken almost one-third of the city of Beccia hostage to make Alric and me give them the obsidian chimera. When we did that, they decided to keep the people, and us, for snacks for the long journey to wherever their home hellhole was. Necromancy took a lot of death to work.

I ignored the twitch that hit Alric's left eye at almost every mention of Glorinal. Alric rarely found himself bested—but both Jovan and Glorinal had done that. Jovan, an ancient elf from before the time of the Breaking, had easily rampaged through Alric's will and psyche. If Glorinal hadn't stabbed Jovan through the heart in a brutal coup for power, Alric would probably be Jovan's docile lap kitten now. The fight against Glorinal hadn't been as clear-cut; had Alric been at full magic power at the time, then maybe he could have won. But he wasn't. Had the mine we were in not collapsed due to a few too many pot shots of serious magic striking its walls, I had a feeling Glorinal would have won.

Alric didn't talk about his past much, but it was clear that losing was a foreign concept to him. And losing to another elf definitely didn't sit well with him.

"Your eye is going to stick like that." I grabbed the last sandwich and wolfed it down. I'd been practicing my on-again, off-again magic this morning and I needed something more than some fancy little sandwiches. I found myself missing the huge meals Foxy used to foist on me. Maybe if I asked him nicely I could get a decent lunch out of him.

"My eye is fine."

However, I noticed he'd reached up to stop the twitching. Before he could try and defend his physiological tic, the tiny waitress came back, curtsied, and placed a platter of sandwiches almost as big as she was on our table. She also refilled my tea, brought him a cup, and blushed when Alric flashed a grin.

I narrowed my eyes. "Your glamour is slipping."

He swallowed a sandwich in a single bite and washed it down with tea. "What are you talking about?"

"Your glamour." I filched a pair of sandwiches and pulled them to my empty plate. "Either you're losing control of it, or you are deliberately letting it slip. For your own gain."

His bright green eyes, looking a little less bright than they did naturally, but still impressive, widened in feigned innocence. "Why would I do that?" He waved his hand to indicate the passing people in front of us. "They're not too riled up about an elf in their midst, as long as I don't remind them of it. But I have a feeling they'd feel different about who I really am."

I looked down to my plate, but my two stolen sandwiches were gone. I stole two more. "No, you wouldn't let it drop completely, but let it weaken a bit? To get extra sandwiches perhaps?"

His laugh was something I hadn't heard very often. We hadn't been doing things that led to laughter. It was nice to hear though. "You mean like trying to help you out by finagling a few extra sandwiches so you wouldn't get a magic backlash headache? What an evil man I am."

His relaxed smile reminded me why he was dangerous for me. Even without trying, and against my better judgement, I found myself pulled back in. There was no doubt of the attraction between us. I just wasn't sure I would survive the outcome.

I didn't respond to either his comment, or the thoughts going on in my head, but did take another bite of the ill-gotten sandwich.

Alric ducked as Bunky the chimera dove at his head. Too bad. Alric had been getting faster and Bunky hadn't gotten a good hit in days. Bunky liked Alric, but had taken to my faeries' habit of slamming into my head in greeting. Of course, a four-inch faery hit with a lot less impact than a chimera construct the size of a flying cat. No one knew much about the chimeras, aside from the fact that some long dead master mage created them. Almost no one knew they existed until a group of them burst out of the ground at my patroness' dig site. She had been looking for them, but even she really knew nothing about them.

Bunky swung back up into the air giving his latest war cry—he didn't know words but mimicked any animal he could find. The goat he was doing now was fitting. Like all of the chimeras we'd seen, Bunky was a round, all-black flyer. Each chimera had different attributes however, and Bunky's was having a goat-like set of legs, improbably tiny wings, and his very goat-like head. The other chimeras had vanished after the fight with Glorinal and Jovan. Fortunately, so had the surviving sceanra anam—the other creatures who had come out of the ground when the chimeras appeared. Whereas the chimeras seemed mostly harmless, except for having the good taste to go after Glorinal before we knew what he was, the sceanra anam were vicious flying snake-like creatures with an unholy amount of teeth. No one had reported seeing either type of flyer, except for Bunky, in the last three weeks.

Bunky hadn't shown any interest in leaving town, and seemed to think he was simply a giant, all black faery. I didn't have proof, but I figured he also helped the faeries with their illegal cat racing. Yesterday afternoon, I'd caught him herding a pair of cats out toward the old barns. When Alric and I went out there and looked a few weeks ago, the racing track they'd had up before was gone, but I knew those hooligans were still racing somewhere.

Finally tired of dive-bombing Alric, Bunky flew off toward the ruins. Some of the remaining wild faeries stayed out there, just past the old ruins. They avoided most everyone. Only their queen appeared from time to time to meet with my own faeries and the ones who had come to live in the city. Those meetings were usually short and terse and ended up with the city faeries all in the pub getting drunk faster than previously thought possible. It had happened enough that Foxy made a special drawer for them to sleep it off behind the bar.

Bunky seemed to be undisturbed by whatever was going on between the two groups and went back and forth regularly.

Another pile of sandwiches appeared as if by magic and I noticed with a start that we'd polished off all the others. This magic user business was going to cost me a fortune in food.

Since the cave-in at the mine, Alric, Covey, and even Harlan, had decided once and for all that my days as a

magic sink were over and somehow I had become a
magic user. That I wasn't sure I *wanted* to be a magic
user, and that whatever magic I did have seemed to go
from massive bursts to nothing, without warning, didn't
stop them.

"Once you're finished, we need another magic
lesson." Alric said. "Without dragon bane."

That was an issue and an ongoing argument between
us. For some reason whisky, also known as dragon bane,
had an unusual effect on me. Which was putting it
mildly. If I drank it, I became aggressive in all senses of
the word and scared the hell out of Alric. If it touched
my skin, I became a killing machine and that scared the
hell out of me.

I would love to stop using dragon bane, but without
it, magic was painful. Literally. I could do a few things
but it felt like an army of fire ants ripping my skull apart.
However, Foxy, the barkeeper and owner of the
Shimmering Dewdrop, had a hard time keeping me
supplied with the stuff. It seemed that his usual sources
either weren't responding or were out of it. Not to
mention the smell made me so violently sick at this point,
that Alric started slapping an anti-nausea spell on me
each day before our practice.

Therefore, it was horrible smell, potential nausea,
dwindling and increasingly expensive supplies—or
millions of bugs burning their way through my skull.

My friends wondered why I wasn't excited about my
newfound magic.

"Is this a good idea?" I dropped my voice when it
appeared the couple at the neighboring table were
leaning a bit more in our direction. "We're not even sure
where my skills came from." One thing we all agreed on:
like my previous magic-sink status, it would probably be
a good idea to keep my new magical status as secret as
possible.

Alric scowled and let that scowl drift, along with a raised eyebrow, toward the couple listening in. They quickly righted themselves and became engrossed in their own tiny sandwiches. "Covey can say what she will, but for good or bad, those skills have become yours. You are far more dangerous to others and yourself if you don't know what you're doing.

I quickly busied myself with more tea as an image of a battered and broken Slim Jankins popped into my head. The stubborn satyr had survived his attempt at flying when I flung him away from me in the ruins a few months ago. However, almost every bone in his body had been broken.

Lucky for me, he had no idea what had happened, and I wasn't telling anyone. But while Slim had been trying to kill me, and probably deserved a sound thrashing for all of his criminal activities, what if that had happened to a friend? Or an innocent? I had no control over what I did to him.

"Fine. But I won't like it. And if my head explodes I am coming back from the dead to haunt you for the rest of your long life." I waved the flittering waitress over. "He'll be paying."

Alric handed her a handful of coins—I still had no idea where he got funding from, and I didn't know that I wanted to know—then we left.

We were a few pubs down the street when the ground started shaking.

CHAPTER TWO

We were too close to one of the more ramshackle pubs on the lane, so both Alric and I ran for the center of the street before parts of the buildings could drop on us. By the time the shaking stopped five minutes later, everyone from inside the pubs had joined us.

Parts of the Kingdom of Lindor regularly had earthquakes—Beccia wasn't one.

"Ach, Taryn, what be that?" Foxy was the last person to join us in the street, most likely making sure all the stragglers were out of his pub.

"An earthquake?" the minotaur next to us answered. Which started a major argument between a dozen or so other Beccian citizens as to how impossible that was since Beccia didn't get those and clearly magic was involved.

At which point they all looked at Alric.

"It wasn't me, and I agree, it was an earthquake." When Alric had saved the town the first time from the ravages of the glass gargoyle and my former patron Thaddeus, everyone thought he was dead and a martyr. When they realized he was not dead, had come back, and again saved the town, they celebrated him for hours. Until someone pointed out that he was an elf and put that together with the fact that two elves had kidnapped good Beccian citizens, killed over sixty of them, and again tried to destroy the town. At that point, they collectively decided they weren't sure what to think of him. Well, straight women and gay men ignored the drama and just gave him mooneyes.

They muttered at Alric's comment, but regardless of how they felt about him, the entire town agreed he was not someone to be messed with. They dispersed and went back to their early Saturday afternoon drinking.

"I thought we don't get earthquakes." I said.

Alric took my arm and changed direction, so we were going further into town. "We don't. That wasn't an earthquake."

Damn. I would have hoped that in the last five months of knowing Alric I'd get used to the lies. Nope, he got me again.

"Then what was it?"

He grinned. Anything mysterious and possibly deadly seemed to make him do that. "I have no idea, but we should go check."

"Checking what? We go, too." Garbage Blossom, my orange faery, said as she flew past while riding Bunky like a flying goat.

"Bumbling rumbles!" Crusty Bucket chirped as she flew around Bunky.

"Not our fault!" That was Leaf Grub's contribution as she too flew over Bunky.

As usual, Bunky said nothing but seemed content to be with his faeries.

Before I could respond to anyone, the ground shook again. Instead of the long, slow rumble of a few minutes ago, this one was sharp enough to knock Alric and me to the ground. Then it stopped.

Alric's grin vanished as he got to his feet and helped me up as well.

Garbage Blossom's scowl matched his as she glared from atop her obsidian steed.

"That was not an earthquake either." He picked up speed and almost started running when a second sharp jolt hit. This time neither of us fell, but the faeries and even Bunky tumbled about in the air as an invisible pressure wave hit them.

"What the hell is going on?" I said to anyone or anything that had an answer.

Alric didn't say anything but increased his pace. Unfortunately, everyone who had gone back to their pubs and homes after the first quake, were now back in the street. Running evolved into dodging at this point.

"That was an explosion, a big one," Alric finally said as we reached the end of the pubs and he turned down a narrow lane to the left. There were a few businesses at this end, scattered among a collection of tiny gnome houses. The only big thing down here was the Antiquities Museum.

Or rather, the only big thing down here *had been* the museum.

A huge wall of dust and airborne debris brought us to a stop before we could see the end of the lane, or the building. Bunky and the girls dropped lower in flight, and all four hovered a bit behind us.

I thought Alric would keep going anyway, but instead he muttered a few words and threw his left hand in the air. A wind came from behind us and thinned out the dust.

"I thought you said not to use magic for simple things?"

He scowled at the dust still hanging in the air. "No, I said don't waste magic. This isn't wasting it. We need to see what happened. Now." He flung his right hand up this time and the dust vanished.

So had the museum.

The Antiquities Museum had been built about sixty years ago. An offshoot of the university, no big elven ruins had been found at that point. Since then, each administration added onto it until it had become almost as large as some of the massive ruins below the city. It was ugly, awkward, and ill designed.

It was also missing.

"You didn't accidentally do that, did you?" I didn't think he would have, but one never knew.

Alric's glare said volumes. "If I destroy a building it wouldn't be by accident." He went to the far side of the hole where the museum had been.

A group of unconscious people were in a pile at the bottom of the ruined steps that had led into the museum. While Alric stalked around the hole, I ran over to see if any of them were alive. There were two museum guards and two of the employees, all still breathing but very battered and bloody. They must have been running out of the museum when it collapsed into the hole before us.

I stepped past them and peered into the giant hole. If anyone had still been inside when it went down, they were dead now. From the pile of bricks and debris, the building must have crumbled as it fell into the hole beneath it. As if the ground under the center of it vanished and the building followed. Even the nearby trees looked crooked.

"These people need help," I said to Alric but he was busy frowning at something in the dirt a few feet away from me.

"It's coming." Alric waved a hand behind us. Foxy, his fiancé, Amara, and half a dozen townsfolk came up the path. Foxy and Amara were an interesting pair. Foxy was about seven feet tall, with long floppy ears and tusks that jutted up from his lower jaw. Amara was a pureblooded dryad, so tiny and frail she continuously looked like a faint breeze could lift her up. The faeries and Bunky led them and I hadn't even noticed that they left us.

Foxy thanked the faeries, then came to where I stood and motioned to the handful of townsfolk with him. "Gather around, we be needing to get these people to a healer." Foxy was in his new take-charge mode, one that started after he fell for Amara a few months ago. I had no idea how the relationship between he and Amara had finally been settled. She had been originally using him to get information about us and the relics for the people she worked for. Who, unbeknownst to her, happened to be Jovan and Glorinal. Foxy had taken the betrayal hard, but it looked like love had managed to overcome it.

"What happened?" Foxy stepped beside me and peered down the hole. Then he shuddered and took a step backwards.

Alric joined us as he wiped his hands on his black pants. He'd been messing around with the dirt again. "I found a number of smaller holes and, judging by the age of the debris, someone spent weeks tunneling under the museum."

"So this was a natural collapse? Well, not natural if someone dug the ground out from underneath it, but this wasn't an explosion?" I had my doubts.

"Oh no," Alric peered down the hole and shook his head. "There was an explosion. A bunch of them I'd say. The others were too far away for us to feel them, and they were probably smaller. They ended here."

Foxy folded his arms and nodded. "Then where it be starting?"

Alric shook his head, and the frown on his face carved a few more lines. "I'm not certain, but judging from the collapsing trees, I'd say it started in that direction." He pointed out to the forest behind the former museum. Trees, huge old gapens, tilted unnaturally. "If I had to guess I'd say it started about two miles from here. At the mine."

CHAPTER THREE

I regretted eating all of those sandwiches now. "What do you mean, *mine*?" While Beccia hadn't mined for the last thirty or so years, plenty of former ones were around. It didn't have to be *that* one.

"That mine. The one that collapsed two months ago, taking that bastard with it." Alric looked ready to jump down in the hole in front of us to find answers, but he shook himself and stepped back instead.

One of the guards was too big for the others to carry, so Foxy nodded to us and went to help.

I waited until he was out of earshot. "Are you trying to say that *he* caused this?" The townsfolk were almost as wary of Glorinal's name as Alric was. "How could that be? That mine was huge and it collapsed. I don't care how strong a magic user you are, if an entire mine falls on you, you are dead." He needed to be dead. I still woke up at night in terror of him and what he tried to do. And what he threatened to do. Both he and Jovan had been working for someone else, someone they both called Master. However, Glorinal went crazy and decided that with me at his side, willing or not, we could overthrow everyone. Including Jovan and the Master.

Alric bent down, sifted the dirt through his fingers, and then looked up into the trees. They were denser here than I recalled, but then I didn't think I'd ever studied them as I was doing now. "I don't know. What I do know is that magic was used—a lot of it—to displace the ground under the museum. And judging by the tracks, some people escaped into the woods afterwards."

"But it doesn't have to have been him. Besides, how can you even make a guess about what happened?" I was worried that someone destroyed the Antiquities Museum, but I was terrified that Glorinal might not be dead. Denial was a fine place, and I was staying there.

Alric gave me a look as he rose to his feet. "I'm a scout, remember? I was trained in tracking." He dusted his hands off again and put an arm around me. I slipped my arm around his waist and leaned close. He rubbed my shoulder for a few moments, then lowered his voice. "We have no idea if he survived. Most likely these were just treasure hunters looking for the chimera." He dropped a kiss on top of my head.

I looked up into those amazing green eyes. "Liar."

"I tried." He shrugged, gave my shoulder a final squeeze, and headed back to the main road.

I should have accepted the lie.

The people carrying the injured had gone, but more townsfolk headed our way. More folks who looked like they would ask questions.

Alric grabbed my arm and briskly started walking away. Harlan had been in the new crowd, but he broke free of them and followed us. He was a good friend, fellow digger, and possibly the nosiest person I knew. He hated me to say it, but I'd long ago decided his insatiable curiosity was a throwback to his feline ancestors. Harlan was a chataling, a species that looked like a house cat had mated with a human. Chatalings hated being called cats.

"You two are up to something. Now, what really happened back there?" Harlan's whiskers twitched.

"We need to get to the mine. Now." Alric dropped his voice low. As soon as we were out of sight from anyone at the collapsed museum, he turned us down another lane, and then twisted back through two alleys.

"Mine? What mine?" Harlan kept up with us, but he had missed the earlier conversation.

"Keep it down." Alric shot him a look and gave a quick shake of his head.

Harlan, sensing a great conspiracy at work, simply smiled and laid one claw aside his nose with a wink.

"Alric thinks the explosion that took out the museum started at the mine," I said then held up a hand to stop him. "Yes, *that* mine." I looked around to make sure no one was listening; I was now sure I saw Glorinal everywhere.

Harlan froze, his eyes wide, and his tail lashing about. Glorinal and Jovan had kidnapped him and Covey when they'd grabbed townsfolk.

I was sure Harlan's nightmares were at least as bad as mine.

"No." That was the most succinct I'd ever heard Harlan, but I agreed with the sentiment.

"I need both of you to calm down. We've no idea what happened, but I can almost guarantee that the magic shields around the mine fell with those earthquakes. We need to get there and see what really happened before the council realizes their shields are gone." Alric turned down a few more alleys, one nothing more than a two-foot-wide gap between two old stone buildings, then to a trail into the woods.

I shoved Glorinal out of my head. With any luck we'd find his skeletal remains in the mine and I could sleep better at night. Finding the chimera artifact would be a bonus.

It wasn't hard to follow the line of destruction once you knew what you were looking at. The explosions out here hadn't been as large as the one that swallowed the Antiquities Museum, but they left a brand-new ravine in the woods. Trees tipped over or hung out over the edge, their roots reaching out toward the abyss.

The mine had already collapsed, thanks to the fight with Glorinal, so the new damage was even further down. I hadn't been near the mine, none of us had, since that horrific day, but it looked like the hole was deeper and wider now.

The fact that all three of us could walk right up to it told me Alric was right about the shield being down. Magic of that sort would have been tied to a nearby object. Chances were the tether was down in the hole now.

"Who is going down there?" Harlan peered over the edge, but the look on his face said it wouldn't be him.

"Me."

CHAPTER FOUR

I looked around trying to see who said that and realized it came from me. Possibly the last place I wanted to go was down there. Yet, there it was.

"No, I'll go." Alric looked around for somewhere to tie his rope.

I hadn't even noticed he had a rope.

Most likely, the enterprising former thief stole it as we moved between houses on the way here. Good to know he kept his skills up.

I hadn't meant to volunteer myself, but I knew why I did. "I need to go. I'm the best one at rummaging through debris and rocks. Especially considering where Qianru has me digging lately." I tried to take the rope, but he moved it out of reach. "I'm the trained digger, remember? You're just the trained spy and tracker. Not so helpful here."

"I'm stronger than you, both physically and magically. If there is anything unexpected down there—"

"I'll yell for help." I yanked the rope out of his hands. He had already secured it around a heavy gapen tree that looked far enough from the newly exploded ravine to still be stable. I wished I had my digger tools, but we couldn't waste time going back for them. The Hill council were politicians at heart, which meant they'd be arguing about the collapsed museum, and how to get their stored treasures out of the mess, for a while. It might take time before they looked to check on their shields on the mine. However, we couldn't be sure that other folks didn't make the same connection Alric had.

Alric and Harlan held the rope and let it out as I slowly descended. The walls of the pit were jagged and uneven, a testament to their violent birth. I dodged a giant tree root blocking my path and focused on the dig. This was just a dig. I was looking for an artifact in a dig, not the body of my murderous former boyfriend.

I figured if I kept telling myself that eventually I'd give in and believe it.

The metal corral that Jovan and Glorinal had used to keep their kidnapped prisoners contained lay in a massive twisted heap not far below the exposed tree roots. Although he couldn't see them from the top, I was sure Harlan would be glad to hear of their demise.

I was almost to what could be considered the bottom—there were a lot of layers here— when a second, thinner rope dropped down along side of me. Followed moments later by Alric. The rope didn't look strong enough to hold him, and it was an odd green color, faintly glowing.

"First off, I said I was doing this. You were going to stay up top. Secondly, what the hell is that?" I swear the rope was slowly moving of its own accord, even caressing Alric's hand when he let go of it.

"I never actually said I would stay." Alric smiled and looked around where we landed. "And the rope is made up of magic and tree leaves, something you might be able to make in a few dozen years or so." He pointed to the rope near me. "I stole that one for you."

I settled on giving him a scowl and turned toward the collapsed cavern before us.

A deep half-dome carved in the wall ahead of us looked like a likely place to start. It looked fresh, as if the recent explosion had cracked it open. It was also so dark that nothing beyond the first few feet could be seen. I waited for Alric to magic us some light; finally I turned around to him. "We don't have much time, remember?"

"I think you should try casting a light spell. It's one of the first ones we teach babies." He handed me a small rock. "It helps if you have a focus to pin it on."

I shifted the rock in my hand and shook my head. "I seriously doubt you elves trained babies to fling lit rocks around. What if something goes wrong? I could have a massive headache and pass out." Granted, that hadn't happened yet, but whenever he'd tried to get me to do magic without dragon bane, it sure felt like it would.

"Then it's a good thing I'm with you, isn't it?"

I wanted to smack the grin off his face. Instead, I turned my back to him and focused on the spell for light. It had some long-winded elven name that meant luminesce. I called it glow magic. I shut my eyes— something else Alric was trying to break me of, but my back was to him for a reason—and pulled in energy to fuel the spell. My temples started throbbing first, and then a buzzing filled my head. I took a deep breath and concentrated on the spell, just the spell, the spell was all.

"Another problem of closing your eyes." Alric's voice was right next to my ear and I almost jumped a foot in the air.

I also opened my eyes. The blinding glow bathed the entire area in an eerie greenish gold light.

"What's going on down there?" Harlan used his yelling but trying to be quiet about it voice.

Which meant they probably heard him back in town.

"Taryn is playing around. Nothing to worry about." Alric covered the hand holding the rock with his own and muttered a few spell words. The pressure in my head lessened and the glow dimmed down to a manageable level.

"We probably want to move along before Harlan brings in the whole town," Alric said as he started into the dark cavern.

I swore under my breath at his back and followed him in.

And swore some more after about ten minutes of scrambling over rocks. The ones near the entrance were jagged and blown outward. But further in...even to my magic-novice eyes it was clear magic caused the condition of the cavern. Neither tools nor nature molded rocks this way. It was as if a giant bubble had forced the rocks to curve around it. The further we got, the more evidence of magic showed in the rocks. Something, or someone, had magically pushed a giant bubble into the rocks as the mine had fallen in on itself.

There wasn't much space in the rock bubble. The original mine had been huge, but this was almost like a pocket of it that had stayed near the surface and burst open with the recent explosion. Before that, it would have been dark and almost airless.

Lucky for me, I now had enough light to see the decimated corpse.

From the clothing it was Jovan.

"Was he drained...?" I couldn't even finish my question.

"Yes." The anger in Alric's voice didn't need any other words to emphasize it. Whoever had been down here had used death magic to drain any remaining energy from the corpse. Even though it most likely happened right after the collapse two months ago, waves of the spells used still permeated the area. A heavy feeling of evil lingered over the corpse and boulders near it.

Three more decimated bodies, all wearing the gray uniforms of Glorinal's guards, were dumped behind the boulder closest to Jovan's corpse. The magic stench from their corpses almost made me throw up. They had been fed on while still alive.

If Glorinal had been the one behind the magic rock bubble, he had survived down here for two months with nothing but four corpses and his magic to sustain him.

I so wanted to run screaming out of there right now.

Alric silently turned me away from the bodies, and kept his hand on my shoulder after we moved away. I wouldn't admit it out loud, but I was now glad he had come down here with me. I probably could have handled seeing the dead remains of Glorinal. Dead and drained remains that gave evidence that Glorinal might still be alive, and had used these bodies to stay that way wasn't really what I was up for.

"He had to have created a magic bubble to survive the cave in, then whoever got him out, inadvertently pushed the bubble to the surface when everything exploded." Alric walked over to see the remains of a partially collapsed tunnel. Then he went to the end of the cavern, having to scramble over large boulders to do so. He peered down into something I couldn't see and shook his head. "I can't imagine he would have gone through all of this only to leave the obsidian chimera behind. So either it is with him, or it's down there."

I scrambled over to him. I was a good digger and not afraid of deep finds. However, there was no way any digger could get down there. The huge pit in front of me was so wide and deep that even holding my glow rock out over it, I couldn't see the far side, or the bottom.

Glorinal was alive. He escaped with help. And he possibly had a little relic of potential world destruction with him.

I wondered if moving to the other end of the world was an option. Maybe some obscure and hard to find mountain top somewhere where Bunky, the girls, and I could raise goats.

Then Alric started swearing.

There had already been plenty of things to swear about in here, so I was almost afraid to see what this newest one was.

He'd moved back toward the collapsed tunnel someone had used to free Glorinal and had brushed away some dust on the right edge of it.

I stepped closer just as he turned to me, his face pale. "We have to leave *now*." He grabbed my arm, but I pulled back to see what was on the rock face. A two-inch-long dark green shape had been stamped into the rock about as high as my shoulder, with enough force to send cracks radiating out from the design. An odd magical stench gave evidence of how someone embedded it into solid stone.

"A green dragon?" I'd seen Alric face down any number of horrors and laugh them off. However, he was about to pick me up and carry me out by force if I didn't follow him right then and there.

I let him pull me away this time. "Fine, but why are you so disturbed? It's kinda weird, I'll admit. Do you think Glorinal did it?"

"No. I know he didn't." Alric pulled me until we were almost running. "It's not a green dragon, it's the emerald dragon. The mark of a group called the rakasa. They almost destroyed my people. They were wiped out over five hundred years before the Breaking."

CHAPTER FIVE

That brought mixed feelings. A supposedly long-dead murderous group who liked to kill elves had managed to dig their way through at least a mile of dirt and rock—to free an elf. I knew the elves were mostly still in hiding, at least Alric's clan was, but that seemed a little extreme.

I blinked as Alric dragged us back into the sunlight. "Um, they weren't actually dragons were they?" I had a hard time thinking of any self-respecting dragon, if they weren't just mythological bugaboos anyway, fitting in the remains of that tunnel. Harlan was probably the largest I could see fitting in there. Even Foxy would have been too big.

"No, but they worshipped a large emerald that had been carved into the shape of a dragon, and that was their symbol." He quickly went over to the ropes and handed mine to me. "You go up first." He didn't have his sword with him, but he did have his dagger. I wasn't sure at what point in our rushed journey he'd taken it out, but it was out now as he turned to face the cavern entrance.

I wanted to ask more questions, and I would, but his fear was something I could almost taste. I didn't think he was this upset when Jovan tortured him.

My scramble up the rope probably wasn't graceful, but it got me up the side of the rocks in record time. I looked back and Alric was still watching the cavern mouth. "I'm up." He nodded but didn't look toward me for a few tense minutes, then turned back to the cliff face, sheathed his dagger and quickly, and with disgusting grace, climbed up the rope. His boots barely touched the rocks.

"Did you find the artifact?" Harlan had clearly been bored while we were down there as he'd been making little designs in the dirt.

Alric said nothing, but untied the rope I'd used, and then said a few words over the rope he'd created and it dissolved into a pile of leaves. He then used his foot to wipe out all of Harlan's dirt doodles. "We were never here. No one can know we were here."

Harlan opened his mouth to ask probably the same questions I was about to, but Alric stopped us both with a look. "Not. Here." He turned and headed down a narrow, unused trail. One that didn't seem to be heading back toward town.

Harlan looked at me but I shrugged and followed Alric.

I could almost feel Harlan's bottled-up questions pushing at my back as we made our way through the trees. Alric changed trails at least five times, one time leading us through a stream to do so. Harlan was not amused.

Finally, the city was within sight, and Alric slowed down. "I'm sorry, but we needed to get away from there immediately and without anyone seeing us come from there."

"I have a question—wait, that's not true; I have a lot of them. And Harlan here is going to explode with them. But my first one is how can a race of people who have forgotten a lot of things since the Breaking have such a vivid memory of ...them?" The look in Alric's eyes told me I didn't want to say dragons, green, or rakasa out here.

"Because they were that horrible. I'll explain more when we find Covey, but the story of the rakasa and their green dragon cult," he even winced when he said it, but he also dropped his voice, "was one so traumatic to our people it was never forgotten. They almost slaughtered the entire elven race."

Harlan's eyes got round at that and I did fear he would explode if he couldn't ask his questions. I leaned forward and whispered in his ear as we headed toward the university. "Glorinal had been down there until recently, but some group found him. We don't know if they took him or killed him." I thought about that crater in the cavern; if they had dumped his body down that, we wouldn't have seen anything. "They are from the elves' past."

"Oh! But—"

Alric turned and shook his head at both of us. "Not now."

We stayed silent until we got to the campus, but at least Harlan didn't look quite as ready to explode now. He did look like his brain was working overtime on what I gave him though.

The university was a beautiful place—providing school wasn't in session. Few students roamed the halls on weekends and even fewer faculty. However, Alric thought as I did—Covey would be there.

Harlan's tail lashed and a full scowl had grown on his face by the time we got to Covey's office. "Can we talk *now*?"

"Almost." Alric looked around each corridor we crossed as if he thought we'd been followed. Finally, we reached Covey's office and he knocked on her door.

I thought she wasn't in there at first. Her office wasn't that big, and she didn't respond for two full sets of knocks. Eventually, the door swung open.

"Covey?" I stuck my head in, as while the door had opened there was no one behind it. She was already going back to her desk, her nose buried in a book. Covey was a trellian, a reptilian-based biped race that lived in the deserts for the most part. Her limbs were longer than an average person, and although extremely slender, she was insanely strong.

"Yes, yes, go ahead and clean the room, I'll stay out of your way."

Alric shoved me into the office, with himself and Harlan close behind, then shut and locked the door behind us.

Covey still hadn't looked up.

"Covey, we apparently need to talk to you," I finally said.

She looked up and it took a few moments for her brain to pull itself free of whatever she was reading, and focus on all of us standing in her tiny office.

"Do you have anything on the emerald dragon cult, the rakasa?" Alric wasn't beating around the bush on this one. However, it was good that he looked a tiny bit less upset.

"I can't say I've...wait a minute." That was Covey, didn't even ask why we were there, or what this cult was. Ask her about something she could research and she was like a hawk with a mouse.

Alric followed Covey to a new painting with a heavy frame. Which was weird, Covey never decorated her office; she focused on packing it full of scrolls, books, and relics. The question was resolved when she pulled the painting away from the wall and revealed a safe.

"People keep taking things of mine that they shouldn't." She shot a look over her shoulder at Alric. The first time they'd met had been when he stole a scroll from her. They were friends now, but she did like to remind him of it from time to time.

"It's odd that you mention an emerald dragon. I don't think I've seen anything about a cult, nor anyone called the rakasa, but there's mention of a relic. It's an older scroll, probably a good thousand years before your people vanished from here."

"I thought you said this was a cult and somehow related to Glorinal possibly being alive?" Harlan had been incredibly patient on the way over, but he'd finally had enough.

Only years of training kept Covey from dropping the pile of scrolls she had taken out of her safe. She did, however, fling them at me and turn to Alric.

"That bastard is alive? And you're doing research? We need to find him. Kill him." That was very Covey. Most academics were meek and stayed in their world of academia. Covey was a hunter at heart, and occasionally that prey was living. Granted, she only went after people who deserved to be killed, but she had no problem doing the deed herself.

From the look in her eyes she was already planning Glorinal's demise. Along with kidnapping Harlan, Glorinal had also taken Covey. She had extreme control issues, and Glorinal had shown that he, most likely with a lot of magical back up from Jovan, had been able to render her immobile. Their victims could only move when one of the two elves commanded it, but they were aware the entire time of their capture. Covey had been furious that a cave-in had taken out Glorinal before she could rip him into shreds.

Alric glared at Harlan. "We have no idea if he is alive or not. He *was* alive, but the people that might have found him hate elves. Most likely his body was in that cavern somewhere. The focus here needs to be on this cult and that they very possibly have the obsidian chimera." He briefly explained everything that happened in the cavern, and what we thought happened a few days ago. That went well.

"Two days?" I wasn't sure who said it first, but both Harlan and Covey looked ready to bust a vessel.

"Their spells triggered a delayed explosive collapse. That's what caused those earthquakes." Alric grabbed Covey as she started to push past him. "They have a two-day lead, and we have no idea where they went."

Covey usually didn't use weapons. Although fully trained in multiple forms of combat, she was enough of a weapon by herself. She shook free of his grasp and raced around her office, pulling out small knives and throwing stars she had hidden away and stashing them upon her person. "If there is even the slightest chance that murdering bastard is alive and not being tortured as we speak, I need to find him. I will find him. You said they escaped by the Antiquities Museum? That's where I'm starting. Take what you need of the scrolls, lock up afterwards." With that, she vanished down the hall.

I started to go after her, she was my best friend after all, and we shouldn't have let her dash off like that. When I turned to ask Alric and Harlan how best we could stop her I noticed both of them were busy reading the scrolls I'd dumped on her desk.

"Don't you two think we should stop her? Those rakasa things are probably dangerous to everyone, right?"

Harlan looked up briefly, and then went back to skimming one of the smaller scrolls. "I have no idea how to stop her."

"She won't listen and needs to get it out of her system." Alric spoke without looking up. "Besides, her people used to hunt the rakasa for sport. At least once the elves fought them off and chased them out to the Trellian desert."

An awful thought crossed my mind. "You didn't only come here for the scrolls, you came here in hopes Covey would do just what she did." In the last two months, I'd begun to think Alric had toned down his spy life. He seemed like he treated us, all of us, like people he cared about, not pawns. I started to believe there might be a chance for us to build a relationship. This blew that to hell.

"I needed to see these scrolls, or at least see if they gave us any clues." He looked contrite, but I noticed he hadn't denied my accusation.

"Look me in the eye, and tell me that you never thought of using Covey to find those rakasa." Even Harlan looked up at the tone of my voice, but it took Alric a few moments longer.

"I can't." He shook his head. "Well, I could, but as you point out on a regular basis, I lie. Yes, I did think she might react the way she did. Having a pissed-off, semi-berserker trellian hounding the rakasa might make them sloppy."

I felt like I'd been punched in the gut. I'd accused him of it, but somewhere in my mind I'd hoped I'd been wrong. I couldn't play this game anymore. He was risking my friends' lives as well as my heart. "You know what? Why don't you go back to your damn elven kingdom and play your games there. Death and destruction have followed you around since you came stalking through here, and you don't even care. You push people around like playing pieces to get what you want at any cost." I turned for the door. "I'm done."

"Taryn," Alric dropped the scroll to follow me, but I spun on him.

"No. You stay and see what you can find. I need to be somewhere else."

His beautiful green eyes looked hurt, but he was a damn skilled actor, so I wasn't taken in. Without saying another word—I couldn't think of any I could say without yelling or crying—

I stomped out.

Part of my brain said that even though Alric was still first and foremost a scout for his people, he also wasn't the soulless bastard I was making him out to be. And if I was honest with myself, my money was on Covey in any fight as long as death magic wasn't involved. However, it was the principle. Not to mention if he was manipulating her, was he still doing that to me?

I was so annoyed and concerned, I didn't even notice the sceanra anam until it hit me in the face.

CHAPTER SIX

I was too shocked to scream, and I think it felt the same.

Its tail hit me in the face as it tried to turn around. However, it was now trapped between me and a group of pissed-off faeries.

At first I thought they were the wild faeries come back, but a closer look as they buzzed around blocking the flying snake's escape showed me they were all wearing tiny overalls. I was saddened that the wild ones hadn't come back, but glad to see the domesticated ones actually doing something. The sceanra anam had vanished, or so we thought. But if the faeries were hunting down the last of the vicious killer flying snakes, I wouldn't try to dissuade them. I still had nightmares about one of their victims who had ended up on my doorstep.

Garbage Blossom, still riding Bunky, came up from the rear of the flying mass. "We hunt it." She waved her war stick in the air and the other faeries mimicked her even though only some had sticks. Bunky seemed more interested in coming to me, and wasn't watching the sceanra anam.

It watched him though.

With a lightning fast move, the sceanra anam dove up toward Bunky's middle. I knew if they lost their head, the chimera constructs would effectively die, and I was fond of my little flying goat. I jumped forward to smack the sceanra anam aside, but twenty faeries beat me to it. With war cries they had to have learned from Garbage, they charged forward and started stabbing the thing.

The sceanra anam must have already been injured by the way it turned around when it saw me instead of just eating its way through me. It was hard to read emotions on its snake-like face, but it had seemed as terrified of me as it had been of the faeries.

However, even injured, I would have thought it would have been able to fight off more than twenty faeries. The swirl of bright colors and madness that were the faeries quickly engulfed it.

In under a minute, nothing but shredded bits of sceanra anam drifted to the ground.

I motioned Crusty Bucket over to me since all of the others were focused on the dead creature. Crusty had been looking at a bright light down one of the darker hallways. She was always easily distracted.

"We bring gift." She waved her arm toward the rest of the faeries.

"Um, thank you? Where did you find it?" The rest of the attack squad surrounded the twenty 'warriors' and gave rounds of cheers.

"Out. Out, out, out, very far out." A scowl flittered across her face at the number of 'outs' but she shook it off.

I could ask the others where they'd found it, but I doubted I'd get a better answer. We hadn't seen the sceanra anam for two months and the hope was they were dead. If not dead, then maybe back into hibernation. The academics had been trying to find any reference to them, to find out how they came out of the ground, and from where. Not to mention how many there were. I'd seen five originally, but we'd already accounted for more than that just by sightings. But aside from them mentioned almost as a grim elven fairy tale, there was nothing to find so far.

Garbage, Leaf, and the rest of this hunting party surrounded me at that point. "We train, we fight!" Garbage waved her war stick in the air and I was immediately in the middle of a faery war cry.

If they yelled like that to the sceanra anam, the thing had been fleeing the cries more than the sticks.

"That's great." I looked around; luckily the hallways were still empty. "Uncle Harlan and Alric are in Covey's office." I pointed to the gruesome pile of former sceanra anam on the ground. "You need to go get them and tell them to collect this; someone may be able to use it. Oh, and try to tell them where you found the thing. In detail. Give them lots of detail."

I smiled as I walked away. I did my good deed. They *should* try to see if the academics could do anything with the remains. That I'd instructed Garbage and the others to drive Alric crazy while trying to explain where "out-out-out" was, was simply a bonus.

I stood at the edge of the campus, put my hands on my hips, and tried to figure out exactly how my finding her would help Covey in any way. There was no way I was ready to admit Alric was right about not going after her, I was still too upset about his duplicity. However, there also wasn't anything I could do to help her. My burgeoning magic was more likely to hurt her than help her. And my weapons training hadn't gotten much further than my magic.

I surrendered that idea and headed for The Shimmering Dewdrop. It was technically too early in the day for drinking, just a little over two hours had passed since I'd been sitting there drinking tea, but that was my place. No matter how weird life got, that one place was always there for me. That, I could count on.

Unless it was closed?

I was surprised to see no one sitting outside in the café as I approached, but thought maybe folks had wised up to the superiority of a dark pub. Nope, a rarely used sign hung on the door: 'Closed-gone to shopping'.

"Gone to shopping?" I hadn't meant to say it aloud, it just happened that way.

"Aye, sorrowful, ain't it?" The voice was so low; literally, I had to look around for the speaker. One of the daytime bar gnomes sat against the wall. He didn't look like one of those who had joined us in the fight for the glass gargoyle, but they all sort of looked the same so it was hard to tell.

"They be off to a wedding person." He waved one small hand in the air and a whiff of stale booze hit me. "Disgusting."

I shook my head. I knew the two of them were getting married, but a wedding person? That was a new trend come down from the big city of Kenithworth a few weeks' ride north of us. I knew it wouldn't have been Foxy's idea.

I could either sit here with a drunken waste of a gnome, commiserating life's cruelties, or go home where a repair crew finished fixing all the damage caused by Glorinal and his henchmen while they were looking for the obsidian chimera a few months ago. Going to another bar wasn't an option, as I didn't want to drink; I just wanted to whine a bit.

When Amara got stressed, she climbed into a tree. Not the replacement clone of her original tree—he wasn't big enough yet even if the seedling they used to grow him was fed magic spells along with his water every day. But any of the larger trees out near the ruins. Amara was a dryad, and being in nature, especially a tree, helped calm her down.

Growing up, my mother had told me we had dryad somewhere in our family line. Hence my hair picking up an odd shade of green in the summer. Now was as good a time as ever to test that.

I turned and headed off toward the trees. Ten minutes later, I found them. No idea what to do next.

I stood in a clump of seven trees, all more or less looking the same. "Should one of you be calling to me?" I kept my voice low. Even though no one was around, I didn't want it to get back to anyone that I stood in a clump of trees talking to them.

The trees gave no response.

"Fine." I marched up to the first one, and scrambled up it with only one scratch. Not too bad since I didn't even have memories of climbing trees as a child.

This one seemed nice enough, even had a few branches higher up that looked relatively seat-like.

I climbed up onto the largest and steadiest, and settled in. Nothing. Maybe I needed to touch the tree more. I leaned in so that my entire forearm touched the tree. Still nothing. I seriously wouldn't strip to come to peace with this tree.

Voices interrupted my musing about tree bonding.

"I tol' you, I ain't paying that." The voice was a bit whiney and high, although slurred. And familiar. Grimwold hadn't had the same length of jail time as his boss, but I was sure he wasn't supposed to be out yet.

"You want out of town or ya want folks questioning why you're out drinking in the woods instead of locked up where you should be?"

I carefully peered down below me. I didn't recognize the other voice, but now that I was no longer forced to bounty hunt for a living, I made it a point to avoid staying up to date on Beccia's criminal element. The man was close to Grimwold, but his hat was too broad for me to see his face.

Maybe if I moved closer. I froze the moment after that thought hit me. I could see them well even if I couldn't see who the other person was. Which meant all they had to do was look up and they'd see me just as easily.

I really needed a faery. One of their more recent new powers was the ability to make a stationary person invisible by landing on them. But since there were none about, I held my breath and prayed to any deity I could think of that neither of them would happen to look up.

"Take this," Grimwold shoved a small bag at the other person. "Just get me out. Now." There was a terror in his voice I'd never heard in all the years he annoyed me. Unless the faeries were chasing him. That was a nice memory.

"Not enough. If you want to get to Kenithworth, you are going to need triple this." The voice was cold.

"I can pay your people more when I get there, I promise. I need out of this place." Funny how terror had chased away his drunken slur.

I was caught up eavesdropping and shifted a bit without thinking. I swore as a few tree bits drifted down to the heads below. I knew I couldn't jump out of this tree and get away from them. And climbing higher wasn't an option. Those branches might hold Amara, but they wouldn't hold me.

I felt a thunk hit my head and for a second was afraid the man below had seen me and shot me. The second thunk, and a flittering of faery wings to the side of my face, told me it was my faeries.

Just in time. Both Grimwold and the mysterious hat man looked up when my falling tree bits hit them.

"Who's there?" Grimwold sounded much older and more frightened than he had before going into jail.

"No one, you idiot." The man with the hat quickly looked back down, but he wasn't anyone I knew. "It's the wind. Leaves fall off."

Grimwold was rattled now. "We need to move, somewhere deeper in the forest." Without waiting for the second man, he turned and stumbled deeper into the trees. Fear may have sobered his speech, but it didn't help with his walking.

The man with the hat looked up to where the faeries hid me one more time, swore, and then went after Grimwold. "Wait, I know another way for you to get there, a job." The rest of their discussion was lost as they moved out of range.

I had never been so happy to see my little flying maniacs in my life.

Crusty and Leaf had been the two who landed on me. Garbage flew surveillance over us.

"Thanks, girls. You have great timing." Although I doubted they'd been annoying Alric nearly long enough if they were out prowling the forest now.

"We hear you," Crusty said from her perch on my head. "You call, we come. Boom."

Now, that was weird. I had no way of calling them, not to mention they used 'boom' for a lot of things, most of which were not healthy for any living being.

I reached up with one hand, keeping the other securely on my branch, and pulled her off my hair. It was sometimes easier for Crusty to focus if she looked right at you.

"Honey, how did you hear me?"

"In here, silly." She tapped the side of her head and laughed.

"Garbage? Leaf? You all heard me in your head?" They both nodded. "But I didn't call you." I was happy they'd come by, caught spying in a tree by any criminal element wasn't a good thing. But how they did it was starting to weird me out.

"You think us, we hear you, we come." Garbage was obviously quite proud of her explanation and the other two faeries nodded enthusiastically.

I thought *them*? "You mean when I was thinking I needed you, you heard that? Can you hear everything I'm thinking?" Weirded out factor went a few levels higher now. The idea of having those flying loons inside my head all the time? Shudder.

Leaf looped in front of my face and landed on my hand. "No, you think *us* we hear we come. It always this way."

I almost fell out of the tree as I tried to grab her in shock. "How about we get out of this tree, then you three explain this?"

Garbage rolled her eyes, but all three faeries lifted off me so I could scramble out of the tree.

They flew around near the bottom until I joined them.

"Faster if you boom." Crusty shook her head after I finally reached the ground. Climbing down was a lot harder than going up. No wonder so many cats got stuck in trees.

"Boom?" I didn't like the sound of that.

Crusty made a tiny fist, held it high, then dropped it. "Boom." The maniacal grin on her face was disturbing.

"Uh, yes." I turned away from her and faced Garbage. "How long have you been able to hear me in your heads?" I waved my hands as I noticed all three about to give me a useless answer. "Without actually hearing the words come out of my mouth with your ears." I tried thinking back to any time they'd done something like this, but while sometimes they did show up about when they might be handy, plenty of times they didn't.

"Always hear." Leaf drifted down to try to communicate, since obviously I was dafter than the rock Crusty stared at. "Then we didn't." She frowned and shook her head. "Then we did." Big grin on this one.

Great. Most likely this was another one of their mysterious powers they had a long time ago, like hiding people, that was now coming back. I wasn't sure how I felt about these powers popping up. Not to mention I was still weirded out about them being in my head. I focused hard on thinking of a huge pile of sweets next to a giant bottle of ale.

None of the faeries even responded.

I added them to the thought by name.

"You give us now!" Garbage was an inch in front of my face in an instant. The other two were not far behind her.

That was reassuring. So they could hear me in their heads, but only if I thought of them. I'd have to watch my thoughts.

"Can you hear everybody?"

Garbage, realizing that I wouldn't magically supply them with sweets and booze in the midst of a bunch of trees, pulled back. "No. Was we could. Now. Boom. No."

"We hear *you*." Leaf added.

Clearly, that was the extent of their answers. We were back to boom. For a second I thought about running and telling Covey, but then I remembered her taking off was part of why I'd been in that tree in the first place.

"You give us now!" Garbage wasn't letting go of the sweets and alcohol idea. I should have made my test thought a little less appealing.

"I can't. The Shimmering Dewdrop is closed right now, and I don't know if they're done with the house yet." The final repairs should have been finished today, but knowing the crew I had working on it, they probably took a two-hour break after the earthquakes. A repair job that should have taken about two weeks ended with almost a full, two-month-long rebuild of my entire house.

The reasons I'd been in the tree all slammed back into place. Damn. I'd managed to push the fact that Glorinal was possibly alive and running around with a bunch of murderous rakasa out of my head.

"Girls." I waved all three faeries closer and lowered my voice. "Have you ever heard of the emerald dragon cult? Or of the rakasa?"

Crusty looked studiously blank. I'd say it was an act but I wasn't even sure she heard me. Leaf and Garbage looked worried for the merest of seconds, and then both shook their heads.

That was something new. They were deliberately lying to me. Most times they were too vague for others to understand, but they didn't outright lie.

"Not cult, no." Crusty paid attention after all. And judging from the tiny glare Garbage shot her, she told me the truth.

"So you have heard of the emerald dragon then?"

Crusty, suddenly realizing that she said something she shouldn't, took a deep breath, as if she was holding it under water, and then did a backwards summersault away from me. The other two quickly followed, then flew off over the trees.

Life was so much easier when all I had to do each day was dig through elven ruins.

I drifted back toward the ruins. Not where the standard dig sites were, but the side near the Forgotten Plains. The plains were unnaturally created eons ago when a bunch of bad magic went horribly wrong. Or so some of the stories went. Other stories stated that the plains were natural, and the land around them had been flung five hundred feet in the air. However, no one had evidence of any disaster having caused them. Of course no one who tried to go through them ever came back out to say one way or another, so who knew what the truth was.

Until recently, this area had been off-limits as the cliffs weren't stable. Last month some dilettante patron had paid to have the whole area magically shored up, then vanished. Leaving a nice big mostly unexplored area for folks like me to wander about.

The trees here weren't as big as the gapen trees in the rest of the ruins, and there was little evidence that any big finds were out here. However, it was nice and quiet.

I'd found a nice area and was just starting to relax and let my annoyance at Alric wander off when Covey burst into my clearing, looking like she'd just done battle with an army.

CHAPTER SEVEN

"Do you have any weapons?" She looked around the trees, then tossed me one of her daggers when she realized there weren't any weapons hanging around. Her eyes were wild and her short hair stuck up in ridiculous clumps. "Come on, we have to stop them!"

She stopped dancing around long enough for me to grab her arm. The cliffs over the Forgotten Plains were only about ten feet behind us; I didn't want her to decide to race in that direction. It had only been about an hour since she'd taken off, but her clothes were ragged and streaks of blood ran across her face and arms.

She'd found something.

"You found, *him*?" I didn't want to say his name out loud. I wanted Glorinal's body to be lying dead in the dark depths of that pit in the cavern. Even though that dream was fading, I wasn't ready to let go of it yet.

"The sahlins are coming!" She pulled free of my arm and looked around a pair of trees.

Sahlins? I couldn't pinpoint where I'd heard the name, but I was sure I had. Maybe ages ago, growing up. However, I couldn't think of what they were or why their coming would cause someone like Covey to fall apart.

Covey froze as someone rustled the bushes to the side of us.

"Hello? What's all this about then?" Harlan's voice entered the clearing a second before he did. Just in time to get a knife flung at him.

The world slowed down as I realized Covey might be impaired, but her aim wasn't. I immediately reached out with my magic to grab it, then threw both Covey and I to the ground as the knife spun back toward us and thunked into a tree.

I looked up to see Harlan crouching behind a tree. "I thought you were mad at Alric, not me."

Covey shook her head and looked around as if just waking up. "What is going on, and why did you tackle me? I mean it, if there is a chance that bastard is still alive I need to find him."

Harlan and I looked at each other as she got to her feet. She looked far more like herself than the hysterical and raving woman she'd been moments before. Except for the fact that she didn't act as if she knew she'd been gone for an hour.

Harlan studied her for a few moments, then came out from behind his tree. "You left us an hour ago, looking for the rakasa and Glorinal if he's still alive."

Covey shot Harlan a look that university students everywhere feared—the 'what lies are you trying to feed me now', look.

Harlan was made of far sterner stuff than the average student was and glared right back. "It's not my fault you forgot what you were doing."

"I didn't forget. I was...." Covey rocked back on her feet and really looked where she was. "We were in my office. Why are we in the ruins?"

Harlan scowled. "She doesn't remember anything after leaving the office."

Covey rolled her eyes and looked a little less rattled. "I can speak for myself you know. Moreover, I do remember a bit more, slowly bits are coming back.

Leaving the campus and heading toward the Antiquities Museum." She shook her head. "Or rather what's left of it. You weren't kidding that it was destroyed. I don't recall anything after that except Taryn tackling me."

I really didn't want to stay out here having this discussion. "How about we go somewhere else?"

"Sure, Foxy and Amara should be back by now," Harlan said as we walked out of the ruins.

I nodded. Some serious food and a nice glass of ale would settle this day down nicely.

Covey had been scowling at the trees around us, then aimed the scowl at us. "This is wonderful. However, I have somehow lost an hour of time, I have scrapes and cuts that I have no memory of getting, and I need answers. I'll even go to that place, if it will get you two to talk."

Covey wasn't a big fan of pubs in general, and The Shimmering Dewdrop in particular, since she felt I spent too much time there.

She didn't wait for either of us to respond, but stomped down the path to the pub.

Neither Harlan nor I were motivated to try to catch up with her. She was in a foul mood and those were never healthy for folks around her. Maybe, if I was lucky, Alric would be at the pub and she could take him down a few pegs.

"Where did you leave Alric?"

"I knew you weren't that mad at him," Harlan said with a chuckle. "But I was about to ask you how you managed to stop that knife, since I don't think that would be good talk for the pub."

Damn it. "I'd hoped maybe you hadn't noticed that." I lowered my voice. "Yes, I used magic. No, I have no idea what spell it was. Yes, you're welcome for saving that thick head of yours."

Harlan gave me a polite sniff. "No dragon bane?"

"Of course not. I didn't know Covey would turn into a knife-flinging monster before my eyes. I...." I let my words drift. No dragon bane, yet no fire ants in my skull. That was an improvement. And hopefully not the start of some new side effect that just hadn't shown up yet.

"Ah." Harlan's smirk told me all I needed to know— he made the connection too since I wasn't bitching about my head.

"We can talk about it later." Much, much later, if I had my way. I had no idea where this magic came from, or what I could do with it. Harlan was certain I would become some mighty mage and live a life of power and wealth. Or something equally ridiculous.

"Now where's Alric? Did he find anything of interest?" We were approaching the pub so we both had to watch our words. Not that it would last long with Harlan. He could spread gossip faster than an entire henhouse of grandmothers.

"He found something. But he wouldn't tell me what it was; just rolled up the scroll he'd been looking at and left." Harlan held the door to the pub open for me. "I had to put the mess away, but I will not be the one telling Covey about the missing one."

"He stole another scroll?" Obviously, the hopes I had for a reformed Alric were completely unfounded.

Harlan scowled but the way he tapped his teeth told me he was scowling about something in his head, not me. "He muttered something. No, I simply can't recall it."

Covey had gotten to the pub first and commandeered one of the best tables. From the disgruntled but trying-not-to-let-her-see-it looks on the faces of the people at the tables around her, it may not have been empty when she took it.

I couldn't blame folks for getting out of her way. She had clearly been trying to find her missing time on the walk over here, and just as clearly hadn't been able to.

She looked ready to spit nails, and then hammer them into someone with her fist.

"This is acceptable?" At the nods from both Harlan and me as we sat, she nodded as well. "Then talk. I already told Foxy to bring you both whatever it is you drink. But you need to talk now."

Harlan jumped right in. "You left your office, then an hour or more later, you threw a knife at my head in the ruins."

"That was not helpful." She started to turn toward me but then twisted back to him. "I do apologize about the knife however. I wonder how I missed." She wasn't saying she had hoped to hit Harlan, although if she knew he didn't stop Alric from stealing another scroll, she probably would change that thought. However, Covey had impeccable aim. She turned to me. "I see you and I may have more to talk about, later."

The look she gave me said that she may have lost time, but like Harlan, she had an almost obsessive issue with my magic. She knew darn well why she missed.

Foxy walked up then, bringing two ales and one very clear water in a fancy glass. "Fresh spring water from the Longhan Mountains. Amara sends it with her best regards." He put the water in front of Covey. Then gave Harlan and me the ales. He looked ready to chat, but a ruckus from the kitchen pulled his attention and he nodded and left.

I didn't know when he'd be back, so I quickly told Covey about her sudden appearance in the ruins.

The telling of it had been brief, it all had happened in a few minutes, but Covey's face changed from annoyance to worry.

"Sahlins?" She took a long drink of the spring water before her. "Are you certain? That was the exact word I used?"

Now she was making me worried. I hadn't been sure if I heard of the term before, but when she used it I was trying to get her to stop throwing sharp weapons around. "As far as I know, yeah, that's what it sounded like. You said they were coming and we needed weapons."

Covey drained the rest of her glass in a single gulp, and then studied the drops inside as if they had answers.

"The sahlins were desert dwellers. None survived after decades of being hunted by my people—before we became civilized. They were mindless, vicious things, little more than animals that could talk. And kill. Tales were passed down to trellian children that one day the sahlins would come back and repay our race for what we did."

The three of us were silent. First, a cult thought to be extinct, but one that had tried to destroy the elves, left evidence they were back. Now nightmares from a long-lost trellian past were haunting Covey. Of course, since Covey had no idea what had happened to her during her missing time, there was no way to know if the threat from them was real or not. Or if the two were connected.

Harlan coughed and looked embarrassed. "Ah, this isn't pertinent to this discussion, but I just remembered the other thing about Alric. He was going to break into your patroness' home."

CHAPTER EIGHT

Sadly, I had just taken a sip of ale when he spoke. Sadder for Harlan, since I couldn't control it when he made me choke and he got hit with a bit. Served him right for not telling me Alric's plans right off the bat.

"He's doing what?" Covey and I managed to say it at the same moment. At least Alric's newest exercise in stupidity had drawn her out of her worry about her missing time, and potential killers stalking her.

"Why is he doing that?" I knew we should be out trying to stop him, but I also knew that with that slippery bastard, he was probably already gone now. I looked closely at Harlan. He was a bit of a blowhard, and definitely a gossip. He was not, however, a scatterbrain.

Alric had been teaching me more than how to use magic. He was also training me to read signs to see if others had been using magic or had been hit with some.

"Hold still." I peered into Harlan's eyes. Yup, a faint shadow flashed across his eyes. It could be something else, but most likely he was recently spelled. "That bastard."

Harlan pulled his head back and looked between Covey and me. "What? What did he do?"

"Alric spelled you. That's why you didn't remember until now that he was breaking in."

Harlan downed his ale then rolled to his feet. "We need to stop him."

I flagged down Lehua, the half-giant barmaid. "Can we get some food to go? Doesn't matter what." When she'd nodded and jogged into the kitchen, I looked to the others. "Going there won't help. He would have timed it so the spell broke as he finished. We need to catch him at home."

"His apartment? He's rarely ever there," Harlan said.

"I know." I smiled. "Not there. He had a spot in the ruins before, but I think he's found another one recently." Again, another thing I'd hoped I'd been wrong about. "I think we may even get there before him."

Lehua came back with a few bags of food that I shoved into Harlan's arms. "Thanks. Tell Foxy to put it all on Alric's tab." In the last few hours, Alric had unraveled all of the changes I thought he'd made. Obviously, he never ever made them, but was making it seem that way to get whatever he was after. As usual. If I wasn't so worried about whatever he might have taken from my patron, I would have found a nice corner of the pub and sat there wallowing in ale for a few hours. I really had horrible taste in men.

Covey grabbed my arm as I turned to go. "If you can tell Harlan was spelled, look in my eyes."

I didn't know which answer would be worse, that someone took her memories with magic or without.

"I may not be able to tell, and even if I see something it may not mean anything." I ignored the fact I was leading us on a hunting trip based on what I saw in Harlan's eyes.

Covey shook her head. "I don't care. Check."

I knew we couldn't leave until I did it, and while I was sure where Alric was hiding, I wanted to make sure we got there before him. Besides, the pub patrons were looking at us oddly.

Covey had to bend down, since we were both standing and she's a good foot taller than I am. It was weird looking in Harlan's eyes; it was positively bizarre looking in Covey's. Her eyes were those of a true predator, and somewhere thousands of lifetimes back in my family tree, an ancestor of mine shook in fear.

I took a deep breath, pulled in whatever skills I had, ignored the screaming voices, and looked.

A spell slammed into me and tore the air from my lungs. I dragged in another breath, trying to sort out what I was seeing, or at least pull away from Covey's eyes, but neither attempt worked. Finally, I collapsed to the floor.

Covey and Harlan were around me in moments, with the rest of the pub hovering around on the edges. Not wanting to be involved, but desperate to know what weirdness I'd fallen into this time.

"Are you sure you're all right?" Covey's question sounded like she'd asked it before and didn't like the answer.

I forced a nod, as I didn't recall giving her an answer before.

She and Harlan pulled me off the floor and sat me back on a chair. Then Covey turned to the gaping masses.

"Don't you all have something far more important you should be doing?" Her hands were on her hips and the do-not-mess-with-me tone flew strong.

Even the drunkest person around us fled within a minute under that glare.

I felt bad for Covey's students.

"I was spelled, wasn't I?" That was Covey's concern. I'd been knocked on my ass, had no idea what I'd really just seen, and she was worried that she had been spelled.

"Yeah." I took a sip of the ale in front of me. "I have no idea what happened, but I'd say someone messed with your head." And mine, but I didn't say that out loud.

"Could you tell anything else?" Covey shoved another ale at me and nodded. "You looked like you needed another. Now, what else did you see? You didn't collapse about Harlan." The look on her face said she was wishing she drank about now.

"It's my wonkie magic." I tried to shrug it off and took another long drink of the free ale. "Sometimes it goes badly."

"You are a terrible liar, Taryn. But I won't pry now, you still don't look good," Covey said.

I finished my ale, then stood up. Proud when I only wobbled slightly. Whoever had spelled Covey was of a far different type of magic user than Alric. "Now, can we go find out what that pointy-eared bastard is doing this time?"

Harlan looked like he wanted to ask more questions, but Covey got to her feet and pulled him up with her.

And fell back to their seats when the pub rattled its walls.

I might have thought the bouncing around was another added bonus from peering into Covey's eyes, except that everyone who had been upright in the pub had taken a tumble.

"Another earthquake!" one of the patrons shouted from under his table. He had been under it since we came in, so most likely he was just upset the shaking ground woke him up.

Considering that the first two earthquakes we had today were actually delayed explosions from spells, I hoped he was right and this was natural. If I kept telling myself that, eventually I might believe it.

When more faeries started living in town, Foxy had made a tiny entrance above the top of the doorframe for them. When it had only been my three, they had to wait for someone to open the doors to let them in or out, but now faeries could come and go at will.

Three blurs of color shot in through the hole over the door and headed right for me.

"Not our fault!" Garbage yelled defiantly to anyone who would listen.

A horrific rattling at the door made many folks dive for cover again. Harlan went over and opened the door to let Bunky in.

The crazily flying chimera listed to one side and seemed a bit stunned. If constructs could be stunned. Crusty Bucket flew over to him and patted him comfortingly.

I shook my head and focused on Garbage. "What wasn't your fault?"

"Boom." Leaf buzzed forward with a serious look. "We no boom."

Garbage pushed ahead of her. "Things out there go boom. We not out there. Not our fault."

I pinched the bridge of my nose and shut my eyes. "Do you know where the boom is?" I ignored the worried looks from both Harlan and Covey.

All three faeries shared a look and Bunky buzzed around behind them. While they were conferring, I motioned for him to come closer. I wanted to get a look at the side he favored.

I found out the first time I saw him, that I couldn't touch Bunky without a flood of strange images filling my head. It didn't seem to happen to others, and Alric said it was related to my odd magic. Since I didn't have my gloves with me, I motioned for Bunky to turn a bit.

A long shallow gash marred his left side. I had no idea what would do that to magical obsidian, but it probably wasn't good. And it confirmed that the faeries and Bunky had been in the center of something.

The three faeries were still arguing, but then Garbage pushed the other two aside and flew back to me. "We no faulted. But we go there." She was clearly not happy, but then none of them looked happy.

"Aren't we going after Alric?" Harlan regained his annoyance at being spelled. His tail lashed back and forth a few times. Not a good idea in a crowded pub.

"I have a feeling whatever caused that shake might be a bit more important." I was hesitant to say 'explosion' in the pub. The rattling had shaken folks up, but for the most part they went back to their drinking. The quakes of earlier in the day had shown them the buildings probably wouldn't collapse.

"Same." Crusty looked up from where she was petting Bunky.

Garbage waved at her to stay quiet, but Crusty completely missed it.

"Him and boom. Same." She patted Bunky and I swore I saw the injury heal a tiny bit.

I shook my head as her words hit. "Wait, Alric exploded?" I doubted their 'boom' was that literal, but I needed to be as clear as possible.

"Silly." Leaf shook her head. She also ignored Garbage's waving off. "He there. *It* boom."

I finally gave up and turned to Garbage. "Look, I know you didn't do it, whatever it was. But I need to know where it was." I held up one hand as Crusty started excitedly bouncing around. "Not just 'out'. I need to know where. You need to take us there."

Garbage didn't answer me at first but turned to the other two and chittered something that sounded very angry in native faery. Finally, after a few more strong words, she turned back to me.

"Fine. We take." She started toward the door but then spun around quickly. "Just remember not our fault." The way her lower lip stuck out I knew something of what we were about to see was definitely their fault.

The rest of the patrons were carefully not looking our way, and I'd already added all of our drinks and food onto Alric's bill. We followed the faeries out the door.

Bunky stayed by me as we left. He listed less, but whatever had happened had left him rattled. The faeries were his friends, but I was his protector. In his mind anyway.

Covey and Harlan were silent at first, but then started talking once we were clear of the pubs.

"Is this where we were going anyway?" Harlan said as we turned toward the outer edge of the ruins. "I need to give Alric a piece of my mind."

I refrained from pointing out Alric took a piece already—or rather blocked the memory of part of it.

The girls were still buzzing ahead, clearly annoyed by how slow we were going.

"Unfortunately, yes." Alric seemed to favor this one side of the ruins. Not popular with patrons or diggers, it was rocky and jutted out over a cliff that led down to the Forgotten Plains. Most of the ruins were safely far from this edge.

It was late on a weekend so not too many people were around. The ones that were peered down over the cliff. A cliff edge that was quite a bit closer to us than it had been previously.

"Oh crap." I started running toward the huge section where the former cliff had decided to join the plains below. The plains way below. If Alric had been in there—it looked like the approximate location of his most recent hovel—he was too far down for us to recover his body.

"Alric!" My heart started pounding. Yes, I'd been pissed off that all the changes I thought he'd made, he hadn't. But the idea that he was gone for good terrified me. My heart wasn't ready to lose him.

"What?" He stood in between a few of the lookie-loos and I hadn't even seen him. The fact he had his black cloak on and the hood pulled up hadn't helped.

"I thought you were in there." I ran to get to him before Harlan and Covey could have their words.

As I got closer, I noticed his hands were bloody and he had scrapes on his face and up his left arm where his sleeve was pushed up. He was also dusty and was hanging on to a large pack on his back so tightly his knuckles were white.

"I was." His face was grim and furious. He shook his head tightly as Harlan and Covey got closer. "Not here."

"Look, whatever you did to me, was completely uncalled for—" Harlan stepped around a rock to get a better angle for his tirade. He also got a much better look at Alric's condition.

"Not. Here." Alric watched the people around us for a few moments, and then shook his head. "We need a private place to go."

I had been watching the faeries loop around in the air over the plains. I had to believe their claimed innocence on this—even they couldn't do this much destruction.

Covey had been silent, but her eyes narrowed at the sight of Alric's pack. "My place will be fine." She held up one hand as Harlan started to speak. "No. My place. Now." Without waiting, she turned and stalked away from the collapsed cliff.

Alric started to follow her, and then froze when he saw a rock her foot had flipped over. He grabbed it fast, almost too fast for me to see. However, not fast enough.

Etched in the stone was a tiny green dragon.

CHAPTER NINE

Covey was a fast walker. Alric gave her a run for her money, with Harlan and me almost running to catch up.

Alric had dropped the stone in his pocket, but quickly pulled his hand free. He did, however, keep his hand right next to the pocket.

I sped up so that I could keep my voice low. "So were they after you? Or just an unfortunate coincidence?"

He shot me a glare that repeated his earlier words about not here, but must have realized no one was near us, nor was anyone paying attention to us. "I would say coincidence. But I know you'd never believe me."

I looked around for the girls, but we were rapidly moving away from the forest and they were air dancing over the plains below. Nothing like now to test my new skill. Rather, the faeries' new skill. I thought about them joining us.

Nothing. They were still whooping and flying around, playing on air drafts coming up the new sharper cliff face.

I envisioned a big bottle of ale and all three of them with it.

Yup, that did it. The whooping came our way and Alric had to dodge as Bunky, following the faeries, made a detour for his head.

I waved the others on ahead; I knew where they were going. Covey didn't slow down. Harlan looked at me, shrugged, and kept following her. Alric stopped.

"Girls, I need you to look over the boom area."

Garbage immediately stuck her lip back out. "Not our fault!"

"I know, I know. But we need you to look around for any more markings like this." I turned to Alric and pointed to his pocket. He looked around quickly, and then pulled out the rock.

Garbage flew over first, and shook her head as if she'd smelled something nasty. "No good, we no want."

Crusty came by and tilted her head. "We saw."

This launched Garbage into another round of pissed-off faery arguing.

"Look, girls? I don't want you to touch them, but I need you to fly around and see if you find any more marks like this. And make a note of where they are." I'd noticed they could recall things they saw; you just had to make sure they knew they were supposed to recall them.

Garbage looked ready to continue her argument, but then Bunky flew next to her and nudged her. The change in my little perpetually cranky faery was amazing. She smiled and petted him. Then scowled and started to pull away. Her face softened as I'd never seen before as he flew closer to her.

"Fine." She petted Bunky a few more times. "We go see. Want us look for sneaky little men too?"

Alric had been mostly watching the crowd behind us but started at her comment. "Sneaky little men?"

I was curious too, but he didn't look curious, he looked freaked out.

Garbage focused on Bunky, but pulled herself away. "Yes. Little. Sneaky. Smell bad." Then she went back to petting Bunky.

I waited to see if Alric would ask more questions, but he had retreated into his own sneaky head. He looked like he'd found something deadly in his shoe and wasn't sure it hadn't already bit him.

"I think you should look for the men too, but," I held up a hand as all four started to buzz around, "do not leave the area. Just look around here where the collapse happened."

"Where cave, yes." Garbage had one of her own trying-to-be-sneaky looks.

It took me a minute to get what she was talking about. "Where it was up here, not on the plains."

All three faeries looked disappointed but nodded. Bunky buzzed around waiting for instructions. Which might be a good idea.

"Bunky? Keep the girls from going down to the plains, okay?"

His buzz increased a bit and moved into his purr sound. He bobbed up and down. When you didn't have much of a neck, nodding was a full body endeavor.

Not sure why I never thought of this sooner. Bunky loved the girls, they loved him, and he was good at following orders.

The girls must have realized what had happened as all three tiny faces went from disappointed to downright petulant. Without another word, all four of my flyers took off.

Alric had started slowly walking away while I dealt with my delinquent faeries. He was so lost in some dark thought, I doubted he knew I wasn't next to him.

I ran to catch up. "Let me guess, the folks you think rescued our friend are supposed to be little, stinky, and sneaky?"

Alric still looked like he was frightened and angry. Even on his disgustingly handsome face that look wasn't a good option. "I don't know. We had different myths about them. The more recent made them like giants, huge creatures who could devour entire towns. I liked that myth. It meant they couldn't have gotten him out because they never would have fit in that tunnel." He went back into his head again.

"I take it there were other myths?" He was starting to freak me out. This distracted and worried Alric wasn't one I'd had the pleasure of meeting yet. And I can't say I was enjoying the experience.

He shook his head. "Yes. Tiny, evil beings, no more than chest high to you or me with mouths full of teeth and three-inch-long claws for hands. And they follow dark magic."

I thought about how high that green dragon emblem had been in the mine. A person about that height would have to reach up a bit, but no more than someone my height would when hanging a picture. A shiver went down my back. Next time that look on his face showed up, I wasn't asking about anything. These little monsters might have only been after elves in the past, however, most of the other races were still living in caves to the far south back then. Who knew what else they'd like now that there were more races to hunt from?

Harlan came huffing down the path toward us. "What are you two doing? Covey's about to come drag you both in by your hair." He didn't even pause to wait for us to respond, just turned back and trudged toward Covey's side of town.

"Not to change the subject," which of course was what I was doing, "but I think Harlan and Covey are going to rip you a new one."

That shook him out of whatever was crawling around in his head. "What? I didn't do anything."

I managed to fold my arms, tilt him an eyebrow raise, and keep walking. Not as easy as it sounds. "They know."

"Know what?" Whatever was going on in his head about those rakasa still had him off his game. He wasn't even trying.

"That you spelled Harlan, stole one of Covey's scrolls, and broke into Qianru's house and most likely stole something from there too."

Silence stalked us for a good five minutes before he finally responded. "Oh."

Wow, even when his magic had been stolen from him I hadn't seen him this out of sorts.

We'd slowed down enough that Harlan was nowhere in sight as we walked down the twilight darkened street to Covey's house. Unlike me, Covey lived in a decent part of town. Not fancy and overblown like the folks on The Hill, but a nice, quiet, respectable neighborhood. Her house being thrashed a few times in the last few months was about the only criminal element probably ever seen here.

So I could not be blamed for screaming out in shock when two masked thugs, holding mini-crossbows jumped in front of us.

CHAPTER TEN

Alric froze, and let his hands drift down by his sides, but still kept the bag he carried pinned behind him. I'd not seen his sword, but he most likely had a few other weapons on him. He didn't favor billowy black shirts just for a fashion statement.

"You don't want to be doing this." His voice was low and dangerous, one I hadn't heard for a while.

If our robbers were impressed, they weren't showing it. I'd never seen either one before, as far as I could tell. They both had ridiculous cloths tied around the lower part of their faces. Of course, that made their eyes more memorable. Neither had particularly bright-looking orbs.

"Listen, old man. We'll be the ones saying what we'll be doing. Now hand over that bag and any valuables you have, and we'll let you go without hurting ya none." The lead goon was a bit taller than I was, but not as tall as Alric. He was quite a bit wider though.

Alric looked to me and sighed. "Do you want to do the honors or me?"

The goons shared a look; this wasn't how victims were supposed to behave.

I had no idea what Alric's plan was, but he could easily take these two. Along with my struggling magic, Covey and he were back to trying to teach me to fight.

My skill set in either group wasn't what anyone would call trustworthy.

"Oh, why don't you? I took the last ones." It was easy to be cocky when I was standing with a serious fighter at my back.

"I'll give them one more chance." Alric looked ready to play along until Garbage flew into view. Even I could see the scowl on her face. Alric could too. "Okay, change in plans—no more chances." He pushed back his hood and hair on one side to show his elven ear, then flipped back his cloak to show a familiar large sword that I knew hadn't been there moments ago. One of these days, I would find out how he did that.

"Now do you know why you shouldn't mess with us?" He wasn't paying attention; his eyes were on Garbage who frantically motioned us toward Covey's house.

The goon's eyes didn't change at Alric's elven ear, they did get bigger at the sword. But the one in front was smarter than I'd given him credit for and also clearly noticed Alric's distraction.

"Don't know why you think them ears will be scaring us, but we will take what you have." The goon lunged forward to grab Alric's bag.

I was in between and reacted without thinking and pushed the would-be thief away.

I'd been startled by both Alric's inattention and the thief's gall, so my reaction wasn't controlled. My head filled with fire ants and I dropped to the ground. After I'd sent the thief ass over head into the next block.

The remaining thief shook and ran off. In the opposite direction. They may have been working together, but there was no camaraderie between them. Especially since I'd just displayed an unreasonable amount of magic.

Alric spun around, looking for any other attackers, and it wasn't lost that his left hand was down near the hilt of his sword. His eyes were better than mine and night was falling quickly, once he was certain no other attackers were around, he helped me to my feet.

"Please tell me this was one of your testing situations, and that I didn't just save your ass?" I dusted myself off, but it was more to hide my shaking hands than any real fear of dirt.

Alric was still distracted, even though Garbage had flown to Covey's house. "What? Yeah, sure. And we need to talk. But not here."

I was getting sick and tired of his 'not here' comments. But I followed him down the street in silence.

The fire ants in my head dissipated faster than ever, which was a good thing. I hoped. With my luck it meant something worse was coming down the line.

"Here. Now. Hurry." Garbage was agitated and she kept flying up to us, then back to Covey's door. The fact that clearly Bunky and the other girls weren't with her finally settled in my agitated brain.

"Where are the others?" We walked up to the door and I heard Covey and Harlan arguing, but I didn't hear or see the faeries.

"Not here." This time Garbage said it, but the tone was almost exactly like Alric. Great, now I'd be hearing that annoying phrase from two sources.

I knocked on the door, but Covey had left it partially open and it swung further at my knock. Garbage flew in over my head, and Alric, with one final look behind us, followed. He pointedly shut and locked the door behind us.

"Come here. Now." Garbage was more upset than I'd ever seen her, and she didn't wait for our response before flying into Covey's kitchen.

Alric looked almost as upset as she was but his looks kept drifting toward me.

"Thank the gods you're both here." Harlan said from an adversarial position at one end of the kitchen table. "Covey has gone completely beyond the bend."

Covey spun toward us. "I am completely justified. Someone spelled me, and that shall not be—"

Garbage cut her off by flying in front of her and sternly placing her hand over Covey's mouth. Surprise alone kept Covey from launching her tirade again.

"No, you all listen. This serious." Once Garbage was certain we'd all been cowed by her fierce glare, she continued. "They have been stolen. You need fix."

A chill went down my spine and I hoped she was talking about some rocks in her collection. "What has been stolen, sweetie?"

Then Garbage did something I'd never seen—she started crying. "My friends. They stole my friends! Bring them back!"

I almost started crying as well. Someone stole the girls and Bunky? I always counted on them being able to protect themselves, and Bunky as well.

Alric looked almost as upset as I felt. "Come here, sweetling, and tell me what happened." Now that was a voice I'd never heard from him. Confident and secure, and far older than he looked. This voice could belong to an elven high lord.

Garbage wiped her tears and flew over to land on his outstretched hand. I'd never seen her so distraught.

"We go over boom. Crusty see something. Then Leaf go too. I see something over plains. I come back, they gone." She sat down on his hand. "No feel them!" She pounded both sides of her head.

Covey and Harlan both moved closer. "You can feel them in your head?" Covey may have been yelling at

Harlan moments before but Garbage's fear and sadness was contagious.

"Not anymore. They gone." Garbage ignored the sugar Harlan put down in front of her. I'd have to re-think my opinion of the faeries. Garbage always seemed like she tolerated the other two but now it was clear she was having a major breakdown at their loss.

I tried thinking of both Leaf and Crusty specifically. I wasn't sure how to tell if the image went out since I avoided adding Garbage to the image. I thought harder, adding a feeling of come here now and images of as many treats as I could think of.

A huge wall of black engulfed me, and I found myself lying on the floor of Covey's kitchen. Surrounded by the others looking concerned, freaked out, and trying to help me back into my chair.

Garbage watched me from the table and shook her head. "You tried calling. Not work."

"Calling?" Harlan was the one who finally got me into my chair. "Calling who?"

"Today I found out that if I think of them specifically, I can call the girls to me. And yes, Garbage is right, I tried calling Leaf and Crusty and it slammed back and smacked me down." I shook.

"We need to try to find them. Whoever has them is blocking both of you from feeling them." Alric had shaken off his worried look. "And no, I don't think they are dead."

I wasn't sure how he knew it, but I didn't want to ask about it. Right now I needed to believe my little friends were still alive.

"No." Garbage sat down and shook her head. "They no go." She pointed to Covey, Harlan, and me. "Me no go." Her scowl overwhelmed her tears at that point. "Only you." She pointed to Alric.

"Agreed, it's too risky for the others to go." Alric dug through the bag he carried, pulled out a few small items, most likely weapons, then handed it to me. "Guard this." It felt remarkably smooth for the weight of it. Most likely a magic bag, a larger version of the tiny ones the girls carried. I was sure there'd be no way I'd open it without him.

"They're my faeries; I should be the one to go." I sounded tough. But whatever had happened in my head when I flung that thief had now combined with whatever had smacked me down when I tried to reach the girls. I doubted I could even get out of this chair right now.

As usual, Alric knew me too well. "Can you even move?" When I finally shook my head, he gave a quick nod and turned to Harlan and Covey. "She did some unexpected magic earlier and I have a feeling the reaction is now getting to her. You all need to stay here. Sorry, Harlan, maybe Covey can put you up on the sofa. Something odd is happening tonight, and I need you all here. I'll get the girls back."

He was at the door before anyone could argue.

"Oh and someone should grab her." He looked at me, but before I could point out I was fine, a wall of black rose up, and the last thing I heard was Covey yelling my name.

CHAPTER ELEVEN

I found myself in a destroyed building. It wasn't Covey's house, but filled with broken things from the people I knew and loved, like someone had dug them out of a dig site as mementos. As if someone had been hoarding these items. I wandered through endless tunnels, filled with broken items. A tiny part of my mind told me I wasn't awake, but had fallen into a nightmare. Even as part of me knew this wasn't real, another part equally knew it was. That I had lost everyone and everything, and this was my life.

I screamed myself awake.

To find Garbage sitting on my chest peering down at me, her arm back for what was probably another strike at my face. "You go bad place. No go again." She started the slap, but I blocked her tiny hand.

"Stop it. I'm awake." It took my brain a few minutes to shake completely free of the images and feelings. Those were worse than the images—the bone-deep feeling that what I'd dreamed was real. If this was a new side effect of my using magic, or in last night's case, over using magic, I think I wanted to go back to throwing up.

"How did you know where I was?"

Garbage scowled and stomped around on my chest some more. "You tell me in head. Bad place. Not good."

Light trickled in through a gap in the curtains, but it wasn't a full bright sunlight. It had felt like I had been asleep for days, but clearly it was earlier than I usually woke up on a weekend.

It took me three tries to fall out of bed, and every part of my body felt like it had been beaten by a gang of thugs with sticks. I looked down where Garbage was now stomping around my pillow. "Did you beat me up?"

"No, I try to wake you up. Face only."

I lifted my shirt, but where it felt like I should have massive black and purple bruises, my skin was surprisingly unmarked.

"Is Alric back?" It had taken a few minutes to mentally catch up with the final events of last night, but Garbage looked more mad than sad, so I figured that must be a good thing.

The door popped open before Garbage could respond. "Ah, you're awake?" Harlan peered in further and noticed Garbage. "I told her to leave you alone."

I shivered as I thought of the scary place I'd found myself in. "Actually, I'm glad she woke me up." At Harlan's raised eyebrow, I added, "Nightmares."

"I see. By the way, your nose is bleeding."

I put my hand up and sure enough it came back with blood. Harlan gave me a concerned look, but then handed me a handkerchief without question.

Covey was hunched over a mug of coffee in the kitchen, and two more half-empty mugs of tea told me someone else had been with her. Most likely, Alric. Who was gone again.

"You're bleeding." Covey was far more of a morning person than I was, but you wouldn't know it by looking at her right now. Her eyes were haggard and half-open and she clutched her cup of coffee as if it was a lifeline.

I held the cloth back up to my nose and took a seat. "Where's Alric?" Might as well cut to the chase.

"He's gone back out. He found where the girls were grabbed, but hasn't found them. She seems better though." She nodded to Garbage who had followed us out of the bedroom and was sticking her head in Alric's abandoned teacup. I'd never seen any of them drink anything with caffeine, and wasn't sure it was a good idea to start. However, it was good not to see her as heartbroken as she had been.

"Garbage? Sweetie? How are you doing?" I removed the cloth from my nose; whatever caused the bleeding seemed to have finally stopped. Probably one of Garbage's slaps hit with a bit too much force. The faeries were far stronger than they looked.

Garbage looked up at me, happily licking dribbles of tea off her lips. "Is better. They okay. Tell me."

Harlan and Covey looked surprised at that so I gathered she hadn't made this known earlier.

"How did they tell you? Can you find out where they are?" I felt better that she wasn't so upset, but I still was worried they could be in danger. The faeries were *almost* indestructible and sometimes they forgot they weren't.

"In head. High thing rustled the peoples. They dropped things. I hear them." Her scowl came back. "They still be hidden." She seemed satisfied and dipped herself back into the teacup.

I looked to the other two, but they both looked as lost as me. High thing was most likely Alric; the girls had an ongoing refusal to call people by their names. "What did Alric do last night? And where is he now?"

Harlan got up and poured me some tea. "He came back briefly about an hour ago. He said that more was going on at the cliffs than we thought, grabbed the bag he had left, and took off again."

"Damn it. I should have known. Whatever he took from Qianru was most likely in that bag. Plus whatever scrolls he borrowed from you." Last night I figured I couldn't get into the bag; this morning I was more optimistic. I wanted a crack at it. Whatever he stole he needed to return to Qianru, but not before I saw what it was and why he took it. I wouldn't have stolen anything from her, but since the deed was already done, might as well get some answers.

Covey finished off her coffee, then poured herself another before speaking. "I can't say what he took from your patroness, he had a lot of things in there. It's magically enhanced, by the way." She waved her hand at me and I noticed two of her fingers had bandages. Obviously not only was it enhanced, that bag was armed.

She reached under the table and pulled out a scroll. "But it wasn't fast enough to stop me. I spent a few hours making a dummy that should fool him for a bit." She looked down at the original scroll with a smile.

Good to know we were back to her not trusting Alric.

I wandered over to the larder and pulled out some nuts and seeds. I'd found in my time at Covey's place they were the safest breakfast option. "So do we know why he was looking at that one? Oh, did he tell you some jerks tried to rob us last night? Just a few houses down the street from here."

"Alric mentioned it. He said it had to do with your collapse?" Harlan's words indicated he knew what caused the collapse, but as usual he hoped for more details from me.

"Guess so, he'd be the one who knew."

Covey finished her coffee, and then nodded. "I've heard talk around the university about more robberies. Word of the recent high-end magical artifacts have reached the criminal element."

That made me feel a bit better. Run-of-the-mill thieves were one thing; magical beasties after us was something I wanted to be done with. "That explains a bit. They didn't recognize Alric, even when he showed his ears." Another thought struck me. "Did either of you see his sword on him? Either when we came in or when he came back?"

They both shook their heads.

"I haven't seen that blade in months. I was afraid to ask since I thought maybe it was taken when he lost his magic." Harlan shook his head in regret at not asking. He always regretted not asking things, which was why it rarely happened.

I simply nodded, but didn't elaborate. There was something about our fair-haired elven lad and his sword. Something he wasn't telling us.

We had enough other problems going around. We didn't need one about a disappearing and reappearing sword. I shook my head, sipped some more tea, and tried to focus.

"Did you guys find out anything from the sceanra anam's body?" I tried to sound innocent, but I had wanted the girls to bug Harlan as well. However, we did need to know why they were back.

Harlan scowled; he knew what I'd done with sending the girls to him and Alric. "Not really. There weren't enough parts. We left it in her office."

That perked Covey right up. Unfortunately, she perked right up into Harlan's face. Unfortunate for him anyway. I was safely on the other side of the table.

"You left a sceanra anam in my office? Are you daft?" She darted to the hook where she kept her coat.

Harlan cleaned up his tea where he'd spilled it when she jumped at him. "It was a few piles of what looks like ash. And, I assure you, it was locked up in one of your specimen jars." He switched his glare to me, as Covey replaced her coat on the hook and resumed her seat. "What we did get was a long, detailed, and useless explanation of where out-out-out was."

I hid my smirk behind my tea and briefly told Covey about the sceanra anam and the girls' dispatching of it. She was more annoyed about Harlan and Alric leaving the thing in her office than she was about the fact there had been a live one flying around the city after months of no sign.

"So where was out-out-out?"

Still scowling, Harlan mollified himself with a piece of bread and jam. He took his time responding. "Near as Alric gathered, over the plains somewhere. There's no life down there, but maybe in the air above it?"

No one knew what caused Forgotten Plains, or why there was no life to be found anywhere within them. And only idiots tried to cross them.

Idiots and flying nightmares.

Ones that I couldn't deal with right now, but we'd have to look into once we got the faeries back.

Yesterday had been a long, weird, not-good day and it was taking a while for my brain to sort things. "Do we think everything is connected?"

Both of them looked up at that.

"How can we not? I'm afraid the glass gargoyle started a chain of actions that we're only seeing a small part of so far." Covey unrolled the scroll she'd recovered from Alric. "I know Alric is an asset, and in some regards a friend." The look she shot me told me she knew more than that. "But we can't completely trust him. He's still focused on the good of his people at any cost. If what we want dovetails with that, great. If not?"

I nodded. There had been a time recently where I thought that was changing, but yesterday slammed that back into my face.

Harlan hovered over the scroll. At first his expression had been curious, then pensive, then annoyed. "This is covering the Spheres. Where did you get it?" The tone of his voice made me realize his annoyance was at Covey, not Alric.

I glanced down, but I still couldn't read much elven. I seemed to be better with Ancient, but still not as good as Alric. The Spheres were some gigantic ruins to the far south, a trip that required a long detour to go around the Forbidden Plains. Six huge spheres in a circle, each one easily a hundred-feet tall, made of six-foot-high rounded blocks. No exact age given to them as far as I knew—but they were rumored to be thousands of years old.

Before Covey could answer, the slightly rocking teacup on the table exploded.

Garbage Blossom had flown out of it with such force, that the entire cup split into a dozen pieces on its way up in the air, then rained down like some twisted porcelain storm on the table.

Garbage was nowhere to be seen.

Then an orange streak flew back into the kitchen, never mind that none of us had seen her go out. She slowed down long enough to drop an enormous amount of berries on the table, chitter something so fast that all I heard was a whine, and then shot back outside again.

Leaving the three of us to look at the berries, the shattered teacup, and the new hole in Covey's window in shock.

Harlan recovered first. "She said, 'Here's breakfast. Let me get meat for the cat.'" The wrinkle of his nose told me his opinion of being called a cat.

"What did she do?" Covey didn't seem upset about the teacup at all—knowing her, she wasn't letting any of us use her good stuff—but the hole in the kitchen window was impressive. Covey's window had a perfect faery-sized circle in it. No shattering, breaking, or cracks. Just a circle. One that would have fit Garbage well enough but not the pound or so of wild berries she brought in with her.

Before I could move, the orange blur raced back in with a live crow and flung it at the table.

Covey yelled. Harlan stumbled back out of his chair as the stunned, and very much alive, bird fluttered about trying to figure out what happened. Garbage vanished again.

I ran to the front room and opened the door. Hopefully the poor bird could figure out which way to go.

Actually, the way it was trying to stay clear of both Covey and Harlan, who clearly looked far too predatory for its liking, I think it was willing to try and get out.

With a flutter of black feathers and a loud, indignant caw, the crow fled past me.

I shut the door and ran back to the kitchen. Either Garbage had been spelled, or it was the tea. I'd never seen her like this, but to be honest, I was more shocked at her trying to feed us and be helpful than her speed.

Garbage never helped anyone.

"Harlan, do you have any more chocolate?" A new substance to Beccia, the girls and I both loved it. I've found it helped to get them to sleep when they were too wired. Maybe it could get Garbage off her caffeine high before she destroyed Covey's house.

Harlan nodded and went down the hall where his coat was.

"Do you know what she said this time?" I yelled down at him. I'd heard her buzz again, but again it was too fast and too high for my hearing.

Covey locked up all of her breakables by the time Harlan came back to the kitchen. She'd also tried to block the hole in her window with a pot. "Aye, she said 'this time would be a prize'. I'm assuming she meant surprise, but she spoke very fast." He broke off a large piece of chocolate and carefully sat it in the middle of the table. That much could knock out a dozen faeries.

Which, considering what Garbage was doing now was probably the right amount.

A series of large thumps came from the wall around Covey's kitchen, then over the top of the roof, then slammed through the front door.

At least Covey didn't have to worry about the kitchen window any more. Of course there was now a hole in the door.

And a still-bouncy Garbage zipping around with something in a bag that logically could not have fit through that hole.

The bag squirmed, but I couldn't tell if it was an animal, or if Garbage had tracked down a wayward cherub.

She flew in a circle and dumped out the bag.

A pissed-off brownie faced us all. Large for one of his ilk, and they were rare this far south, preferring the colder northern climates. But we had two and a half feet of angry, beard-jutting, pointed-hat-wearing brownie looking like he was already planning what part he would cut off first from each one of us.

Before he could act though, Garbage darted forward, grabbed something from him, managing to stay clear of some fast moving hands on his part, and came to the kitchen and dropped a rock on Covey's table.

She also noticed the chocolate for the first time and swooped down to get it.

"No!" I grabbed the bag the brownie came in and ran for the kitchen. "Don't let her eat that! She needs to take that thing back first!"

I was too late.

CHAPTER TWELVE

Garbage spun in a winding circle like a wobbling flying top with chocolate all over her face. She'd only been about a foot over the table, which was good, because when she crashed, she crashed hard.

She landed next to the rock she'd brought in, and I admired her ability to focus on it with the tea and chocolate battling for control of her head.

"Is good," she said as she doubled over in laughter—at what I had no idea—then leaned her entire body into the rock to push it my way. The tea must have previously helped with her strength, since she'd had no trouble stealing the rock from the brownie. Or stealing the brownie.

The brownie in question leaned around a lot, but couldn't seem to move from where Garbage put him. The faeries had some limited spell tricks they could use, and I had a feeling Garbage had trapped him where he stood. Probably a good thing given the words he muttered just loud enough for us to hear. Whoever said wee folks were happy, helpful folks never met one.

I grabbed the rock before Harlan could. Covey guarded her scroll and glared at the brownie. It might be best for his safety as well if he couldn't break free of whatever Garbage Blossom had put him under.

The rock I snatched out of Harlan's paw took both hands to hold. It was also very old, and while the edges around it were still rougher than say a stone worn down by water or ice for a few thousand years, they were still timeworn.

I flipped it over and started swearing almost as loudly as our little friend in the front room.

Another emerald dragon.

However, this one looked different from the other two. Like them, the image had been magically pushed into the stone about half an inch. But the image was larger and far more detailed. As if the others we saw were imitations of this one, but no one was around to make one this fancy any more.

I looked back at the brownie.

He was quite a bit smaller than what I'd thought the cult members would be. And while rumored to be vicious in a pack, brownies didn't have jagged pointed teeth or anything else attributed to the rakasa.

The digger in me wanted to keep things academic, but the rest of my mind screamed that this was a relic from long before the Breaking. It couldn't be a coincidence that it showed up at the same time we thought a long-dead cult had resurrected itself.

The brownie pulled at his feet when I turned to him, but his shoes must have been spelled. No matter how hard he pulled, he couldn't get his feet out of them.

"Do you want to explain this?" I waved the stone at him, and then I hooked a thumb over at Harlan and Covey. "Or do I let these two big, bad predators remind themselves brownies were prey?" I was pushing it. Covey was fierce when the mood hit her, but Harlan was more a fluffy lap cat than predator. I doubted the chatalings ever hunted anything larger than a mouse. And brownies were too ornery to be prey for most species, not to mention the whole living in the frozen north bit. But hopefully the two of them were behind me looking fierce.

"You can't make me talk! I demand to be let free! I demand...keep it away from me!" The brownie almost broke both legs trying to pull backwards to get away from something behind me coming out of the kitchen.

I'd expected Covey to be stalking along behind me, but was surprised when a wobbly Garbage came out walking on the ground. Chocolate was not just smeared on her face, but it appeared she'd rolled in it.

I turned back to the brownie. I had no idea the little things were that bendable. Trained contortionists wouldn't be able to bend like that. "Keep it away!" he yelled.

"You're afraid of a tiny faery?"

"It's the collector of souls! It has the souls of the dead on its face!"

I looked back and shared a look with Harlan who simply shrugged. Not only was this new chocolate stuff tasty, and calming to the faeries, it also collected souls. Good to know.

Garbage stumbled a few more steps forward, then collapsed and sat cross-legged on the carpet about a foot away from the brownie. "You tell nice lady what she wanna know."

I was now nice lady? Clearly, whatever effect the tea had on her personality it was still messing with it.

She gave a huge yawn and stretched. "You tell her now...." And she tumbled over asleep.

There was a lot of weirdness going on right now and I was reaching the edge of dealing with it.

Garbage's collapse seemed to give the brownie more courage. "I am stronger than all of you! I have the path of the righteous on my side! I have—"

He cut off as Garbage, with what was probably her final burst of energy, woke up, yelled a bunch of vulgar faery swear words and ran toward him waving her arms.

"I found it! I found it! I came looking for *them*. We follow them to take over the world!" He squealed as Garbage jumped for him. "I lie! I lie! I'm just a baker!"

Garbage shook her fist at him, then passed out at his feet, a little pile of chocolate-covered, drooling faery goodness. I scooped her up and took her into the kitchen to wash her off.

I motioned to the other two to join me at the sink. "I believe him. And we're not going to get any answers out of her until she comes off her chocolate high. I think she stole him because she could sense the emerald dragon rock."

Covey and Harlan both started talking at the same time, but I couldn't focus since our brownie friend, emboldened by the collapse of his faery nemesis, was now back to yelling to be released.

Alric had come into the house without any of us noticing and nodded to the screaming brownie. "Why are you collecting brownies? Or is this a special one?"

"Long story, but Garbage brought him as a prize for us, she also cannot have tea ever again, and he had this with him." I tossed Alric the rock. Part of me didn't want to because of his recent tricks, but like Covey said, if any new disasters came our way, we needed to have our resident expert on board.

Alric caught the rock without even a slight jiggle of the bag he carried. He looked at it, but wasn't as impressed as I expected him to be.

"It's like ones you have, only older. Much older." I hadn't expected him to react the same way as he had to the more recent marks, but he acted as if I'd handed him a mildly interesting flower. "He said he found it, and was coming to Beccia to find the rest of them."

Alric looked back at the brownie, who had stopped yelling for the moment and was intently watching Alric, then went the rest of the way into the kitchen and sat down. "We're going to see more of them. The new marks are for their followers, not us." He put the rock in his bag and pulled out two bottles of ale.

"This isn't the time for drinking, you know." Harlan's tail lashed back and forth. Good reason or not, he was not going to forgive and forget about the spell Alric had pulled.

"I thought you might want these two back." He settled the bottles on the table and I noticed they both were empty of beer, but full of faery.

Passed out little faeries.

"Where did you find them?" I rushed forward to grab the bottles. I'd felt better when Garbage said she could hear them again, but seeing them was much better. Both of them slept the sleep of the justifiably drunk. Even with the lids still on their bottles, I could hear Crusty snoring.

"I wouldn't open those lids yet, they both just passed out. They were at The Shimmering Dewdrop, drunk like I've never seen. Both of them were chittering so fast even I couldn't understand them. The rest of the bar faeries were in the same shape."

"So whoever had them just let them go?" I nodded over toward his bag. "You don't happen to have Bunky in there do you?"

"I guess they got tired of them." Alric was distracted by trying to slide Covey's scroll over to him. I'd never seen him be so blatant about his thievery. "What? Um, no."

A pounding at the front door pulled me away from Alric's odd behavior. Covey waved her hand for me to get the door. From the way her eyes narrowed as she watched Alric, I'd say I wasn't the only one concerned.

Bunky almost knocked me over. Only a bit of a dance to the side saved me. His buzz was the angriest I'd ever heard it as he pulled back and studied me from head to toe. His buzz reduced a bit when he realized who I was, but then increased when he spun toward the kitchen.

I was used to Bunky playfully trying to head butt Alric, but there was nothing at all playful in the way he charged forward. His buzzing was loud enough to cause Garbage Blossom to stir a bit on the cloth we'd left her on at the table. He hit Alric with enough force to slam him out of his chair and across the kitchen floor.

"Bunky! Knock it off!" I ran forward as Harlan and Covey ran to stand between Alric and my pissed-off chimera. They blocked Bunky for the time, but I had a feeling unless we were willing to disable him, we couldn't stop him for long.

Alric staggered to his feet and clutched his duffle bag to his chest.

I had seen Alric in many different moods in the five months I'd known him. Cowardly and terrified were not ones I was familiar with. Nor did it look good on him.

"Everyone back off." I grabbed the two bottles that held the faeries. Harlan picked up Garbage and came to my side of the table. Covey was still scowling and trying to block an increasingly agitated Bunky from an increasingly frantic Alric.

"Covey, you too. Alric? Why is Bunky trying to hurt you?" I debated opening up the bottles and seeing if a dunk in cold tea could revive Crusty and Leaf. Something was wrong here and even hyperactive faeries might be more of a help than none at all.

"Trying?" Alric pulled his terror-filled eyes away from the enraged chimera before him for only a second, but it was enough. With a speed I'd never seen him exhibit before, Bunky dove forward and ripped the bag out of Alric's hands with his teeth. He then flew to me, dropped it at my feet, and flew back to hover over Alric. Every single move Alric made, Bunky matched.

Covey had gotten bit by the spell Alric had on the bag previously. There didn't seem to be any spell on it that I could feel now, but I was still careful as I opened it.

To find a bag full of rags.

"I told them I couldn't do this!" Alric, or whatever was pretending to be him, started shrinking and growing thin and gray. Huge, eerie, green-blue eyes took over half of its face, and the look of fear and terror looked much more at home there. His gray skin was covered by a shabby-looking coat made up of rags and pockets and he reached into pocket and pulled out a spell ball before I could move to stop him.

"Bunky! Get him!" I made a dive for the former-Alric just as Bunky dove down at him. Neither of us caught him as he slammed the spell ball on the ground and vanished.

CHAPTER THIRTEEN

"I know I'm new to the whole magic thing, but still, what just happened?" I knew for a fact that Covey had a spell breaker ball in her window, one possibly as strong as the spell Alric, the real one, had put on my house a few months ago. The disguised creature should have been exposed the minute he came inside.

Instead, the only thing that exposed him was my little chimera construct. I reached in my pocket and pulled out a pair of thin wool gloves, then called Bunky over to me. He was still buzzing around the area the stranger had been in, but came rushing over when he realized I had the gloves on.

For some reason, if I touched Bunky I ran the risk of getting knocked ass over head with a slew of images. They didn't always hit, nor did anyone else seem to be affected, but after the third time of being knocked on my butt, I never touched Bunky without gloves. However, he deserved some scratches for what he did.

"I'd say we saw an elven changeling." Far from being disturbed about having someone come into her home and pretend to be Alric, Covey seemed fascinated. She went to her spell breaker ball, and then shook her head. "He didn't even rattle it. Amazing. Or rather it didn't. Changelings don't have gender, as we know it. Fragile beings, I would have thought they wouldn't have survived the Breaking."

I kept patting Bunky. Focusing on him kept the screaming words away. "If that thing replaced Alric, where is the real one?" Or almost kept them away.

"If Covey is right and that thing was a changeling, then I'd say Alric is long gone." Harlan said. "The whole point of changelings, from a historical view, was to fool other species into taking one of them in, thus giving the elves a chance to get away with the real one. The rumor had it they usually took children. But someone must have taken Alric, then left a replacement."

Covey shook her head. "Those were unfounded myths, most likely created to scare chataling children. None of the current races, mine excluded, were advanced enough for the elves to have cared about taking them."

"But still—"

A wild scream coming from the brownie in the living room cut off Harlan's defense. Which woke up Garbage who also started screaming and running toward the brownie—like earlier, for some reason she didn't fly. The brownie had managed to free itself from its shoes which were still stuck solidly to the living room floor, but that didn't slow him down as he raced in his stocking feet for the door.

He got there before she did, then ran out into the late morning.

Garbage skidded to a halt, then turned and flew back to us. She was still a little groggy from her bout with the chocolate, but her flying was straight.

"Why didn't you fly after him?" When your legs were only a few inches high, running was not a great mode of transportation.

"Then what do with him?" The look she gave me told me the old Garbage was back in place. "He not good. Just wanted rock."

She flew over to where I'd laid down the bottles and started pulling off a cap. "They need up."

This was already one of the strangest mornings I'd ever had. I went to help Garbage with the bottles as I tried to think back over Alric's behavior. How long had that thing been in his place?

I got both bottles open while Covey and Harlan kept their academic debate going. Garbage slapped both of her friends around until they shook themselves out of their stupor.

I turned back to my other two friends. "I don't care whether changelings are purple, ten feet tall, and run the underground city to the north; we need to find out where Alric is."

"Is true, they lost high thing." Garbage nodded to Leaf and Crusty, and then shot all three of us a disgusted look. Clearly, she was *very* much back to her old self.

"Why you lose him?" Crusty's voice still had a bit of her drunken warble, like at any moment she would burst into song.

Leaf nodded slowly, and then listed to the side. "He pretty, no should be losted."

Obviously, neither one had gone through their reset or whatever sobering mechanism the faeries had. Both were still quite tipsy.

Garbage marched around the two of them like a tiny and annoyed general. Before any of us could act, she grabbed both by an arm, flew them over to Covey's teapot, and dropped them in.

I had been thinking of taking that action myself, but only when I thought I might need backup of any sort. The crisis of the moment was over. We didn't need to find out if tea had the same effect on all three faeries.

Covey had still been arguing with Harlan, but with a hawk-like skill only the really good professors had, she'd seen Garbage's trick, and felt the same way I did.

She was also faster than me.

"No!" She grabbed the teapot and dumped the tea and the faeries into her sink and was pouring water over them before I even got there.

"They no be this. Must get up." Garbage buzzed around Covey but not too close.

"Not with tea." I pulled over Covey's half-finished coffee cup and dumped it down the drain as well. Better to be safe.

They weren't hyperactive, but both Leaf and Crusty looked far more sober than they had been. Garbage nodded in approval. "We go find, they lose."

Without waiting for me to explain that we didn't lose Alric, and find out more about why she brought in the brownie, and who took the others, all three zipped out through the hole in Covey's kitchen window. Which had mysteriously become open again. Bunky buzzed to the front door for me to let him out. "Try to keep them out of trouble?" He gave what sounded to my hopeful ears a positive sounding buzz, and then vanished down the street.

"Well, that takes care of that." I turned back to the kitchen and the others. "So, the question is who took Alric, how did they take him, and when did they take him?" I pulled the rags out of the bag the fake-Alric had been carrying, but found nothing other than the relic emerald dragon stone we got from the brownie. "If I had to guess, I'd say they'd grabbed Alric at some point after he'd started carrying the duffle bag, and had it to be consistent, but didn't know, or want to replicate, what was in there. Which meant the real Alric still has the real bag and, more importantly, everything in it."

"I'd say they copied him after he left a few hours ago." Covey said as she wiggled her injured fingers at me. "That was when he took his bag back. Had they copied him the first time he left, they wouldn't have needed it."

"Do either of you know where he went?"

"He said he found where the girls and Bunky were grabbed, but that was all," Harlan said. "He only came back to see how you were."

"I know you two don't agree on what the changelings are." If we didn't know where he was grabbed, maybe we could figure out who took him. "But it is agreed that the changelings were part of the elvish community?"

Harlan opened his mouth, most likely to argue judging by the look on his face, but Covey cut him off.

"They were created by the elves long ago, but more as servants. They were similar to being a construct but more autonomous. And as you saw, they are excellent shapeshifters." She had returned to making a barricade to block the faeries, or any other odd flying creature, from her kitchen window so she missed the flapping tail from Harlan.

"So if only the elves used changelings, then another *elf* grabbed Alric. Alric, who was here as a spy for his people." I nudged through the bowl of nuts I'd pulled down earlier. "Why? Who took the faeries, and then let them go, and grabbed Alric? And how long was that replacement supposed to fool us?"

As we saw with Jovan and Glorinal elves were more prevalent in other parts of the world than here, but still uncommon. But the closest clan here was Alric's and they'd been hiding for over a thousand years. Why would they send a changeling out to replace him, when they were the ones who sent him out here in the first place?

Or they weren't the ones who grabbed him, which was worse.

CHAPTER FOURTEEN

"I think the best thing we can do today is go to where Alric had been hiding, or rather what's left of it." That was such a proactive and non-research related comment I was almost shocked it came from Covey. I must really look freaked out.

A scowl crossed her face. "I'm still unable to recall what happened to me during the hour I was missing, or why I was worried about an invasion from sahlins, but we may find answers to my mystery over there as well."

"Agreed." I looked over to where Harlan was lashing his tail again. "What is it, Harlan?"

He shook his head. "I feel like we are missing something important. Perhaps I should go look into these questions about the Spheres and see how they tie into everything...." He trickled off when I folded my arms and glared at him. Clearly, in Harlan's mind, far more interesting mysteries were afoot than who took Alric. I hoped it was simply because he felt Alric could fend for himself and not that he just wanted to get his hands on Covey's scroll on the Spheres.

"You know I won't be much help if there are hooligans about." He tried looking small and meek. Didn't work. However, he was right. He'd never been a fighter and sadly getting his butt kicked during the fight with the city guards when he and Covey had rescued

Alric and I had left him even more wary. In addition, I think getting caught up in yesterday's mishap at the mine was more than enough excitement for him for a while. Harlan wanted to know what was going on; he just wanted to find out about it from a safe pub.

"It's the middle of the day, who is going to attack you in the middle of the day?" Covey said as she stomped around her kitchen and living room. She had clearly divested herself of all of her weapons that she'd loaded up on yesterday. Either that or she had spares stashed around her house. Finally, she shook her head at Harlan. "Never mind, go research." She reached for the scroll that Alric had previously stolen, then paused. "I'm lending you this, solely so you can see if you can figure out why he took it, and what he thought it tied into. That is all. I get it right back."

Harlan's eyes remained on the scroll as she waved it around, but eventually he looked to her face. The shaky grin he gave her told me he'd only partially listened to her, but picked up on the gist of it from her expression.

"I promise." He gave himself a delicate sniff. "I also believe it would be best if I went home and bathed. I will report what I find." He tucked the scroll inside his waistcoat and left the house with a jaunty step.

"He thinks he tricked you into lending him that scroll." I said as I gathered my stuff together.

I'd been staying at Covey's while my house was under repairs, but sadly I didn't have much in the way of weapons. Besides the dagger I carried, I had a short sword I hadn't completely mastered yet and a pair of knives. I took the knives and their sheaths. A sword was like magic: if the person wielding it wasn't well trained it could do more harm than good. I knew enough about sword play to probably not hurt someone unless I intended it, but better to be safe than sorry for now.

Twenty minutes later, Covey and I skirted along the edge of the crumbling cliff face where Alric's most recent hidey-hole had been.

A good fifteen-foot-wide chunk of land still hung to this end of the cliff near where his cave had been, and it looked solid. At least I kept telling myself that. I wasn't afraid of heights. It was the whole falling to the plains below that had me worried. If there was a magic spell to make someone without wings fly, no one had mentioned it to me yet.

Tree roots stuck out at odd angles, their twisted forms giving testimony to how they felt about the entire thing. It rather reflected my life. One day you're going along fine, then all of a sudden your world gets shaken up and you're left dangling in the wind.

I guess the moral is to be grateful you're not one of the ones smashed five hundred feet below.

Covey dropped down to the ground, almost sniffing the dirt, then rose back to her feet and prowled around the tree we'd stopped in front of. Covey's people were very good hunters with an exaggeratedly talented sense of smell. She usually put that skill aside as one akin to her berserker ancestors and rarely displayed it. It spoke to how concerned she was about Alric, that she was willing to drag it out now.

"I believe whoever took the faeries waited at this tree." Covey shook her head. "No. They waited in this tree, up there." She scowled up into the leafy branches above us as if they would tell her their secrets. She stepped forward; her eyes still locked on the branches, and stepped on something. Swearing, she stepped backwards and picked up a cracked spell ball. This one was bright orange and yellow, made of something clear, but stronger than regular glass, and had the remains of a string and twig tied to it. She held it to her nose then pulled back in disgust and shoved it in my face.

An overwhelming stench of sugar, ale, and what smelled like rusted nails slapped me in the face. "Gah! What is that?" I shoved it back at her but she let it drop to the ground. Then she shattered it by pounding on it with her right foot a few times.

"They used an old faery trapper; I'm surprised anyone still knew the recipe. One whiff of that and the faeries would have been easy to grab."

I looked around. The girls would have been right around here since I told them to investigate but not go over the plains. "So whoever grabbed them did so...why exactly?"

"Probably to use them to grab Alric. Or you. But considering Garbage was insistent only he come searching for the rest of them, I'd say it was him."

"She wouldn't have set him up." I knew my little orange faery was a pain in the ass, but she wouldn't betray Alric like that.

Covey stomped around the tree some more, but shook her head as she walked. "No, she wouldn't. Nevertheless, that spell ball could have been used to plant a suggestion in her head. She thought she missed being taken, but I doubt that was the case." Covey picked up the shreds of a spell wrapper. Pre-made spells weren't that uncommon. Before my newfound magic had kicked in, I'd had to use them myself. Unfortunately, this wrapper was too shredded to see what spell it had held.

"Wait, they went through this elaborate abduction set-up, then are messy enough to leave evidence behind? Sloppy. And why would someone want to take Alric?" I didn't have either the tracking skills of Alric, or the scenting skills of Covey, but I looked around as well. It really didn't make sense that someone, or ones, would take the girls with the idea they could get Alric.

Covey shrugged. "That is a damn good question, but someone did. Most likely he'd been up to something he didn't tell us about." She made one more pass around the area. When she found nothing, she turned and headed back to town.

"Wait, so that's it? Someone took him, and we're just leaving?" I jogged to keep up, as she was moving quickly. My worry at him being gone was overlaid with the fact that Glorinal had once been able to strip Alric of his magic. What if Glorinal had taken him again?

Covey stopped and turned to face me, but kept her voice extremely low. It was a trick she was trying to teach me, you spoke on your outward breath in a whisper. "No, that's not it. But we can't find out anything more here. And we've been watched for the last five minutes."

She glanced over her shoulder quickly, and then smacked me when I made to do the same. "They are still following us, I can't see who they are, and no, don't look."

We headed to a break in the trees. The right path went back into town, the left went toward the ruins.

"At the break, you go left. I'll go right. I'll follow behind once they follow you." She didn't give me a chance to respond as she made a sharp right turn with a wave. "I'll see you later, then!"

I didn't have much of a chance to do anything else. So I went toward the ruins.

The path here was narrow and overgrown; this wasn't a common way to get to the dig sites. I went a full minute before I heard a rustling behind me.

I didn't turn at first, in case the person following me was just that incompetent, but changed my mind when the sounds grew louder.

And saw Covey wrestling Alric in the forest path.

CHAPTER FIFTEEN

"What are you doing?" I wasn't sure if I was yelling at Covey or Alric.

Covey had Alric pinned and was pulling at his hair. Considering I'd seen her fight many times, that tactic was unfamiliar to me.

"Who are you?" She punched him when he tried to squirm away.

That was another thing. I'd seen Alric fight, and this thing wearing Alric's face wasn't doing anything but trying to get away.

"Another changeling?" An army of Alrics might be handy if they could fight in a battle, but so far these seemed to look like him but not have any of his skills. "Why isn't he vanishing like the other one did?"

Covey nodded back behind her. A pack similar to the one Alric had previously been carrying lay in the bushes behind her.

"Search it. I bet you'll find the spell ball inside." Covey grunted as the fake Alric managed to get a strike in with his flailing.

I stepped around them and grabbed the bag. Yup, nothing but rags, and an unbroken spell ball. I turned back to the wrestling match. "What are we going to do with him? Or it?"

"It is going to tell us who sent it here and what it was supposed to do." Covey accented her words with a few well-placed punches, and I saw the changeling flicker between Alric and the skinny gray thing I'd see in Covey's house.

"I'm Alric! I am him!" The thing's voice was sort of Alric's, but whereas the first changeling had sounded exactly like him, this one was muted, like it was a copy of a copy. I peered down closer to see his face and it looked a bit off too. The features were more rounded than Alric's.

"Look, we saw you drop your disguise, and we already caught the other one of your kind. You might as well fess up if you don't want to meet the same fate." With any luck, it would think we killed the first one.

The thing gave one final burst of strength, which was met by a few more punches from Covey. Finally, it lay still.

"I am a changeling, yes, but I was hired to take the previous form." The thing's speech was now refined and crisp. The accent was unrecognizable. "I do not know who hired me, it was through another party. I have never been in this...city...before, and I can assure if you let me go, I will never return." Its superior attitude dropped a bit. "So you have killed my brother?"

Research may say they didn't have genders but they obviously thought they did. At least they'd adopted them to communicate relationships.

Covey remained sitting on him, but hadn't hit him again since he changed. She finally shrugged. "I don't think the other one is dead. It used its spell ball to escape."

I took the ball out of the bag and threw it down next to the changeling, but too far for it to reach. "No, you can't have this one back." I squatted down next to it. "You were wearing the face of someone I care about.

That doesn't make me happy, especially since he's gone missing. So you can either give my friend some answers, or you can see how angry I can get." I narrowed my eyes. "Did you hear what happened to the last two groups of people who tried to mess with this town?"

He shook his head, but there was a big dose of fear in those strange ice blue eyes. He knew something.

"They aren't alive anymore and suffered horribly before they died." Now granted that was a stretch, a big one. I was there, but I didn't directly kill any of them.

"You are the terror of Beccia?" If possible, he now shrunk even further into himself and was even skinnier than he was before.

I had never heard of the terror of Beccia, but I could work with it. "What do you think?" I leaned forward looking as fierce as I could. I also started to pull one of my knives out of its sheath.

"Now, you know how messy it was the last time you went after someone like this. We don't need that kind of trouble again." Covey winked; she was having fun playing with this changeling.

"I'm telling you—I don't know anything. We were hired to make it seem like this elf was still in town. Started yesterday. There were two of us in different areas."

He paused, as if trying to recall something, then shook his head when it didn't surface. "The person we're playing is gone. We stepped in to make sure that it looks like he is still here." He managed to snake one hand out from under Covey. "No, we don't know where the person has gone to. They leave us imprint, money, and instructions."

Imprint? During the start of my magic training, Alric had briefly spoken of magical imprints. Unfortunately, he hadn't gotten far beyond the basic concept. A magical image of a person was hard to capture and very difficult to work with. "So the imprint was what you copied. How do they leave it for you? He looked at me as if I was an idiot. "In a spell ball. We have two in our package: the maker and the escape."

He looked like he said something he shouldn't have. The escape? That was what the one that escaped from Covey's house used.

Covey looked like she agreed. She leaned forward a bit to grab the spell ball and the changeling took advantage of her distraction and kicked her off. Covey was on her feet immediately and after the fake Alric.

I tried to catch up, but she had much longer legs and was built to run. The best I could do was try to keep her in sight. At least until I rounded a bend and slammed right into her.

"Dang it, don't stop like that." I fought to untangle limbs and push myself away.

Covey swore and dusted herself off. "It got away."

"That wasn't my fault; you're the one who stopped in front of me. I could have caught up on my own." Doubtful, but beside the point right now.

"I know," Covey said as she peered up into the trees above us. "It went up. Damn it, we've lost it for good."

A thought hit me. That changeling hadn't been just running to get away, he seemed to be heading somewhere specifically. "Do changelings pick up anything from their targets? Like, anything they might have been rattling in their heads when the imprint was taken?" I was running off an assumption based on where Alric was when they saw him, and how the changeling appeared to have a specific destination in mind as he took off.

Covey resumed walking the way she'd been running but still looked up in the trees. "I have no proof, but I'd think they'd have to get something from them."

I nodded down the path the changeling had gone. "So, could another hiding place have been in Alric's mind when the spell was cast? Like one of the many we know he's had in the ruins?"

"I wouldn't know for certain, but I could make an educated guess, that yes, that may very well be the case. Since we thwarted this one from vanishing," She held up the spell ball in her hand, "he may be looking for anything else to help him get out of here."

Covey tilted her head, either listening or—knowing her—smelling for our friend. I was about to tell her I knew where all of Alric's known hidey-holes were when she nodded to herself and started down one of the lesser-known trails. One that wasn't near any of Alric's places. There went my theory about the changeling.

Anyone else I would have badgered until she told me where we were going. I'd learned years ago that when Covey hunted something, in a book or in a forest, to let her be. Within about fifteen feet, she lost whatever she'd been following.

Covey paused a split-second, then barged forward through some bushes. I think she stopped just to make sure I followed, as she seemed far surer than someone with no trail on the ground should be.

I'd never been this way before, but it seemed to be leading us around to the older ruins, the ones the Antiquities Museum, or rather the money behind them, had decided wasn't worth the effort to try to excavate.

The trees here were even older and more massive than the ones in the rest of the ruins, and considering the roots on the gapen trees in the main part of the ruins were often wider than me, that said something. Many of the above ground roots we climbed over were wider than five of me. And they took some serious scrambling.

"I think he's stopped, the scent is drifting here." Covey kept her voice down and I peered around to see if

anything was moving. Problem with massive trees—
their equally massive tree canopies. It felt like a
permanent twilight in here and visibility for folks like me
wasn't great.

Leaves dropped on my head. Not surprising given
where we were, but this was a lot of leaves. What was it
with these changelings and trees? I looked up, but only
caught his foot as he vanished into another tree. I
followed, but trying to climb over giant roots and still
watching the branches above wasn't easy. Then I
realized Covey wasn't behind me.

"Covey! He's getting away!" I didn't want to shout;
best way to get lots of folks coming to you when you
didn't want them was to yell that something interesting
was going on.

"Here." Years of teaching had given Covey the magic
art of raising one's voice loud enough to be heard
without actually yelling. Of course more than a single
word would have been helpful.

The branches overhead had stopped moving, so either
our changeling had moved on, or he'd heard us and was
being smart and froze in place. I recently explored the
dryad line of my family, but I think only a full-blooded
one could climb one of these beastly trees.

So much for following our lead. With a sigh, I turned
around and trekked my way back to Covey. She'd gone
a few more feet away from where I'd left her, standing
in what looked like a huge, ancient, and prickly, mass of
bushes. Or one very large one.

"How did you get in there and why in the hell would
you think I would follow?" The monster pile of
shrubbery was at least up to my chest and looked meaner
and more potentially outright aggressive the closer I got
to it. Three-inch-long thorns curved in the best way to
pierce skin, and if they didn't get you, the thousands of
tiny barbs in the branches and even on the leaves would.

I'd been digging in Beccia for fifteen years and I'd never seen a plant like this. "Another question, what the hell is this?"

Covey smiled and nodded as if we were out for tea at the café. "You noticed. Very good. There may be hope for you yet. This is a Flomixinian Rose bush. Deadly, poisonous, and some history books say carnivorous. It also died out thousands of years ago." As she spoke she swung her hand right through the middle of it. I held my breath waiting for blood and screams, but she pulled her hand up with no bloody wounds that I could see. "It's a spell placed on an ordinary crumpet bush. Just walk right through."

Alric might as well put out a sign for Covey that said, 'here's my hiding place'. Before she'd become obsessed with elves, Covey had been extremely into plants. New ones, old ones, fictional ones. Growing up in a land mostly filled with deserts, she loved plants. Normal people would take one look at the beastie before me and do what I still wanted to, run in the opposite direction. However, it was a green flag for Covey.

I started walking through the mirage. Even knowing it wasn't real still didn't stop me from cringing as I took the first step in, then almost got knocked over by a suspicious whap to the side of my head.

"We here! We help!" Garbage was the one who hit me. Leaf and Crusty had overshot and were tumbling in the air past us, both giggling and laughing like mad fiends. And both going way too fast.

I started to shout as they were aiming right for one of the giant gapen trees, but both changed course, split around the tree and crashed into a smaller one behind it.

"Is okay! We good!"

They almost flew past me again, but spun at the last minute. I ducked so instead of hitting me they slammed into the crumpet bush.

"Let me guess, the three of you found some more tea?"

"Yes. Nice people leave cups for us." Crusty answered this time. It took her three fly-bys to finally land on me.

"You stole tea from the café?"

Garbage stuck out her lower lip. "We no steal. They give. When they leave."

I didn't want to know what they did to make the people leave their tea. But I probably needed to. I would be back to my ostracized status if I couldn't let them go anywhere that might serve tea.

"Okay, what did you do?"

"Is this the time for this?" Covey had been patient for her, but she was on the hunt and wanted to keep going. "We lost the changeling, but there is definitely something hidden here. It may give us insight on Alric's disappearance."

I waved at the giggling, hyperactive blurs of color zipping around us. "I'd say I need to know what kind of trouble I'm looking at."

Garbage hadn't joined the other two as they played dodge and weave with the trees in the area. At least hitting them fifty percent of the time didn't slow them down. "We no...fine. Bunky scare them we take drink."

I rubbed my forehead. This was even worse. Now people would be afraid of poor innocent Bunky. "Where is he anyway?"

That killed Garbage's buzz, even Leaf and Crusty slowed down and looked more serious. I was terrified that someone had hurt him while he helped the girls get their fix.

"He go with Queen Mungoosey. She come by, said need talk."

Crusty flew up in front of me, a tiny frown on her face. "But she no talk at us."

That wasn't good, but not surprising. The wild faeries, led by their tiny, flying cat-faery queen, had stepped in to help save the town when the glass gargoyle, or rather the people behind it, tried to open a portal to another dimension. The problem was that the faeries had their own prophesies, and helping us wasn't on the list. The situation got worse when more of the wild faeries started hanging out with my three troublemakers and became domesticated.

There was now a big divide between the wild faeries and the local ones.

At least Bunky was okay, but I would have to try to get it through his little construct head that he didn't need to do everything the girls told him to. Telling the faeries not to use him like that would be akin to telling a boulder rolling downhill not to roll on you.

"We'll deal with that later. I don't see how you three can help us though." I turned back to Covey only to find she'd vanished. "Covey?"

Her head appeared out of nothingness, or so it looked. "He has way more disguise spells on here than I even knew existed." She nodded to the faeries who had resumed their game of tree dancing. "But we may need them." Then she ducked back behind whatever was camouflaging her.

I held my hand up and for once all three little maniacs came right to me. Only one missed this time, but that wasn't uncommon for Crusty. "I need you three to stay with us. We're looking for one of Alric's secret spots."

Garbage flew in a loop. "We know! We help. We always help him get there."

Leaf and Crusty were all smiles and nods.

"Always help him?" I should have known he'd been using them; he used the rest of us.

"Yes, yes, yes. But this one best." Leaf spun in a circle. They must not have had as much tea as Garbage did the first time; they all were slowing down a bit. "Come. We show."

All three little flying bundles of mayhem zipped over to where I'd seen Covey's head a moment ago then vanished. Followed by some very Covey-style swearing. Clearly, they hadn't sobered up enough to regain full navigation.

I stomped my way through the vicious-looking bush illusion and went through to where they'd all vanished. And almost fell over.

CHAPTER SIXTEEN

It was a cottage. But one that looked like it had been made by an army of gnome and dwarven craftsmen with a clan of elves doing the designs. It wasn't big; it might have a full second story, otherwise a loft. A bit smaller than my house, but the walls were carved in graceful designs looking like an exotic garden. The windows were more works of art filled with color than a way to see out, or in, in this case. The intricately carved door would have launched a huge bidding war for any of the rich folks up on The Hill.

However, it didn't have anything that remotely looked like a handle.

"How did he get this here?" Covey stood extremely close to the cottage, but I noticed she wasn't touching anything. "Oh, and don't touch it. He's got an alarm spell on it." She held up her left hand. Faint smudge marks showed that she hadn't moved fast enough. Considering how quickly she could move, I would have been fried. She didn't have to tell me twice not to touch anything.

"See? Need us." Crusty was the first to fly up to the top spire on the roof, then the other two followed. They took up positions hanging on the spire in a circle, then all started to sing.

Thank goodness it was a short song, and no minkies were involved. Faery singing had been known to start riots and minkies, some sort of strange creatures known only to the girls, were usually in the worst songs they had.

The cottage shimmered as the protection spell dropped and the door slowly opened. Covey started to move forward, then stopped and waved at the faeries, "Is there anything else he does before he goes in?"

Garbage let go of the spire first, then all three drifted down to us. Their tea buzz was definitely short lived. "He give us ale."

Mercenary little things. "Girls, we don't have any and we need to get in there."

Garbage shrugged. "Is okay, is inside." She flew in with Leaf and Crusty right behind her. Covey shrugged and followed.

The inside was even more elaborate and beautiful than the outside. The furniture was simple, like a cottage in the woods should be. But it was made so it seamlessly flowed into the walls as if the entire building, furniture and all, had sprung from a single seed. I shook my head. "This doesn't feel like Alric at all." I hadn't necessarily meant to say that out loud, but there it was. This was possibly the most non-Alric place I could think of. Yes, as we recently found out, Alric was actually an elven high lord, one of the elite ruling class of the elves.

However, he was also a thief—and that fit his personality much better. I fought down the pang of fear that hit when I remembered he was still missing. That thief side was resilient. I just had to concentrate on that. "Girls? Are you sure this is where he lives?" They had immediately headed for the back of the cottage behind a tall wooden screen with an elaborate scene of stylized elk hunters. The riders were all elves, but their clothing and headwear designs weren't familiar.

Crusty flew out from behind the screen and nodded. "Yes. Him here. We help him build." Before I could ask anything else, she ducked behind it. Judging from the clinking sounds I gathered it was a kitchen. I looked back but Covey hadn't moved much past the doorway and appeared to be trying to memorize the designs on the frame. She also muttered to herself but I knew better than to ask her what she was saying. With a shrug, I followed the girls behind the screen.

To say this was a kitchen would be to call the entire place a hovel. It was tiny, but beautiful and graceful. The girls were taking turns trying to pull the cap off a bottle of ale, but they were clearly having problems.

I was still trying to take everything in, but I went over and opened their ale. They quickly focused on that as I studied the place. Alric had been living in a hovel in the poor part of town when I started dealing with him months ago. Since then he mostly stayed at my place, Harlan's place, or in a flophouse.

All that time, he had this place? And he never took me here? I shoved that hurt aside. I'd deal with it when we got him back.

I reached over and took the now half-empty bottle away from the girls. Three pairs of faery eyes looked at me with extreme annoyance. Clearly, their idea of helping was getting us inside, and them getting some more ale.

"I'll give it back after you answer some questions." Garbage looked ready to argue, but I held the bottle up to my mouth as if to drink it. Something I'd never do. They often dove into their bottles.

Garbage backed off and sat down on the black countertop. Damn thing even had gold veins, probably real ones, running through it.

"What." Leaf and Crusty flew down next to her, but all three kept a close eye on the bottle in my hand. Never mind that I was sure there were probably more lurking around this kitchen of the gods.

"How long has Alric had this place?" I waved them off as Crusty started to give an answer. "In big people time, not your time." She frowned then stayed silent.

"He always have this." Garbage narrowed her eyes like she thought I was asking a trick question just to get their ale. "He brought it, but we open it."

That was about the end of their information, so I handed them back their bottle and went back out to the front room. Covey had moved past the doorway but was still examining every part like a rare and treasured artifact.

"Did you hear that? Do you have the slightest idea what they meant?"

Covey looked up from an amazing plant carved of the sheerest piece of wood. "Yes and not really. Well, maybe. I'm not sure." She drifted back to studying the plant.

"Make a guess?" I slid down into the small but cushiony sofa. I was beginning to think the best part of this day had been Garbage slapping me awake.

"I think this is a traveling house." Covey said. "They were specially designed houses which elven nobility could carry around in a pack as they traveled. In the height of the elvish empire, their people traveled quite extensively, but they had begun having problems that kept them closer to home a few hundred years before the Breaking. I now have a feeling it was the rakasa starting to hunt the elves, but we hadn't discovered stories of them yet."

She wandered as she spoke, touching everything in the room with a light hand and a look bordering on awe. "Who is Alric that his people gave him one of these?" She said it more to herself than to me, but the place wasn't big enough for me not to have heard her.

"Um, wouldn't a high lord have access to something like this? I mean it's not like they've done any traveling in the last thousand years except for him, there can't be a big call for them." Unless he'd been lying about that as well. I was worried about what may have happened to him, but part of me was also hurt and angry at more duplicity. How could I care about someone I didn't even really know?

"Yes, yes." She waved her hands at the walls. "But this is an artifact. If they still doubted how this world would receive their kind, they probably would have been wary of sending this with him."

I lifted up a cloth strewn across the sofa. Made of the lightest silk, yet just holding it warmed my hands. "Then he probably stole it." That was one thing I did know about him, he was a thief and a damn good one.

None of this was doing anything to help find him though. The place was immaculate, so there was no way to tell the last time he'd been here. There was nothing personal in it, so there was no insight that way.

A crashing sound came from the small kitchen. A chorus of "we okay!" followed the sound. As long as they didn't start singing I was fine to leave the faeries alone. Clearly Alric wasn't worried about them destroying the place if they'd been the ones who helped him get in.

Even when he wasn't around, Alric could manage to give me a headache.

"There still could be clues to him and his people here. We haven't even—"

I had been looking at an ancient map inlaid on a small table as Covey spoke, so I didn't see what made her cut off until I looked up.

To find a sword held an inch under Covey's chin. The wielder was a tall, slender woman of unimaginable grace and beauty.

And sharply pointed elven ears peering out through bright red hair.

CHAPTER SEVENTEEN

"I know beings like you could not have mastered a ghilfhaln house. Tell me where the true owner is and maybe I'll let you live." Her voice was cultured and eloquent, and I was happy to notice that her accent did not sound like it came from the south. The last thing we needed here was another killer elf. I was also perversely happy that she didn't seem to know who owned this house. If Alric had been cheating on me with a beautiful elf girl, I would kill him myself.

Covey barely breathed, but I saw her eyes narrow. This wouldn't end well. Most likely for myself and this tiny cottage. I knew Covey could fight and I was betting the elf lady could also. She looked very at ease with her long curved sword.

"Look, we don't want to damage this, whatever you just called it, house. So why don't you put down the sword, and we can all talk." I kept my voice low and soothing.

"I have heard of the tricks of you outsiders; you have taken things from my people for the last time. Now where is the owner—" She'd turned to me while she was talking, which gave Covey the chance she was looking for. Honestly, Covey would have attacked with or without an opportunity.

But she did take advantage of the one she had. In a fluid movement, that no one outside of her race could do, Covey shoved the elf woman's arm with the sword away, and at the same time she pulled the woman forward. Her blow caused the elf to lose her grip on her sword, and buckle to one knee. However, when she came up, she came up fighting.

"How dare you strike one of the chosen warriors? I will smite you into dust! You will never see the light of day again!" Even with her extremely cultured accent, the threat was somewhat of cheesy.

Covey tussled with her a bit more, steering clear of any furniture. After a minute Covey disarmed the elf again—this time a knife she'd had on her thigh—and hit her on the back of the head with the pommel. Hard.

A pair of lovely and quickly crossing eyes looked at me in surprise, and then the elf crumbled to the floor.

"Youth." Covey dusted her hands off, and then patted down the elf woman for any more weapons. Three more knives were stashed on her. None of the weapons looked well used.

I peered down at her. Yes, in relaxation, her face did look young, but then I knew for a fact that Alric was far older than he looked. And Jovan had been possibly thousands of years old but looked to be in his early fifties. This girl before us could still be hundreds of years old.

"If you'll note the age and lack of use of her weapons, even though trained, her moves were predictable, and the arrogance, while apparently common in elves, is also one found in university students of all races."

Apparently, my thoughts had been visible or Covey felt the need to go on a mini lecture. "Don't you think we should tie her up or something? We need to find out which clan she's from, and I don't want you to keep fighting her while we try to talk."

Covey shrugged, then rustled around until she found some rope and tied the woman's hands behind her back. She also pulled her up on the sofa.

I wanted to get some reinforcements before she woke up. If this woman was from Alric's clan, or at least any clan who hadn't had outside contact like she sounded, she might be as disturbed by the faeries as Alric first was.

"Girls? Can you come in here?"

"No?" It was Leaf who spoke, and she sounded like she was trying the answer on for size.

"Not the right answer. Let me rephrase it. We need you to come out here now." A loud clink filled in for the answer, then some faery swearing and more clinking.

"Stuck now." That was Garbage and she was very put out about something.

I walked around the screen and almost stepped on them. Crusty was in a badly closed ale bottle that was being rolled by the other two and leaking slightly. The leaking caused all three of them distress, and the bottle was now stuck against the screen.

I took a breath. Why couldn't I have had cats instead of faeries? "Why are you two rolling her?"

Garbage flew up to my eye level. "She no come out. You say come now. We being good." The last word sounded like she wasn't sure quite how to say it. I knew she didn't know how to be it, so the entire concept might be messing her up.

I didn't even try to figure out what she meant, so I picked up the bottle and shook it until Crusty looked at me. Her face was bloated and huge. A closer look revealed it was just her mouth. Like she was holding a giant mouthful of something and now her head was too big for the neck of the bottle.

"What is wrong with her?"

Leaf flew up to eye level and joined Garbage. "Don't know. Is stuck." She patted the side of the bottle sadly. "Will be there forever."

I had to think the combination of hyperactive tea and whatever ale did to their brains was killing off brain cells. All three looked at me sadly. I had a feeling that at least on Garbage's end it was half for her friend and half for the fact she now couldn't get in the bottle.

I tapped on the glass. "Crusty? Sweetie? Spit the ale out."

She looked at me, and then went cross-eyed as she tried to look at her own mouth. Then cautiously opened it. She tried to stop it as it came out and managed to swallow some of it.

I pulled off the stopper and she squished out. The faeries fit in the bottle part, but it was only because they were squishy that they could get in and out through the narrow bottleneck.

"You saved her!" All three flew around me in an almost terrifying show of love.

Actually, spitting out ale would be foreign to most of the regulars down at The Shimmering Dewdrop, so I guess I shouldn't be surprised.

"Okay, now that that is done." I waved off the very soggy Crusty who was trying to hug my hair. "I need you three to sit across from our new friend there and look fierce."

"Not fierce, no sticks," Garbage said.

"No feathers," Leaf added.

Crusty looked at us and gave a huge belch.

"You don't need to go to war on her, just watch her."

Garbage looked annoyed—she was quite fond of being able to poke her war sticks at people, and clearly had been hoping I would send them home to get them. Then she buzzed up to eye level again. "It okay, I give her the look."

I had no idea where she'd learned it, but Garbage contorted her face so that one eye was extremely narrow and the other huge and menacing. It looked like she was insane rather than scary, but as long as she was happy with it I wouldn't say anything.

"You go right ahead." I waved them over to where the elf was, and then nodded to Covey to come outside.

"We need to find out if she knows anything about Alric. Maybe he was taken by another elf." I refrained from adding, "again", but it hung there anyway.

"Not all elves know each other, and not all other elves are bad." A bow and arrow sat on a stump across from the doorway. Covey picked up what had to be the elf's longbow, then handed it to me. A lot of very small runes were etched into the wood. "This indicates a clan probably further to the north, far to the north. She's not from the south where Glorinal and Jovan came from."

I wanted to argue, after all a bow wasn't a lot to go on. However, I couldn't think of a good reason why, if our unconscious friend was part of kidnapping Alric, she would come wandering through the woods and accost us. She seemed too arrogant to be doing anything as lowbrow as kidnapping. I handed the bow back to Covey and went back into the cottage.

Our guest hadn't regained consciousness yet, or if she had, she was playing to see if she could gather information about us. Covey laid the bow and quiver next to the sword and knives, and then sat down.

The faeries were still watching the elf, but they were clearly losing interest. Garbage still had her 'face' on, but it was slipping from looking completely insane to only slightly demented.

One way to find out if our friend was faking it or not. I motioned for Garbage to come closer to me, and of course, the other two followed. That was fine; three were more disturbing than one. "When I wave you forward, I want the three of you to fly over to her and start jumping on her. Preferably where she can see you." I spoke in a whisper so low that I didn't even think sharp elven ears could pick it up. Faery ears were sharper.

All three nodded, and of course completely ignored my instructions. They immediately flew over and started bouncing on her legs. The first bounce or two, she held tight. I could see her twitching, so I was right in my guess of her being awake.

Then she slid open an eye, probably to see what new and horrific torture we were using upon her.

Her scream could have awoken the dead.

She kicked her feet to try to get the faeries off of her legs. But Covey had tied her very well and she couldn't free her arms. I thought flinging herself on the floor and trying to roll away from them was a unique, but odd, means of escape.

"Get them away! Demonflyers! Let me free so I can fight them before they take all of our souls!"

Garbage and Leaf pulled back at that outburst and hovered in the air looking at me. Crusty kept running the woman's side like a logrolling contest.

"It's on me! Remove yourself, you spawn of the abyss!" She demonstrated the rumor about elves being agile. But her rolling on the floor trying to escape the tiny blue faery running on her was anything but graceful.

"Okay, Crusty, I think she's learned. You can let her up." I managed to make it sound like her running the elf woman all over the small house was my idea. Crusty looked disappointed. Clearly, this would have been a new favorite game for her, but she flew up and joined the other two standing on the small table. "There, I saved you. Now do you think you can tell us more about why you're here and who you are?"

Covey walked over and lifted the elf to her feet, then walked her back over to the sofa. The woman's naturally huge eyes practically took over her face as she kept them on the three faeries the entire time. Nevertheless, she did give a small nod.

I'd been hoping for a bit of a freak out. I'd thought of them as spawns of the abyss, but usually only in my head when they'd been particularly a pain in the ass. Even back in the day when most of the citizens of Beccia didn't like them, no one ever called them that.

"What's a demonflyer?" I reached over to rub the faeries' backs in gratitude but also to establish who was behind these terrifying little beings.

"Those things. You are working with them, how can you be unaware of what they are? They fly out at night and suck the souls out of the innocent." She adjusted her arms. We'd have to make sure she hadn't loosened anything while rolling around.

"And they wear flower petal caps and overalls while they do this?" I held up Leaf in the palm of my hand. The elf pulled back, but then she looked closer. Leaf smiled and bowed.

"No be nice! We fierce!" Garbage flew up to where I was holding Leaf and glared at the woman. Unfortunately, Crusty decided she wanted to be on my hand as well and just as Garbage was leaning forward to cow her prey with 'the look' Crusty flew right into her and all three tumbled down.

The elf woman laughed. So much for striking fear in her. Even as she laughed though, she kept a wary eye on the three flying around until they were back to their table.

"Maybe they aren't demonflyers, tales from my childhood, but they are still unnatural." She moved her arms behind her back more.

Covey went over and tightened her rope. Sure enough it had come loose in the rolling.

The woman sighed. She'd been stalling until she could free herself. "My name is Orenda. I am from the clan Tjuliate. I have come to find those who stole our sacred relic, the symbol of our survival and longevity."

I thought about what relics kept meaning around here and I wasn't sure I wanted to know the answer. "What was this relic? I am an archeologist. Perhaps I have seen it."

Orenda shook her head. "You would not have found it in the ground, nor with mortal toys. It is an artifact of true power and beauty. The hgythh, the emerald dragon."

I really hated being right.

CHAPTER EIGHTEEN

Covey stepped forward at this, clearly having decided she had observed as much as she could from Orenda, and most likely felt I would screw up our questioning.

"Tell me about the artifact. Has it always been with your people? Did they take it during the Breaking?"

Orenda's eyes flew wide again and she looked quickly back and forth between us. "You are not clan; you are both of the younger races, and how is it you know of the Breaking?"

She was definitely not from Alric's clan. Nor, thank goodness, from wherever the tribe Glorinal and Jovan came from. I was beginning to wonder how we thought the elves had died out, since it seemed there were pockets of them all over the place.

"Let's leave it at I'm a university professor and she's an archeologist specializing in your people. We know," Covey said. I gathered we weren't going to point out that we hadn't known about the Breaking until a murdering elven member of the Dark came to town. Yeah, probably better not to mention that.

I went to sit a bit further away. Alric's odd little hideaway didn't have a lot of seating, but a stool grew out of the wall near the door. Orenda looked toward me; maybe she thought I was nicer or she wanted to make sure the keeper of the demonflyers was in sight at all times.

"Perhaps when you have forgiven me for my assumptions and attack upon your person, you can explain where the knowledge came from." Orenda tilted her head in a well-practiced show of apology.

Covey shrugged. She wasn't the type to care for formalities, what she cared about was information. She hadn't been interested at first when Alric brought up the emerald dragon, but the sheer repetition of it right now was clearly piquing her interest. "The dragon?" The tone was crossing into annoyed professor now.

"I am not one of our religious leaders, but I can tell you the hgythh was rescued from its place in the temple when the Breaking came. It was kept as a sign that we could reclaim our lives as we had saved ourselves from the cult that tried to destroy us."

Covey sat back in her chair and flexed her fingers. It was a predatory move, but for her it was mostly because she was thinking.

Orenda was watching her fingers almost as closely as she'd been watching the faeries. She may have called both of us younger races, but she clearly recognized a trellian.

"Done now?" Garbage and the other two were sitting on the edge of the table swinging their legs. Bored faeries were almost more dangerous than drunken ones and I didn't know how much more Orenda's ill ease about them would help us.

"Fine, go bug Harlan. See if he's found anything about Alric."

All three were out the door before my words ended.

Orenda narrowed her eyes. "That is an elvish name. Have you resorted to calling yourselves by your superiors' names?"

Oh, she was going to be fun. Jovan had that same attitude, along with wanting to destroy the world. However, even he hadn't been quite as annoying as she was.

"Our superiors?" Covey leaned forward now, her eyes narrowing. "My people recall who freed the elves from the sahlins. We know what our *superiors* did by leading them to us."

That was news to me. Alric had mentioned it, but I'd no idea that Covey's people had passed the history along. I guess when some all-powerful magic users try to dump a bunch of murdering maniacs in the middle of your home desert, it stuck with a culture.

Orenda deflated a little bit. Covey was right, she was young. And sheltered.

"You know your history well; my people have not forgotten the aid brought to them by the lesser races."

"I'd stop using that lesser races bit unless you want to see how well I am still in touch with my berserker ancestors."

I couldn't see Covey's face from where I sat, but seeing Orenda's was enough. I knew there was no way Covey would allow herself to slip into that berserker status for someone like Orenda, but the elf didn't know that.

"So, then is Alric now a common name among your people?" She might be young, but she was trained somewhat in diplomacy. However, I still had questions about a people who would send someone like this out into the strange world.

Alric, I could understand. He was trained to be sneaky and deadly. I didn't doubt Orenda could fight in a controlled environment, but it was clear from her reactions that her people had been as sheltered as Alric's over the centuries.

"Alric is an elf, I'm thinking from a different clan." I told myself I'd imagined her eyes lighting up at that. He was more or less *my* elf from another clan. I was not going to go into that with tall, elven, and beautiful.

I waved my hand as she started to ask questions. "Look, save all of that for later. Right now, why did you come here to find the relic?"

"Fair enough, I have treated you both poorly." She gave an extremely graceful bow especially considering we still had her tied up. "Our dragon guardian, the relic, was stolen some time ago. We cannot function properly without it." She pulled herself up proudly. "I took it upon myself to bring back our guardian totem."

Covey got up with a sigh, and motioned for Orenda to turn so she could untie the rope. "So, you decided that regardless of what your people were doing you would make a name for yourself by finding the emerald dragon." She shook her head.

"Now what do we do with her?" I watched as Orenda rubbed her wrists. Most likely the ones who stole the dragon were the actual remnants of the original cult behind it, the rakasa. Or a new breed of devotee. Either way, leaving her to run around looking for them wasn't a good idea.

Covey's look said she'd reached the same conclusion. "We let her go." Orenda jumped up to grab her weapons, but Covey pushed her back onto the sofa. "But, I'll warn you that someone has been leaving emerald dragon stamps all over Beccia the last two days. In stone. I'd advise you to be careful." She gave a thin-lipped smile.

Orenda's face had been full of enthusiasm at the freedom, but it crashed when she heard about the markings. But, she finally nodded and started picking up her things.

Orenda had finished stowing all of her weapons and was putting the bow and quiver back over her shoulder when the ground slammed into itself. It was a single sharp jolt and it knocked all of us to the ground.

"They found me!" Orenda screamed.

I pulled myself off the ground, braced my legs against any other shakes, and looked out the open door. Not a soul in sight.

"Nope, unless whoever is looking for you is coming up from underground, no one has found you." A fair amount of tree debris was drifting down, but this explosion hadn't been close enough to knock down any trees.

Orenda didn't look like she believed me and stayed on all fours. There was no way in hell her people would have let someone like this out into the wild world. Most likely the 'they' she was worried about finding her were the search party out trying to bring her home.

I motioned to Orenda. "Are we really just going to leave her to wander around?"

Covey started to shrug, and then smiled. "Harlan."

That was perfect. Harlan had always wanted to meet a female elf. He could keep an eye on her, and we'd get both of them out of the way.

"Are you certain that wasn't caused by *them*?" Orenda was settling down but she still looked a little white around the eyes.

I had a feeling I didn't want to know what she was talking about, but being rude to her probably wasn't the best idea. We may need her help later on. "Who is them?"

"The Ancients, the ones who almost destroyed the world." She blushed. "I know they are probably tales told to frighten children, but growing up we were told that a race of giants vanished long before we came north, thousands of years before the Breaking. They were dangerous and brutal and held such magic powers that not even the mightiest mage of elven lore could match.

Our elders told us that if we were bad, or tried to go beyond the clan boundaries, they would come back for us." She waved one long hand in the air. "But clearly there were never any such beings."

Covey and I shared a look, which Orenda caught.

"They are real?" Her hand shook as she pointed out the doorway. "And that ground shaking was them moving around?"

I gave her some credit. If I thought giant, all-powerful beings were coming out of childhood stories to smite me down, I probably would have run away screaming.

"There is evidence of a race of beings that we call the Ancients." Covey spoke slowly, as if weighing how much to say. "But we've not seen anything that indicates they were giants, or that they attacked anyone. They did vanish long before your people appeared to have arrived in the area however."

"But our elders seem so sure of the stories. They aren't just tales for children."

Something Alric had once said about those who survived the Breaking came back to me.

"How old are your elders?" Alric had said most of the eldest were either lost in the Breaking or didn't survive long once they had all scattered. The wounds they received in the Breaking destroyed the oldest and the most powerful. I'd assumed that the other clans, if there were any, would have been in the same situation.

"Very old, at least five hundred years."

Which would mean all of their elders were lost, since the Breaking was over a thousand years ago. Something had been shortening the lifespans of those who survived the Breaking if all of them were gone within five hundred years. No time to deal with confused history at this point. Harlan could work with her.

"We have a friend who will be more than happy to help you with this. He might even be able to help you find the emerald dragon. How long ago did it get stolen?" Covey said but her focus was clearly on getting Orenda dropped off as soon as possible.

"A few years ago. Someone tunneled under our defenses to get into our city. They took the artifact, killed many of our people, then vanished." The scowl on her face was more than a reaction to the crime. "Our leaders said that it was other elves that took it. But that is ridiculous. We are all one people."

I knew a few elves that would have fit the bill. We had no idea how long Glorinal and Jovan had been off doing their evil deeds before they came to Beccia. They, and perhaps more of the Dark, could have attacked her clan. However, we were back to me not wanting to discuss all of this now. We needed to find out what exploded this time, and drop off our elvish princess with Harlan and get back to tracking down who took Alric.

I started herding Orenda toward the door. "You're probably right. Now let's go find someone who will help you. Covey and I have to go solve some problems of our own right now."

We all went out of the small cottage, but I wasn't sure how to shut the door. Alric's spells of hiding should still hold, even if he wasn't in the area. But we couldn't help if someone stumbled upon it and saw an open doorway.

When the girls had sung the door had vanished, an issue I hadn't worried about until now.

"Oh, however did you get it open?" Orenda muttered a few words under her breath, and then waved her right hand in an elaborate arc, and the door came back. The house also seemed to fade a bit. If you got this far, and knew it was there, you could see it. Otherwise, you wouldn't notice it.

"I do hope you can figure out how to get back in. It wouldn't be proper if I compromised another elf's home." Now that her bouts of fear were gone, Orenda was back to her superior attitude.

Judging by the way Covey was flexing and un-flexing her hands as she led the way out of the ruins, I had a feeling the sooner we dumped off our elf friend the better.

CHAPTER NINETEEN

Covey stayed out in front a bit, more to get away from Orenda than to act as point for anything. We were out of the ruins and headed into town when Covey finally dropped back. "We still need to find that second changeling again." She'd kept her voice low, but since Orenda was between us, she couldn't miss it.

Her laughter was not what I'd expected. It was far throatier than I would have given her credit for. "You are kidding now. Changelings? Those never even made proper tales to scare children with."

Again, our faces gave us away.

"You simply cannot be serious. Creatures that can change what they look like on a whim? No one has that kind of magic anymore. And I doubt they ever did. Our forefathers would never let such things be created." The superior tone and attitude was something that had to have taken a few hundred years to perfect. Her people, wherever they were, had the brainwashing down to an art.

"Orenda meet reality, reality meet Orenda." I was hoping she and Harlan took a shine to each other, because she was really bugging me. But her reaction to beings who could change their appearance did make me wonder about her clan's magical abilities. Alric could and would glamour himself with ease.

"Not going to explain it here." Covey looked around, but there was still no one at this end of the town close enough to hear us. "But, yes, they exist."

"But—"

"No." Covey cut her off, then turned and marched toward Harlan's new home.

His wives still hadn't let him back into their family home, so he was living in an upscale flat closer to the center of town. From the way he was settling in, it might be a permanent housing change. He still visited his wives from time to time, and they him. However, they'd grown tired of his increasingly eccentric ways and if they didn't have to live with him it was better for everyone.

We were on the edge of the more populated area of town, when I pulled both Covey and Orenda back. I pointed to Orenda's very noticeable ears. "Can you let your hair down enough to cover those?" Even Alric had kept his hair long and loose to help folks forget what he was, and just about everyone in Beccia knew what he was. A strange elf, even a beautiful lady elf with huge doe eyes, wouldn't be well received in town. Not until the attacks from Jovan and Glorinal faded a bit.

"What is wrong with my ears? They show I am of the highest family in my clan, someone to be respected and honored." Orenda pulled back away from me as if I was going to rip off her ears here on the street.

I wouldn't go after her ears or her hair, but she backed right into Covey and her nice knife. With a single swift movement, Covey sliced the leather cord holding back Orenda's hair.

Orenda let out a meep-like squeak and grabbed the cord as it fell. Her red hair tumbled around her face making her look even younger than she already did. "Why did you do that?"

We were starting to see more people, and in minutes we'd be going down the pub lane. I held on to her arm and stopped her from trying to pull her hair back without a cord or ribbon. "Quickly. Until recently, the people of this town thought the elves were all dead or vanished. This city is built upon the ruins of your people. We found a few elves. One, Alric, we think is on our side." I ignored Covey's raised eyebrow at that. "But the other two were brutal murderers. One a member of the Dark, another, an elder from before the Breaking who had helped the Dark in the end. They hurt a lot of people in this town and killed dozens, so I wouldn't go around advertising you're a pure-blooded elf around here."

Orenda was duskier than Alric, but her skin faded to the color of milk when she heard the word 'dark'. Her people may have a messed-up history, but some things got preserved.

She nodded once, pulled down her hair until it practically covered her face, and seemed to hunch down into herself.

She stayed silent through the rest of our trip. Covey skirted the pub lane, but I liked to think it was because it was faster to cut through side streets than any fear on her side that I would wander into The Shimmering Dewdrop.

Harlan was leaving his flat as we approached. He had moved up in his abode choice; the last time he'd picked his own place it had been a falling-down wreck on the poor side of town. This neighborhood made me feel very outclassed.

Orenda started relaxing the further we got into the nicer side. Most of Beccia would be a rude shock for our elf.

"Hello, ladies." Harlan gave a short bow that was strictly because of Orenda, and that was without even knowing she was an elf. He was always looking for new ladies to charm. "I was about to run some errands, see what exploded this time, that sort of thing...hello?"

As he spoke, I reached up and pulled back Orenda's hair.

Harlan grabbed her hands in his and shook them like an elected official on voting day. "My dear, a real live elf woman. Such a nice change from those men, not that they weren't lovely." He scowled as who he was talking about caught up in his head. "Well Alric isn't bad." He shook his head. "But you, oh, you must come inside and tell me your story. I'm Harlan by the way."

Orenda was looking overwhelmed and I wondered if her people had any history that included chatalings.

"She's Orenda, not from Alric's *or the others* clan, and new to the area." I looked up at Harlan's flat. I knew he had multiple extra rooms. "And she needs a place to stay."

"I couldn't possibly." Orenda's voice came back but she was still watching Harlan shaking her hands.

"Of course you can. Where else would you go? Back into the ruins? I can assure you, you wouldn't find them a good place to sleep." Covey jumped in, telling me she felt we'd dawdled enough.

Harlan had already started turning Orenda around and leading her toward his front door. "I can brew some tea and we can have the biscuits my wives delivered, and you can tell me all about you and your clan."

The tea and biscuits might have started her moving, but the chance to talk about herself got Orenda's feet running for the door.

Covey didn't even wait for them to get to the door, before she swung me around and started back down the street.

"What are you so impatient about?" Tea and biscuits sounded lovely about now. Too bad I hadn't thought of raiding Alric's little house for food.

Covey was still pulling my arm, and considering her legs were about six inches longer than mine were, it was fast enough to make me run to keep up. "I saw him."

"Who him?"

"Alric. However, I think it's the second changeling again. Just down that street, came around the corner, saw you and me, then took off." Covey was on the prowl; her head went down a little bit and every few dozen feet she'd slow down.

I followed behind, but my thought was on the last quake. And Alric. I didn't think the two were really connected, but both were starting to freak me out. I completely agreed with Covey on getting rid of Orenda, but we needed to get back out in the ruins and find out what was going on.

There wasn't much I could do about finding out about the most recent quake if I wanted to keep up with Covey. She was already a few feet ahead of me. My magic wasn't much but she might need it if this changeling gave her a bad time.

Covey had darted around a corner, and I did as well, granted, still a few feet behind her. And right into an unconscious Covey with Alric standing over her with a large stick.

"Alric?" It was safer to let the changeling think I was fooled. "Are you okay?"

The changeling spun to me and lowered his stick. The relief on his/its face was a nice touch. "This is a changeling. I don't know where the real one is."

I sighed. Yup. It was a changeling. There was a tinge of fear in the voice. The changeling had the same bag. I wondered what the real Alric had in the damn thing, and if I'd ever see him again to find out. I shoved that thought back into some dark corner. It took a few tries. Now that my mind had grabbed a hold of Glorinal potentially being alive and roaming free, and with Alric now missing, it was coming up with horrific scenarios faster than I could squash them. I wouldn't be able to do anything if I just crawled into a corner weeping.

Covey was down, at least for now. However, I doubted I could keep the changeling here long enough to wait for her to wake up. I didn't want to seriously hurt it, not until we got more information out of it. But I needed to get it away from Covey.

I dropped my head and let out a long slow breath. Hopefully if I calmed my breathing down enough, I wouldn't have my head explode from fire ants when I tried this spell. Or so Covey kept insisting. She'd become an advocate of meditating recently, even if she herself didn't use it much. I think she'd spent too much time with those nuns during her recovery after the battle for the glass gargoyle.

On my final exhale, I pulled in the power, said the spell words, and reached out for the changeling to come away from Covey.

Problem with spending one's entire life as a magic sink and suddenly getting powers? Very little control of those powers. The spell I used wasn't, or rather shouldn't have been, strong enough to do anything except move the changeling a few feet away. Even that was stretching it, as it was a cantrip used for small objects.

Instead, I cast the spell, and then backed up frantically as the changeling and his bag, slammed into me.

CHAPTER TWENTY

It was more than a little disturbing having what looked, sounded, and felt like Alric squirming to get off me.

I got both my legs under him and kicked up as hard as I could. It worked, sort of. I got him free of me, unfortunately the changeling landed right on Covey.

The good thing was, the impact was enough to wake her up, and she came up fighting. The writhing changeling was tied up with an abandoned clothesline in no time.

We'd tried one route of questioning earlier, now for another tactic. We'd left this one's spell ball in Alric's secret cottage, but now I wished we had it for negotiation.

"Tell me who hired you."

The changeling tried looking away but Covey held him still.

"You know what? I don't like you not answering. I also don't like you wearing Alric's form. So change out of it now, or I destroy your spell bubble. Yes, we still have it, and I can destroy it as easily as I brought you to me." Total lie, but hanging around Alric had a benefit— I was getting better at lying.

The changeling panicked something I decided did not work well with Alric's features. It slowly nodded and changed into one of the small shimmery gray forms I'd seen in Covey's house. I was glad Orenda wasn't around. She seemed like a screamer, and we didn't need folks coming back here.

"Quickly tell me who hired you." I kneeled down to get closer to him. "Or I will crush your escape ball." I held my hand in the air as if holding an invisible ball.

Covey didn't say anything, but the small nod she gave me encouraged me.

"You have less than a minute, then that spell bubble is gone." Most of my life, I'd sat back and let other folks be the strong and aggressive ones. Between all the changes I'd gone through physically, as well as the fact that I was getting tired of these people messing around with my life, I was no longer waiting for others.

The changeling looked at me, then at my hand. Distress was clear on his face, but what was also clear was a set to his jaw.

"What do you think, Covey? Can I destroy it in one spell?" This might be better than actually having it; I wouldn't have wanted to destroy the spell ball. Not yet anyway.

Bunky gave a warbling cry as he came through a gap in the fence and flew toward us. He wasn't doing goat impersonations this time, but had clearly been hanging out with some of the songbirds deep in the ruins.

The changeling almost jumped out of his skin. Actually he did jump out, if you call flashing through a dozen different faces, most of them elven but a few distinctively not in about thirty seconds, jumping out of your skin.

"Keep the construct away." The changeling tried to scramble away from Bunky, who was still buzzing around overhead, completely unaware of the effect he was having on the changeling. "I tell you what I know. I will!"

Good to know, elves feared faeries, and changelings feared constructs.

Covey was practically sitting on the changeling to keep him from slithering away, but she seemed as interested in his answer as I was. Predators. Always looking for weaknesses.

"Unclean. Unclean." The changeling was frothing at the mouth now and contorting himself to stay as far from Bunky as he could. He really didn't like constructs.

"Now, who hired you and why?" I waved Bunky a little bit closer. The changeling started to shake in time with Bunky's buzzing.

"I can't...ai! Keep it away from me!"

Bunky was a quick study and had caught on to the game of scare the changeling. He flew forward with a dangerous sounding buzz and hovered right over my shoulder.

"They wore masks. Small."

I tilted my head toward Covey to see if that sounded like anything to her. She shrugged.

"They wore small masks? What did they look like? Where did you meet them?" I had a feeling we weren't going to get a wealth of information out of this thing, but I had to try.

"No. Small men. In masks. Hire us. For someone else. Don't know who else."

Covey's brow went up at that one. We were beginning to see more and more evidence of a bunch of small men. Whether they were the rakasa, the brownies, or something else still remained to be seen. Nevertheless, anything that popped up more than twice wasn't a coincidence.

"So it wasn't the elves? I thought your people lived with the elves?" I hadn't even known of changelings until recently, but Covey and Harlan said they lived with the elves.

The changeling started twitching and hacking. I stood back in case this was some self-destruct thing.

Then I realized it was laughing. Not a happy laugh.

"Elves. We don't live with them." The changeling spit off to the side in case his tone hadn't been clear. "They left us behind. We are free now."

So it wasn't Glorinal. The changelings may have pretended to be an elf, but it was clear none of them would have taken a job directly from one. Of course, a strong magic user could glamour himself not to look like an elf. However, I'd wager the changelings would be able to tell—them being master change artists themselves.

"What else can you tell us?" Bunky had stayed in position over my left shoulder, but I waved him forward. He got within a foot of the changeling and hovered menacingly.

"We are wanderers. We get work where we can. This time a group of small men in masks hired us. They brought us here. We saw elf to copy, we copy. They tell us to make sure elf being seen all over." He winced, then continued. "Elf being taken north and we needed him to be seen here. My brother was sent to gather information from you, I had other tasks."

"What was your specific task?" Covey got up and paced around then she spun toward him, making sure she looked as predatory as possible.

"No." The changeling settled into himself and clammed up.

I nodded for Bunky to pull back a bit. Maybe we could play good digger, bad construct and get some real answers. "What did they ask you to do? And where did you see the elf you were copying?" That might help track down Alric.

"I was told to run around doing things and make sure people see me with the bag." The changeling shrugged.

"Stupid idea, bag just rags. We were given his imprint to copy, but we saw the elf in the ruins; he had a cave that got destroyed. He was supposed to go with it. That didn't happen, so guess he got taken."

He started shaking, but from the look on his face, he wasn't doing it. Covey tried to grab him, but his eyes went wide and a second later, he vanished.

Bunky buzzed around the area that the changeling had been in, but all he found was the laundry line Covey had used to tie him up. It was sliced through in two places as if a sharp blade had cut it. One that cauterized the ends.

Covey and I looked around as well, but saw nothing. We were in an alley of sorts, but the other end of it was nothing more than a narrow walkway between two houses whose owners had obviously been building out over the years. No one could have come through there without us noticing.

I was keeping an eye on Bunky, in case his little construct eyes could see something we couldn't. He kept circling around a spot of stubby grass about a foot behind where we'd kept the changeling. I moved closer. The ground was an odd color, as if it came from somewhere else and didn't match.

I looked around, grabbed a stone and threw it at the grass. I'd like to say I was surprised when the stone passed right through the grass with a slight flicker, but the fact was, Beccia was getting weirder. It was taking more to surprise me these days.

Bunky dove forward and before I could pull him back, he'd vanished into the hole. I ran forward to stick my head in, Covey right behind me, but Bunky flew straight up out of the hole.

He'd almost smacked me in the head so I rocked back on my heels. He kept buzzing around the hole as if he was sniffing, but then as soon as he thought Covey or I would come closer, he buzzed us off. After a minute or two, the image of the stubby grass vanished and the ground bubbled up like water.

Not unlike the way the holes from the chimeras and sceanra anam filled in after they burst out. However, this wasn't a burst out so much as something had come out, grabbed the changeling, and dropped back in before we could see him. Then got away before the tunnel filled in.

The changeling had looked surprised, so that told me it wasn't expecting that sort of rescue, but since it didn't even know who or what hired it, that wasn't helpful. It was probably whoever was behind hiring the changelings and they didn't want us finding out the truth. Whatever that was.

"That was interesting." Covey was studying the area. "I've never seen a hole fill back in before."

"I have." I told her about the chimeras. Bunky did his nodding bobbing behind me. He'd been long gone by the time the holes that birthed him and the others closed, but he was obviously familiar with it.

"We're still not getting any closer to finding out what happened to Alric." I wasn't as worried, now that it looked like someone else had taken him and not Glorinal. That was a sad statement, but he had messed with my emotions enough over the last few months, and I figured he could get out of most things. I was still worried, just not full panic worried.

"Nor where the beings who took Glorinal out of the cave vanished to. We have to assume that they have Glorinal and they have the obsidian chimera." Covey only growled a little when she said his name, so that was an improvement of sorts.

I didn't add that we also had no idea where she'd vanished to yesterday, and why she had insisted we were under attack from mythological beings, but then recalled none of it. I'd have to ask her later if the sahlins of her past were small men.

"True. I think we have to consider that whoever is behind this is probably behind the ground shaking." I hated to keep saying explosions.

"I agree." She scowled. "There were no indications that the rakasa were underground dwellers in the past, but they were never a focus of my study. I think our best course is to track down the most recent underground disturbance. We know they went under to get *him* out, and they went under to try to kill Alric. It can also be assumed that they went under to get their changeling back."

"Where is he?" The voice was loud, demanding, and far closer than it should have been.

Covey and I turned around and found that while we had been discussing going in search of the latest explosion, a walking explosion had snuck up on us.

Or rather a posse of entitled rich snobs snuck up on us. Specifically, the Hill Committee. Five of the richest and most annoying folks you'd never want to meet and they were all looking right at Covey and I.

"I said, Professor, where is that elf? He explained to us late last night that he needed funds to launch a full-scale excavation of the Antiquities Museum. He took our gold fast enough but failed to meet us at the site this morning as planned." The tall, overdressed woman seemed to be ignoring me. In fact, they were all fixated on Covey as the focus of their annoyance. "He mentioned that you would be supervising."

Covey's eyes narrowed and she looked at each one as if they were her students coming in late to class. She then turned to me. "You should continue with that urgent project we discussed. I shall address this situation." She focused all of her professorial annoyance back on the five in front of her and I made a run for the ruins.

Last night may have been the first job of one of the changelings. Granted, Alric was a thief, former or not, and he stayed in practice. Nevertheless, stealing gold out in the open like that wasn't his style.

I picked up speed as the voices behind me increased in volume. Bunky took off with me, but made a small chirp, then buzzed off a different direction. Most likely he had gone off to find the girls. It might be time for the first cat race of the day.

I briefly looked back down the street. There may only be one Covey and five of them, but The Hill folks were grossly outmatched. I was confident in Covey getting far more information out of them than they got out of her.

Which left me walking quickly back toward the ruins. I didn't want to walk past the watcher bird and guard, so I snuck around the side Covey and I had come back down.

This side area was far darker and creepier than the rest of the ruins. It hadn't been that noticeable when Covey and I were chasing the changeling and finding Alric's secret magic elf house. But it was palpable now.

I found myself looking up to see if any trees were askew thanks to the explosion, but the further I went in, the darker, heavier, and less likely to be moved by something as trivial as an underground explosion they got. Some of these monsters looked like they would swallow the explosion and spit back ash.

Looking up as I was, it wasn't too unexpected when I tripped over a smaller root, and crashed to the ground.

CHAPTER TWENTY-ONE

I fell right in front of a nasty long gash in the ground. It went as far as I could see in either direction. Granted, that wasn't very far in this thick part of the jungle, but I could see enough to freak me out. It wasn't more than two feet wide, but the crack looked like it stayed that wide the entire distance I could see.

Had I not tripped on the root, I likely could have found myself lost down a narrow pit. I shivered and scooted back. I was right about the trees though. None of them seemed in the slightest bit disturbed by the crack running through the forest. And it managed to avoid hitting any of them. I'd have to be nice to all the trees out here. If they could manage to deter an act of nature, I had a new respect for what they could do to us mere mortals.

I couldn't see anything in the crack, and it wasn't useful—like, say, a trail to free a raving murdering lunatic out of a collapsed mine would be. Which meant this was a radiating crack side effect of whatever had caused the explosion.

It could be a natural earthquake, but those odds were slim, and getting even more so with each explosion we had.

The split seemed to point like an arrow further into the old ruins. Of course, the other end pointed toward the city and a lovely pub that I'm sure missed me terribly. I didn't think about it for more than a moment. There had been a time I would have run toward The Shimmering Dewdrop. Hell, I wouldn't have been out here in the first place. But like it or not, it seemed that something big was coming our way. And my friends and I had somehow landed right in the middle of it. Actually, I knew how. Alric. Life was so normal before him. Another thing to have him answer for—again—once we rescued him.

The crack maintained the same width as I walked alongside it. The trees for the most part stayed clear of it. I swore the crack zigged to avoid a monster gapen tree.

It took a few minutes to start seeing the old ruins. The trees had created their perpetual twilight even though it was still early in the day. Unlike the ruins that were under exploration through the Antiquities Museum, these were older and deeper. Towers only stuck up a few feet in the air for the most part, and I found myself again wishing for a patron who would buck tradition enough to dig out here. Qianru was quirky enough to do it, but she was still following her own agenda that she wasn't sharing with me.

The trees, excessive rocks, and bad condition of the visible ruins were the reasons for no digging. However, what I could see strongly implied stylistic differences between these and the ones in the main ruin area. That might be an angle; the academic side focused on what was found in the regular part of the ruins. However, if I could convince them to believe there were cultural differences between the two sets of ruins, or even just a rumor of them, they might be the force needed to get this section open.

I'd have to work on Covey when the rest of this mess settled down. If anyone was stubborn enough to push the academics into demanding exploration of the old ruins, it would be her. Then we could work on nudging Qianru that direction too.

The crack I was following stopped at a boulder to the left of me. The crack actually had gone under the rock, and part of the rock had fallen in. However, the crack was far wider now.

Behind the massive boulder was what had to be the source of the explosion.

The crack funneled into a large pit, and if I had had even the slightest thought that the most recent shake was an actual earthquake, this destroyed it. The ground had vanished in a large, almost circular, pit, with only the largest of boulders staying stuck in the ground, but bearing wounds to mark the force of the explosion. It had been concentrated and focused, that and the distance out from town, was most likely why no one in town seemed to notice it.

The edge near me had some paper shreds. I picked up a few for Covey and Harlan, but they looked like the ones found at the mine and the museum, a combination of explosives and pre-packaged spell wrappers. The spells were what was controlling the explosions most likely and meant the people behind this probably weren't strong magic users themselves. I didn't have the training to control something like an explosion, but someone like Alric would have found it an easy task.

I peered down into the pit, but aside from scarred boulders and tree roots I couldn't see much. I shouldn't have let Bunky take off. He would be very helpful right now. I didn't have a rope, and Alric hadn't taught me his make a rope out of leaves trick yet.

Even though I had no way of reaching Bunky, I might have a way of getting the girls. I had no idea how close they had to be for our little mind-calling trick to work. I was at least a few miles out of town, and if they'd moved their cat-racing track where I thought, then they were at the opposite end.

I tried calling for them in my head, gave it a few minutes, then sat down when they didn't respond. I cleared my head. Maybe Covey and her meditation practices might be right. I focused on the faeries, ale, chocolate, the hole in front of me, and me.

Ten minutes later, I was about to give it up and go all the way back into town for some rope when I heard the lovely sounds of faeries arguing, and a loud buzzing overlaying it all.

"Is true! This where happened!" Leaf flew up front near Garbage.

"You wrong, that no happen." Garbage flew faster, but for once, Leaf wasn't dawdling. The fact that she was managing to not only keep up with Garbage, but was flying ahead enough to try to keep arguing—not to mention the fact she *was* arguing with her—said a lot about Leaf's normal pace on things.

She was the slow one because she wanted to be.

The two pulled up a bit before they got to me, but Crusty and Bunky ignored them and kept flying forward.

"Yummies?" Crusty looked around for anything that warranted her being called out here, but then shrugged when she didn't see anything. "No yummies. You right." She patted Bunky and he buzzed happily.

Crusty wasn't upset about the fact I'd used nonexistent treats to get them to come out here, and Garbage and Leaf were still arguing over goddess knew what. It was as if they hadn't expected any treats well before they got here. I knew the faeries and Bunky communicated somehow, but I'd never looked into it.

"Bunky, did you hear me call them?" He did his version of a headshake and Crusty started giggling.

"He no hear like we do from you, but I share with him. He say no treats but we should help."

Wow. Leaf asserting herself with Garbage, and now Crusty was thinking. My faeries were changing. This could be good. Or very bad.

I looked back at the other two, but they were still flying around various trees, pointing at things only they saw, and arguing. Once Garbage got going it would be a while before she backed down. I was impressed with Leaf keeping up with her though.

"Okay, so just you, Bunky, and me on this." I nodded to Bunky and wished I had my gloves with me to scratch him. I'd have to start carrying them around. "I need you two to fly down there and tell me what you see." I was a bit unsure of using Crusty for this, she being the least observant of the three. Hopefully, whatever connection she and Bunky had would work.

Bunky hovered over the pit, slowly tilting from side to side in the air. He buzzed a question and Crusty nodded and turned toward me. "He says bad, little, little men do this. But they gone again." She frowned as he added to his original message. "He said they be back."

I wished I could understand Bunky directly. However, I'd have to take my information filtered through a tiny faery brain. "How does he know all of that?"

"He taste it." Crusty answered as if I'd asked her what the large tree behind me was. Obviously, there was more to it than that, but Crusty wouldn't be able to explain. I'd also need to nag Covey about more research on constructs.

"We'll go with that." I looked up, but the other two faeries had moved even higher in the air, the only real way to tell they were there was by their voices. I turned back to Crusty and Bunky. "Don't go down real far, but see what you can find."

Crusty nodded, and jumped on Bunky's back, and the two of them looped up in the air, and then dove down. I wasn't sure why she rode him, but in this case, and with her track record of smashing into things, this might be safer.

The sound of Garbage and Leaf continuing their animated debate was the only sound in the forest. I hadn't noticed the animal and bird sounds until now that they were gone. Now granted, the faeries and even myself could have made the wildlife go to ground, but faeries came through the forest regularly. The wild ones still spent a fair amount of time somewhere out here, so they should be well known to the local animals.

I looked down the pit but Crusty and Bunky were out of sight, and Garbage and Leaf were now above the leaf line.

It could be nerves, now that I was aware of the silence, but I swore the woods started to feel darker and colder too. I moved closer to a glouster bush and convinced myself I was being paranoid when I crawled down under it and settled myself inside.

The shuffling started to my right, just as I started to think about crawling out from my hidey-hole. Now there was a chance that Covey could have finished up with the committee folks and followed me out here, but as far as I knew I had never heard Covey shuffle in her life.

Then the trees to the right started to move.

The ground had broken open and those trees hadn't budged at all. Nevertheless, something was bending them as if they were saplings. The shuffling sound got louder, and I shrank into the bush covering me and sent a silent prayer to all three of the girls to stay where they were and to stay quiet.

Then I heard the sounds again, just in time for something to break through the trees on that side of the clearing.

CHAPTER TWENTY-TWO

The shuffling sound was coming from a creature easily ten feet high, but it looked like nothing I'd ever seen before. Long, black, decaying strands of something I hoped wasn't flesh dripped off the form as it moved toward the pit. I couldn't make out any features, so I couldn't even tell if we had another troll zombie on our hands. However, if this thing was a zombie, the original owner had died many years ago.

There wasn't much of a wind this deep in the thick forest, but unfortunately what there was changed direction. I was wrong. That thing had died long before even the elves had taken off and had been kept stored in a giant pickling jar of rotten produce. That was the only way I could explain that odor.

The thing twitched as it moved forward, then almost stumbled, but pulled itself back upright, and shambled closer to the pit the explosion had made.

I closed my eyes briefly, and focused on Crusty Bucket, danger, and staying put. I made sure the danger thought was aimed at her and Bunky, not me. I didn't want them flying right into whatever this thing was in a misguided attempt to rescue me.

I needn't have worried too much. The walking pile of decaying plant life was shrinking as it took its steps closer to the pit. Rather, parts of it were dropping off.

By the time it finally made it to the edge of the pit, there was nothing left except a decaying head of cabbage that rolled unceremoniously into the pit. As long as it didn't manage to land on Crusty or Bunky, they should be safe.

I was about to climb out of my hiding spot—again—when a troop of brownies came into view. One of them might have been the one Garbage had brought in, but I couldn't tell for sure. They all looked alike, and even if they hadn't, they were covered in the same disgusting goop as the creature that just disintegrated had been.

They were yelling at each other in a language I didn't understand, but many of the words sounded like swear words. One or two words stood out.

A golem. Those crazy little bastards had managed to make a golem out of rotting tree parts.

Seven brownies all waved at the pit and yelled at each other. Alric had been teaching me some fighting skills along with the magic, but even so, I might need back up. Providing a second giant shambling pile of decaying shrubbery didn't come down the trail, the girls and I should be able to chase them off.

Armed with my knife, I jumped out of the bushes. I also whistled for the girls and Bunky and sent a thought imagining all the brownies as ale bottles.

The brownies turned at my sudden appearance. It was rumored the little guys could smell as well as a bloodhound, but with the layer of ooze on them, I wasn't surprised they didn't know that the girls or I were here.

They were surprised, however. "Ah! Magic! Our enemies have found us!" The muck-covered brownie closest to me shrieked and charged forward with a sword that probably had an earlier life holding appetizers in a high-end restaurant.

I kicked him away before he even got within skewering distance. Then Garbage Blossom and Leaf

Grub swooped down and did a low fly-by over the slime-encrusted brownies. The girls weren't arguing anymore, but it could be a temporary truce. Unfortunately, with their memories it could be a long time, if ever, before I found out what they were fighting about.

The brownies screamed again. Perhaps they should use that high-pitched sound as a weapon instead of the cocktail skewers they were waving around; it was annoying enough that it would make people run away.

They were jabbering in their own language and backing toward the pit. Garbage and Leaf were playing with them, enjoying whatever adversarial relationship the two species had. Until Crusty and Bunky came charging up out of the pit.

Crusty was waving a sharpened piece of root in one hand, and a cloth bag dribbling gold coins and rocks in the other. She was also yelling what I was sure she felt was a fierce war cry but mostly seemed to be about minkies doing their laundry in the brownies' mouths.

I may have misunderstood as the remaining six brownies—the one I kicked was still down but I had a feeling he was faking it to stay out of trouble—all started screeching some more. I had to block my ears with my hands when they hit even higher pitch levels as they got a good look at Bunky.

Crusty swung the bag with the coins and rocks around her head before I realized what she was doing.

"No! Crusty! Don't throw it!" Most likely that was what was left of the bag The Hill folks were looking for, and equally possibly what the brownies had made the golem to go retrieve. Too late, my excitable, but not always the sharpest cheese in the pantry, faery had flung the bag at the lead brownie, bowling him into three of his friends. Judging by the size of it, and the way it was leaking, my only satisfaction was that most of the coins that had been in it were on the ground. Not to mention, it looked like it had far more rocks than coins in it when she brought it up.

The brownies grabbed their fallen comrades and raced out of there.

"We win!" Crusty started dancing on top of Bunky, tumbled off, and almost fell back into the pit before she remembered she could fly.

Garbage and Leaf drifted down and started picking up the coins scattered around the mouth of the pit.

"Okay, girls and Bunky, I need you to gather all of the coins and give them to me." Garbage had her back to me and from her furtive arm movements I was sure she was stuffing one or more coins into one of their bags. The bags could hold just about anything and were so spelled that trying to find anything once it got in there was almost impossible. Unless you were one of the faeries anyway.

"Including those, Garbage."

She turned, shoved the bag back wherever they went when they weren't being used, which meant it looked like she shoved it into thin air to me, and brought three coins to me. Bunky didn't really have arms, so there was nothing for him to grab anything with. His short, stumpy baby goat legs didn't help gathering them on the ground either.

"Bunky, why don't you keep an eye on the ground from up there? You can tell us if we've missed any, and warn us if those brownies come back." These couldn't possibly be the only coins in the original bag. Crusty, or someone, had filled the bag with rocks, with only a few dozen or so coins in the bottom. Judging from what we found anyway. A quick peer down the pit didn't show any more coins.

Bunky buzzed in agreement and flew up to the lowest branch level over the pit. I still wanted him and the girls to go back into the pit and search it more, but I didn't want to take a chance with the gold lying about. Whether it was the real Alric or one of the changelings who swindled it, I figured I'd keep it until we figured out why it was taken and what happened to the rest of it. And I didn't want it going back into cat racing. No one from the criminal world had questioned the faeries' little side business, but we needed to keep it that way.

While they were doing that, I worked on gathering the pieces that had flown over by the trail the brownies had come down. Now that I knew the shambling creature had been a golem, the bits and pieces didn't look as creepy and disturbing. They also didn't smell as bad. Either I had lost all sense of smell, or they were breaking down at an accelerated rate. I found a stick and used it to lift up one of the slimy strands. To my surprise, it wasn't slimy, but rapidly drying and crumbling into itself.

I picked up two more strands and saw the same thing happening. Alric had only barely touched on golems as a concept, but the magic to animate them was supposed to be almost as much as trying to create a zombie. Brownies were also not a well-known topic, since they weren't native to this part of the world. But they weren't reputed to be great spell casters.

So where did a bunch of brownies get enough power to make a golem but not have enough power to keep it running? Even as the thoughts were going through my head, the strand of former golem was passing into dust.

The brownies must have had help. Whether they were the ones behind the explosion that caused the pit was also a question for another day.

Bunky kept a good eye on the girls, buzzing loudly if one of them tried to slip a gold coin into one of their bags. I should have thought of Bunky as faery-nursemaid months ago when he decided to stay with us.

"Do we have them all?" I'd noticed the girls were shuffling around, but hadn't picked up any more coins for almost a full minute. At their nods, I waved them to me. It had only been a few minutes, yet they were clearly bored to tears.

"Crusty? Did you and Bunky find anything down the hole?" I had a feeling that plenty of things were down there, and I belatedly realized I should have narrowed it down for my little wonder-drunk. I was about to clarify when she pointed behind me.

"Them. No see then, but smelled them." She nodded. "Now see them."

I spun around to see three sceanra anam rising out of the pit behind me.

CHAPTER TWENTY-THREE

I would be leaving it out of my telling of this encounter later on, but I screamed so loudly I was surprised no one from the center of town came running to check on me. Hell, it was loud enough I was surprised no one came from the far south to check.

All three were hovering over the pit, not moving quickly, but the way their entire bodies moved like a water snake in the air, even when holding a single position they looked like they were heading for you.

Or they *were* heading for me.

I took two shaky steps backwards, and found they flew forward an equal distance. They weren't doing anything threatening, but when you were long, lean, and had more teeth than anyone could possibly count, you didn't have to do anything to threaten people.

"Girls? Shouldn't you be doing something about them?" Granted it had been larger groups of faeries that had taken out the creatures before, but these three should at least be worried about the faeries.

"Girls?" I didn't want to risk my life to look around but they were being awfully quiet.

"Bunky?" I couldn't count on him. The last flying snake we saw went after Bunky, but at least if I knew he was around, I'd feel better.

Nope, not a single buzz. Bunky and the girls had taken off and left me here.

"It's just you three and me then. Until the roaming gang of wild faeries comes through here." I had no idea if those flying monstrosities could understand me, but I needed to try.

The sceanra anam nearest me tilted its head as if it was listening. Or maybe it was trying to size up its next meal better. I had one knife, against three of them. And they could fly. Not a fair fight by even faery standards.

However, I also had magic. Questionable. Weak. Untrustworthy, but would definitely give me a headache, magic.

I hated to keep trying to use it. All of Alric's warnings about not going further than I was ready to kept bouncing around my head. However, the sceanra anam had finished communing with the pit or whatever it was they were doing and their eyes now narrowed and focused on me.

I'd get one shot, then I knew whatever spell I picked would slam back into me and I'd be down. I had to make the shot count.

I pushed out all the fear of pain and the flying snakes and fashioned a spell of movement. As I wanted those things to move as far from here as possible. This specific spell was about as far over my head as the faeries were to advanced hypothetical calculus. On a surface level, it appeared to be similar to the first spell I did, pushing open a door, or sending an annoying satyr halfway through a forest. But it was far more complex.

I gathered the spell in my head, then, as Alric had tried to teach me, flung the spell outward.

I managed to hit the lead sceanra anam with enough force to burst it in midair. There wasn't even enough of him left to drift to the ground.

Of course that meant I still had two more sceanra anam, a massively building spell headache, and I felt like I was rapidly losing the ability to move.

It only took a few seconds for the remaining two sceanra anam to realize who had blown up their friend, and about another full second before they flew right at me. I held up my knife. It wasn't enough, but I wasn't going down without a fight.

I'd made one swing, which totally missed the flying snake and reminded me how much that spell took out of me, when screeching faeries came swarming down. Bunky stayed above the swarm, which seemed to consist of every single non-wild faery in the area. My three were in the lead, of course. But then they pulled up right before the sceanra anam and waved the others forward.

Both of the flying snakes seemed torn between the easy prey before them—me—and their fear of the crazed faeries.

However, once the first wave of faeries charged forward, the sceanra anam decided to flee.

Unlike the one that had been trapped in the halls of the university, these had many ways to escape.

The faeries let out a wild mixture of calls and yells and took off after them.

Except my three.

The exhaustion from the spell wore off extremely fast, most likely due to adrenaline, which meant it was postponed, not worn off. I waved to the faeries to show I was okay. They flew forward, but didn't seem to be worried about my condition. All three looked toward the direction the swarm had gone.

"Girls? Why did you take off like that? Couldn't you have at least chased those things away?" I was glad for the assist, but it would have been better to have started with it.

"We need to train. Good training." Garbage folded her arms and scowled at the air where the one I blew up had disintegrated. "These hard to find now. No waste them." Her scowl switched to me and I realized that far from being concerned about me, Garbage was upset that I'd destroyed one of their training toys. To save my own life.

"You remember. No waste." With that solid admonishment, including a tiny, stern finger shake, Garbage led the other two and Bunky in pursuit of their students and the soon to be dead sceanra anam.

I wasn't sure if I was more upset about her disregard for my safety or the fact she said they were getting harder to find. The first, and only, birth of them had been witnessed by myself, my patroness Qianru, and a collection of impeccably trained houseboys. But we had only seen five.

Since I was pretty sure that I'd already seen at least that many, and the girls were upset about them vanishing, I had to guess they were in far greater numbers than we thought. Considering that the history books had little on them, and no one had been able to capture an intact sample alive or dead, I doubted I would get my answers anytime soon.

I began to think that I should have stayed with Covey in town. Then an image of the rich politicians she faced came into my head. I shuddered.

Nope, better to deal with badly made golems, misguided brownies, and exploding sceanra anam.

I gathered the coins that had been re-scattered and peered into the pit. I wished I'd been able to get more details of what Crusty and Bunky had seen. Maybe they'd recall some of it when they came home. My house should be finished by now, so we could have a nice quiet night in.

There wasn't much I could see from the top of the pit. There was little doubt it had been the result of a deep explosion. Unlike the radiating crack through the forest, I could see to the bottom here. It was at least forty feet deep, but without a snap-glow or rope, I had no way to be sure.

The only question was what had happened to the dirt. An explosion that large should have flung dirt, rocks, and small plants all around the forest. Yet the pit and the crack had little dirt around them, and even going out a ways into the forest, I didn't see any debris.

Now, granted, I had inadvertently exploded the sceanra anam to such a degree that it disintegrated, but I doubted too many people would be using a spell of that level just to avoid having rocks and debris around.

There appeared to be a layer of something almost two feet down from the edge of the pit. It was hard to see what it was; all I could tell for sure was that it seemed smoother than the rest of the pit and darker. I wanted to call the girls back, but even thinking about calling them caused my head to throb so badly I almost threw up.

I also didn't feel up to walking all the way back to town and getting a rope. I walked around the pit completely, trying to see if I could make out anything in the band.

The far side from where I had been seemed a bit closer to the band, so I lay on the ground and tried to reach down as far as I could. If I couldn't get myself down to the band, maybe part of it could come up to me.

I had enough of a ledge on the pit to feel the band, but I couldn't see it. It had looked like a solid band but it wasn't. I could feel the rough edges where pieces of something cold and hard fit together. Sections of dirt told me where pieces were missing. Feeling around really gave me no clue as to what it was, how most of it had survived whatever explosion caused the pit, or where it came from. I slid my fingers back over to one of the missing areas, trying to pry a piece up.

My plan worked a little too well as I felt the piece I was trying to pull off suddenly gave way and I heard the tinkling noise it made as it fell down into the pit. A round of swearing didn't help, nor did my quickly aborted attempt to call the faeries again. Whatever I'd done when I blew up the flying snake was messing with any magic I had going right now.

I flopped on my back to see if it helped the horrific pounding and nausea caused from trying to call the girls, but also to see if perhaps they were returning on their own.

It helped the spinning, but there wasn't a single faery wing in sight. With my luck, those damn sceanra anam had probably taken off to another county.

I rolled back over and tried reaching down even further but I still couldn't get to the bottom edge. The piece felt like tile and had raised parts. However, beyond trying to convince myself it was not a collection of emerald dragons, I couldn't tell what they were.

So I went back to where I'd lost the previous piece and tried again. Slower this time and with only one hand so that I could hopefully catch the piece before it fell.

It seemed like an hour before I felt something start to come loose. It spoke a lot to whoever put these here that even after a major explosion right next to them they stayed in place.

I wiggled the piece slowly, like a loose tooth, until it came off. After all the time I'd spent on the damn thing, I might have very well jumped in after it if I dropped another one.

The piece looked like aged porcelain, but was cool, and felt more like metal. Tapping on it sounded like metal as well. The backside was scored and covered in dirt from where it had been wedged into the earth.

No emerald dragons. I let out a sigh of relief at that. However, what was there didn't look terribly friendly. The piece was a bit smaller than the palm of my hand, but covered in strange symbols and letters that could only be described as hostile. There was no other way to describe it. The words, if that's what they were, were sharp and jagged. None of the symbols looked at all familiar, but they did look like they'd been made in anger.

That was weird. I obviously couldn't read it; I'd never even seen this form of image writing before in my life. Yet it made the hairs on the back of my neck stand up and an overwhelming urge to throw this back into the pit filled my head.

I think the only reason I didn't toss it away was because I'd worked so hard for the damn thing. I pulled myself away from the edge of the pit, and eased up into a sitting position.

I needed to find something to wrap up this thing; the more I looked at it the less I wanted to touch it. I was surrounded by leaves, any of which would make a great wrap.

I hid the carved tile in the high grass in front of the nearest tree, and started climbing up it. I'd just reached the big leaves when I saw movement below me.

A man completely in brown walked right to where I'd hidden the tile, found it in a matter of seconds, then held it up to me in salute and walked away. He was wearing a large floppy hat, and a mask of some dun-colored fabric. All I could see were coal black eyes that looked far too smug with himself.

I was exhausted from my adventures out here so far, but that gesture wiped out all of the fatigue. After all I went through and someone was going to walk off with it? I don't think so.

I stuffed the leaves in my shirt, then jumped out of the tree and landed on the person in brown.

Based on the size and build, I'd guess it was male, and he had a good foot on me in height. But I had the advantage of falling from a distance, so I managed to take us both down.

Since even a slight thought of maybe trying to use magic on him sent a stabbing pain into my head, I started punching.

He was good. I only got a few good shots in before he rolled to his feet then started blocking my punches when I followed. But when he blocked me, it was every hit. It looked like he had a sword under his cloak, but he wasn't going for it, nor even fighting back.

Then I got in a sneaky shot Covey had taught me to his lower back. He stumbled forward then came up swinging. I danced backwards and realized he wasn't swinging as much as grabbing.

I smacked his hands away, sneaking in a few more jabs. I might have even been able to take him down if a voice behind me hadn't broken my concentration.

"Stop playing and grab her. Thanks to you, the elf girl got away. We'll bring in this one. We need to make the meet."

I spun to see this person I hadn't even heard approach, and my attacker in brown took the brief distraction and pinned my arms. A moment later a bag was over my head, a silencing spell bag unless my attackers had suddenly gone mute, and rough rope was coiled around my hands.

CHAPTER TWENTY-FOUR

A rough nudge to my left shoulder got me walking, then a few more nudges turned me around a half a dozen times until I wasn't even sure which direction we were going. Whoever was working with the man in brown, they weren't keen on my slow walking. After the maze they walked me through to disorient me, someone big and beefy threw me over his shoulder.

Not hearing anything other than my own breathing was more than a little freaky. However, maybe they were being quiet in hopes I'd think it was a silencing bag. I tested the theory with a scream. That did nothing other than echo around the very sound spelled bag and add to the headache I had from my excessive destruction of the sceanra anam.

I wished it wasn't so dark in here so I could at least see what the inside looked like. I'd had a knock-off one of these bags back when I was bounty hunting. But it had been taken when one of my collars, one Gorgeous Sammy the cherub, met with an untimely demise after I'd turned him in. I never asked for my bag back.

However, this bag felt like a real one. The quality of the fabric against my face was akin to something up on The Hill.

Since I couldn't see, couldn't hear, couldn't yell, and trussed up as I was over this monster's shoulder, couldn't move, I did what I could do. Think. I didn't have much. The man in brown had said nothing, but hadn't been trying to hurt me until the other voice came in. He also hadn't acted as if he would let me go, more like a bored cat who'd found a new toy. But I think if I had stayed in the tree he wouldn't have come after me. There wasn't much to be gained from him aside from that he could fight and wasn't in command of whatever this operation was.

The second voice was probably the one in command. He hadn't sounded stressed out or worried about me getting away or even hurting his all-in-brown fighter. He seemed more upset at the games the fighter was playing. He'd said they'd take me instead of a female elf that got away. Unless there was a run on female elves racing around in the ruins, he had to mean Orenda. The fact she hadn't said anything about escaping from someone didn't bode well for whatever her true reason for being in Beccia was. Nor for whatever sort of trouble she might bring down on Harlan and Covey.

And at least a third one, a bruiser, the one carrying me with little care for how many low-hanging tree branches might smack me.

The brains, the player, and the brawn. There could be more, but the three of them were a nice neat little package. One that had been in those woods for a reason. The man in brown must have waited until I freed the tile piece, but whether that was their goal, or it changed when I left the piece on the ground, I wasn't sure. If the tiles had value, they could have stayed to try to free more, with the bag on my head I wouldn't have known. The only way I knew they hadn't done that was the fact we were moving.

The brute carrying me wasn't a picture of grace, that I could tell from being an unwilling passenger. Therefore, I wasn't too surprised when he took a misstep and almost dropped me. He recovered before either of us took a tumble, but the movement sent a knife hilt briefly into my lower side. I hadn't even noticed that they hadn't searched me when they tied me up. It had happened so fast that I hadn't paid attention. Who kidnaps someone and doesn't search them for weapons?

While he'd managed to keep me from falling, the man carrying me must have hurt his ankle, as a limp was noticeable. It started getting worse, and I took a chance and tried squirming. If I could unbalance him enough, maybe I could at least get the damn bag off long enough to figure out where we were going.

It worked, sort of.

The man carrying me did stumble. We'd been going down a slight incline for a few minutes, but it had gotten steeper and he misjudged his step. The leg he'd hurt earlier happened to be on the same side I was on, so my movements sent him falling. Unfortunately, they also caused him to fling me away from him as he tried to break his fall. Which was good and bad. I wouldn't want something that big on top of me, but at the same time, he flung me hard.

Right into a rough wall.

I shook my head as pain flared out. At least my shoulder had taken the brunt of it, not my head, but it still had me seeing stars. My hands were tied behind me, so I reached down as low as I could with my mouth and tried to fling up the spell sack. I twisted a bit to help pull the bag off and kept pulling when the sudden assault of sound that slammed into my ears told me I'd broken the seal. I debated about trying to keep pulling to see if I could get it loose enough to shake off, but the bag was too heavy. Another bad side effect of better quality. I think if Gorgeous Sammy had sneezed while I was carrying him in my spell bag, the entire thing would have shredded. Just my luck to have people who had funding grab me.

At least now I could hear them. Which also meant I could yell, but it also meant I needed to be quiet so they didn't hear me until I had a chance to make the yell worth the risk. I also didn't want them deciding to search for weapons at this point. My knife wouldn't help me now, but if I could get my hands free it might.

Yelling was going on, and not directed at me. There was a good chance that the brute carrying me hadn't accidentally fallen down the steep ramp we'd come down, or at least he seemed to think so. Moreover, the person or persons he was holding responsible took exception to the accusation and were disagreeing loudly. I was surprised they hadn't started hitting each other yet.

I hadn't been able to tell with the bag over my head, but the way the voices were echoing we had to be in a large chamber of some sort. I hadn't a clue which direction we'd gone, for all I knew we could be back in the center of Beccia. Or far away. Thing was, away from Beccia there weren't any structures that could be as big as this thing sounded. At least nothing I knew of.

I tried to shift around my position some more; I needed to see where I was. But my movements were cut short by a vise-like grip on my arm.

"Where did you want to keep her? And more importantly, why do you want to keep her? Like I said on the way over, the elf girl was a good idea. This one, I don't get." I was going to be upset if I'd missed vital information when I'd been under that damn sack. The voice near me was possibly the man in brown. His accent was strange. It took me a moment to realize that like the brownies, he was probably from the far north. Great, what if these people were working with the little monsters? They were all hanging around the same area at pretty close to the same time and it was clear someone other than the brownies had helped put that golem together. Even if it hadn't stayed together for long. What if they were all together and they were going to hold me accountable for their toy collapsing?

"What, this one doesn't meet your standards for a girlfriend?" The laugh was rough, and he sounded big, like possibly the guy who had been carrying me. "You had no problem with our elven princess. At least she was good enough to share your bed for a few weeks. She sounded enthusiastic in fact. Every single night. She cried herself to sleep after you took off."

"My reasons were my own; I had some trash I needed to cut free. As for this one, I like my women pliable— this one is definitely not." A rough laugh from the one who had been carrying me was cut off with what sounded to be a punch. That meant both were still way too close. Who in the hell was Orenda if she was roaming the woods shacking up with a bunch of kidnappers and thieves? Although, while she hadn't said anything about being kidnapped, she had been afraid someone was coming for her. Maybe she'd been held against her will. However, someone being an enthusiastic sex partner didn't make me think of being held against her will. Maybe she'd liked the man in brown, but didn't want to share with the others.

"We kept this one, because in case you two morons failed to notice, she must have defeated that damn golem. And she chased off the brownies, not that we couldn't have once the golem was gone." This voice sounded like the leader. Heavy footsteps on what sounded like gravel or pounded earth came closer. "Not to mention, I'm pretty sure she's one of the diggers from this town. If we're going to get rich, we need her type more than brawn. What was on that tile anyway?"

A shuffling of feet again, and this time the voices were a bit further away.

"Nothing, damn thing was blank, see for yourself."
The man in brown tossed something at the leader. "She can't be that good of a digger if she spent all that time looking for pieces of cracked tile."

I fought to keep any reaction from showing. I knew something had been on there. It had been weird and creepy, and I hadn't been able to make out any of the symbols on it. Therefore, the man in brown lied. Something that wasn't too unusual in kidnappers, I was sure.

"She can hear us." The man in brown swore and ran to me; I could see his boots under the edge of the bag. I must have given myself away somehow. His hands were coarse as he roughly pulled the bag tighter and fastened the ends. He'd almost closed it when the leader spoke up.

"No, let her hear. Hell, she might as well see too. No reason to keep that bag on her head at this point. Maybe this time *I* get a new girlfriend."

The man in brown swore to himself, clearly not agreeing with his leader's choice, but not willing to fight, then ripped the bag off my head and stomped off.

I had been partially correct. I still had no idea where we were, but we weren't inside any type of building in Beccia or out of it. Or rather, we weren't in any building above ground.

CHAPTER TWENTY-FIVE

I was leaning up against a short broken wall, from what I could see it was clearly elven in origin, in a cavern with a very high ceiling. The cavern looked to have been occupied for quite a while and had mage glows set all around it to make it homey. Or maybe it was so they could see their weapons. Pushed against the cavern walls were piles of weapons, some in use, still others simply relics.

The man in brown was stalking away from me and toward yet another cavern which looked even larger and had at least twenty people in it, most were cleaning weapons or relics. Behind them were a collection of gypsy wagons, most likely the bedrooms for the men and women working down here. Even from this distance, I could tell the wagons looked shabby and ill-used. Probably only a few of them could even still be drawn by a horse.

Looking around I couldn't see someone like Orenda staying here of her own accord without a reason. That pissy man in brown must be one hell of a lover.

"Not sure what all you've heard, but I'll give you the rundown. I'm Locksead. My gang and I are looking for some relics, and not just any relics, we want the serious ones. The ones like they had...." He stopped speaking and leaned forward, tilting my face toward one of the glows. "Carlon, you're an idiot. I told everyone to be looking for any of the people involved with that glass gargoyle debacle. What, if a skirt doesn't twitch your pants you don't even look at her face? This is the digger in the middle of it all. Saryn?"

I thought about lying, but the look on his face told me that while his man Carlon didn't recognize me, he did. "Taryn. My name is Taryn. But I can't help you with stolen artifacts." I sat up a bit straighter. "I won't help you with them." I shook my head and dropped my voice. The leader was crude, but hopefully he was smarter than he looked. "Look, those artifacts won't be worth anything. The only thing they can do is destroy things."

Locksead was a human mix, most of his features were human, but he had shock white hair that almost looked like feathers, and cold blue eyes. He nodded and smiled, but his smile was crueler than a syclarion's frown. "They are worth a lot more than your life to the right people. And if you don't help us, we will find another way to make money off of you." He looked me up and down. "Carlon wasn't right when he said you weren't worth it. You're not ugly, but we'd have to run you for a few dozen years in the red district of Kenithworth to even get part of what some folks will pay for just one of those artifacts." He rocked back on his heels. "I wouldn't like that, and I know you wouldn't like it. So how about you help us with identifying some of these pieces?"

I felt like I might throw up, so instead I nodded. There was no way I would help them find these things and sell them to the highest bidder. No wonder there had been so many more robberies and crimes as of late. The criminally rich and terrible of other cities, most likely other lands, had noticed Beccia. And like the way this man looked at me, it wasn't in a good way.

Locksead leaned down closer to my face. He didn't smell bad at all. They might look like crude thieves and kidnappers, but their leader at least believed in hygiene. I pulled back when I thought that he would try to kiss me, but instead, he smiled and pulled out a piece of tile from inside his vest. "Now, see here, keep your eyes on my face like I am the most interesting man in the world and I am trying to woo you to my bed. I want you to look at this and tell me what you see."

He held the tile up but our bodies were so close I had to twist a bit to see it. It was a piece of broken brown tile used in some houses for roofing. No marks, no images, and clearly hadn't been in the ground for a few hundred years. He crumbled the edges of it when I told him that.

"Thank you. So this wasn't what you pulled off the wall of that pit, was it?" His voice was doing a good two-headed snake impression. If I said it wasn't, then that Carlon would have it out for me, and I didn't think he was safe at all. However, if I said it was, Locksead could probably tell and do what he threatened to do.

I finally shook my head no.

I'd expected Locksead to get angry or violent, but he laughed and threw the piece behind him. "I know. But I wanted to make sure you'd keep honest with me." He waved to one of the guys from the back room. "Tag, help our new friend up and show her what we've found so far."

The man who came up was slender, not much taller than me, and almost looked like an innocent kid. Until you saw the eyes. They probably used him to con his way into places. If you put Qianru's livery on him, he could easily pass as one of her houseboys.

"What about my hands?" It was a little awkward for Tag to get me to my feet since my hands were still behind my back. I couldn't help him tied up like this.

"You don't need your hands to look, and that's all we're going to have you do. For now." Locksead got to his feet and walked into the larger cavern.

It took us a few tries but Tag and I got me to my feet. He held onto my arm as he walked me into the cavern. Which was probably good as otherwise I may have fallen back down again.

It wasn't a cavern. We were in a mostly preserved, with the exception of a few hairline cracks radiating from a jagged hole in the middle of the far top, elven ballroom. Maybe it wasn't just Carlon's bedroom skills that had kept Orenda here.

Tag pulled me forward when I kept standing there. "Yup, she's one of them diggers, that's for sure." His accent was almost exactly like Joie and Qianru's other houseboys. Maybe he had been a houseboy from the south who had decided to branch out.

"Carlon, I need to show her the finds," Tag yelled to the cavern in general, but I didn't see the man in brown. His propensity for dark clothing and surly attitude made me think of Alric when I first met him. Except that Carlon was much taller and heavier than Alric.

"The stuff for her to look at is on the far left table. Just write down what she says." One of the gypsy wagons rocked a bit and Carlon's voice came from it. Hopefully he was just moving about and didn't have another doxy in there.

"Eh, don't mind him." Tag smiled and turned me down the hall. "Assassins are always cranky and crazy."

Carlon had almost seemed to be playing with me when I was fighting him for the tile. That wasn't cranky. It could be crazy though. "He's an assassin?"

Tag's smile dropped and he glanced around to see who was nearby. All the workers were either in their own wagons or in the opposite end of the cavern. "He is one of the best. I've only been part of this gang for two years; he's been here longer in fits and starts. Doesn't seem to like to stay in one place for too long, ya see? But he always finds us." Tag drifted off into his own thoughts for a bit, then shook his head and came back. "He's killed more than thirty people just since I've been here. Most were orders from Locksead, but some were for his own pleasure." He shuddered. "I'd stay clear of him if I were you. I do."

I thought back to what I'd heard from him and agreed. He may have been playing with me in the beginning; he wasn't when we got here though.

I nodded. "Now where are your artifacts?" I did not intend to give them correct information, but I could string them along for a while and find out what they knew and what exactly they were looking for. We hadn't even thought of people outside of Beccia hearing about the two deadly artifacts, but we should have.

That made me think of my friends. Someone would have to be missing me by now, right? I tried hard not to think of the faeries. I was sure the shock to my magic system blowing up that sceanra anam was still messing me up. However, the last thing I wanted would be for these maniacs to grab my faeries. In addition, who knew how much an actual Ancient construct could go for these days?

Naturally, the first thing Tag showed me was something I knew the girls would love. A tiny doll carriage. Unlike their castle, which was only a few hundred years old, and not an artifact, this was pure elven design from the top of the domed roof to the filigree decorating the sides. It was big enough for a doll about twice as tall as one of the faeries, so many of them could comfortably fit inside. Actually, the inside was amazing. It wasn't a carriage at all but a traveler's caravan, down to a way to connect it to miniature horses.

"Where did you find this?" It didn't look like anything anyone around here had ever dug up and I found myself envious of the diggers who found it.

"In a house," Tag said then shrugged. They'd stolen it. For a moment I'd allowed myself to forget I was among thieves and not honest diggers. It was hard to do with the piles of relics they had lying around. "We've found some stuff on our own. We were going to dig that pit when they found you and decided to pull back. Did you make it?"

I looked up from my examination of the caravan car, it was truly amazing. "Did I make what?"

"The pit." He looked around and dropped his voice. "Locksead has been freaked out with all the explosions around here. He says none of them were natural and something bigger than us is coming to town."

This kid should give up being a thief and go into storytelling. Just the way he said the last bit made the skin on the back of my neck crawl. It could also be doing that about whatever could freak out a cold man like Locksead.

"What does Carlon think?" Locksead might also be concerned if his profit was in danger. It was clear what his sole motivation was. Carlon however....

Tag shook his head. "I think he's worried too." A hardened thief would never be this chatty with a prisoner. Most likely Tag was younger than he was trying to be. "He took off a few days ago and just came back last night, but looked really worried. He and Locksead were in deep talks for over an hour and both came out looking more upset than when they went in."

Now that was unsettling. I personally didn't know any, but one would think cold-blooded assassins would take a lot to upset.

"So back to this, is this Ancient or elven?" Tag was done chatting and all business. And testing me. I hoped this kid didn't play cards, he'd lose his shirt.

"Obviously elven, probably from the fifth dynasty, or in common speak, about three hundred years before the vanishing." I almost said Breaking, but that term hadn't become common knowledge and I wanted to keep some things to myself.

"Good girl," Tag smiled and set the toy down. "We already knew that. But this one, we don't." Without even looking for approval, he went around me and untied my hands. Obviously, Locksead had already set that up. I wondered what would have happened had I lied.

He picked up a large piece covered in fabric. It was flat and about two feet by three feet. He carefully removed the fabric although I wasn't sure why he was being so cautious. It took a lot more than some linen to damage metal. Especially this metal.

He was holding up a huge piece of that damn sarcophagus.

Unlike the single squares that we'd found floating around, this was a single sheet that contained about fifteen of the squares. Unless there was more than one of these, this thing had been split up and scattered all over Beccia. I examined a few dents and wondered, not for the first time, if this was the damn one I'd almost drowned in, or if there were a bunch of these lingering around in the abandoned aqueducts under Beccia.

"Where did you steal this one from?" I rubbed the edges carefully; they didn't look rough, but it could be deceiving. They were very smooth. Too smooth. I gently picked the sheet up off of Tag's hands, I knew how tough these pieces were, but he obviously felt different.

"We didn't rob that one." He pointed toward the wagon at the far end. "Carlon found it out digging around about three months ago." He dropped his voice into his storyteller mode. "That's what started the rift between him and Locksead. Carlon told him that was all he found, Locksead didn't believe him." He narrowed his eyes and slowly nodded his head as if that said so much more than what he was speaking.

"That, and Locksead liked the elf girl when we found her. Carlon wooed her away immediately and that widened the rift. I'm surprised Carlon came back this last time. That must have been something important he told Locksead when he came back."

I kept my eyes on the sarcophagus as if I was still trying to figure it out, but my mind was whirling. I knew Carlon had lied to Locksead about the tile. Considering I didn't know what was really on the tile, and therefore didn't know if it was worth lying about, I had to assume he did understand part of it. Now he also lied about this metal. There was no way this thing came out of the ground like this, the edges were freshly cut, and probably with a mage blade. One thing I knew, I did not want to get in between Locksead and Carlon when the two finally had a showdown.

"So tell me about this elf girl. Was she like you all?" I pointed toward the workers on the far end. None of them looked like people you'd want to meet in a dark alley, but there were a few women in the group as well. They looked more dangerous than most of the men.

"Orenda? Naw." Tag's blush told me he'd been smitten by the elf maiden but was way too low on the pecking order to even think about it. "Locksead found her up north a bit. He at first thought she was in disguise, or a breed, but turns out she's a full-blooded elf. Her tribe lives far up north somewhere and she escaped to come down here."

There was a huge dose of awe there. Not only was he smitten, he was also in elf-worship mode. That would change if Glorinal was alive and Tag ever had the dubious honor of running into him.

"So she just started hanging out with you all?" I had only been around her for a short while, but I had a difficult time believing she would have hung out here. It was fascinating seeing an actual elven ballroom more or less intact, but the living conditions were far from the room's former glory.

"None of her people had been out of their city before, not since the elves all vanished. But she was looking for something someone stole from her people so she stayed with us until she was certain we didn't take it." His grin turned him about five years younger. "She was so cute how she didn't think we knew what she was doing."

"So you didn't bring her here tied up and against her will?" I knew Tag hadn't been involved in grabbing me, or bringing me here. Nevertheless, he was still part of the gang who did it.

His laugh made me revise his age. He didn't just look young, he was young. I'm sure he could tell an interesting tale as to how he joined this group of assassins and thieves.

"Naw. It was handy having her with us the last couple of weeks, but she was free to come and go as she wanted. She left us yesterday or you could have met her. I think you'd like her a lot."

I had met her, and I wasn't sure I liked her at all. "But I am a prisoner, right?"

His face dropped at that and I hoped he changed his lifestyle before that innocence and caring was gone. "For now. Locksead thinks he needs you. See, we were counting on Orenda sticking around a bit longer and he's got a job set up for up north. Need to have a couple pretend to be some famous high-class digger couple and get us into some ruins. Not going in play for a few weeks, but he was going to ask her to be a part of it, but then she and Carlon had a big fight a few days ago and he took off. I guess he was tired of her, because he started the fight. Wasn't right, you know? She should be with someone kind and funny and handsome." He looked around to make sure no one else was nearby. "Not him."

"He's none of those things I take it?" He'd been wearing a fabric mask when he and I fought over my piece of tile, and he'd stalked away once they removed my hood.

"No." The look on his face was grim and I hoped I could stay far away from Carlon while I was trapped with these people. "He's mean, and rude, and just plain ugly inside and out."

He shook his head and pointed back to the piece of metal. "So what do you know about this?"

I needed to tell him something they didn't know, but not everything I knew or suspected. I would have to walk that line with everything they wanted me to identify. Hopefully my friends would come find me before I ran out of stalling techniques. I decided that going Harlan on them might be the best approach, both for longevity, and annoyance factor. Most people who asked Harlan to explain something only did so once. And they looked like they completely regretted it the entire time he was speaking during that one time.

"As you can see, this is from the early elven period, most likely sometime around the early reign of King Flouridth and Queen Gallifreid. Now what most people don't know is that the queen and king secretly loved each other, but since that was completely out of fashion during that period, considered to be quite gauche by all of the royalty, they had to hide their love and sneak out to see each other. King Flouridth built chambers like this for their secret tete-a-tetes, they were huge rooms covered in these panels. Most I've seen have been in smaller pieces, this is an amazing find to discover it intact like this."

Tag's eyes had started glazing over at my completely fictitious tale of the former king and queen. The names were correct, those were established early kingdom names, but no one had come across anything else.

"So Carlon was right?" His forehead looked so wrinkled from following my tale that I was afraid I had marred him for life. But it did the job.

"I'd say yes, this piece was probably found as we see it here. However Locksead was also correct, it is part of a much larger item. Just not in the way he thought." I held up the piece so Tag could briefly look at the edges, and then pulled it back. "These were the individual pieces that could have been plastered to the walls of the secret love chamber. Did Carlon happen to say where he found it? Perhaps there are more."

Tag scowled. "No, he gave a general area, out far past the meadows. But he said this was the only piece there. He'd seen a corner of it sticking out of the ground when he passed out in the woods after one of his benders when we first got here." He got his protector look back on his face. "That's another thing about him not being good enough for Orenda. He'd spend all night down in the red light district, drinking, and taking whores, then pass out wherever he crawled to. Sometimes we wouldn't see him for days."

I liked this jerk less and less. However, I had to make sure to keep him in a decent light as much as the artifacts and Locksead were concerned. I didn't care what happened to him once I got out of here, but I didn't want to be in the middle of a war between those two.

"Let me show you a few more pieces. I know Locksead will be moving folks around to find you a nice comfy wagon to stay in—alone." He gave a wink, trying to make it seem like his boss was all about my comfort. Fact was, his boss was all about trying to put me in a place with a door that he could lock.

"Let's see what you have." I smiled and tried to make sure it made it up to my eyes. Part of this group or not, Tag seemed like a good kid. I shouldn't take out my anger and fear on him. Besides, I needed to stall until Covey could get some folks together and come find me.

The rest of the pieces were less important from an archeological standpoint but more from a good, old-fashioned, what-we-can-sell standpoint. Most all of them had jewels of some sort and many were made of solid gold. They were from the later elven period and I didn't have to lie about any of them. They were more like art pieces of no cultural value, but that the idle rich of the elven dynasty they came from would have kept in their homes under lock and key. Not something that Covey or I would care about.

It felt like I had been there about three hours, so it was early evening by now. Still no Covey.

I hadn't seen Locksead the entire time I was with Tag. In fact, every one of the gang seemed to be avoiding me. Tag and Locksead were the only two I saw well enough to be identified. Which made sense if most of their faces were fresh off the wanted section of the local or distant prisons.

Then Locksead showed up and called everyone into another smaller room toward the back. My stomach growled as wonderful scents of well-prepared food hit me. Tag and I started walking toward the room, when Locksead blocked me. "Not you. I'll bring out a plate and some ale for you, but the others don't want you seeing their faces up close yet."

That was a nice confirmation of my theory on them all avoiding me, but still annoying. Once I got rescued, I had a strong feeling that I wouldn't be able to find Locksead anywhere, finding Tag wouldn't help me, and I had no idea what any of the others looked like. Even Carlon and the brute who had carried me in.

Tag came up alongside of me, but I noticed he stayed a half-step behind. "I can get both of us food. I'll stay with her to make sure she doesn't get into anything she shouldn't."

Locksead nodded, then grinned when he saw me starting to look around where we'd come in. "Even if you fight off Tag, and he's far feistier than he looks, you wouldn't get out. The entrance is heavily locked and only I have the key." He pulled out an ancient and non-elven key from where it hung on from a chain on his neck along with a few smaller normal-looking ones. "And if you did overcome Tag, steal the key from me, and make it outside, you'd never make it through the tunnels. The people who originally looted this place once the elves did their big vanishing trick made one hell of a maze out there."

Tag came back with a full plate and a mug of ale. He took it down to where we had been looking through their relics, and then went to get another set for him.

Locksead watched him go, and if I knew him better I might say the man was thoughtful. Then he turned back to me. "Tag's taken a liking to you. It'd be easier for everyone if you'd go along with our plan, help us out, and not try to escape. Nothing bad will happen to you, but we need you. I think in more ways than one." He looked around and dropped his voice. "I will let you go once we finish our task. I promise." Those ice blue eyes were chilling even though I could tell he was trying to be sincere.

"I don't want to be here. You took me against my will." I stood up and tried to reach for my magic but deflated a bit when the headache came slamming back. I'd done a good job earlier. "But I will try to help you within reason." I didn't have a choice. Who knew when my on-again, off-again magic would come back, or how exactly it would help me once I got out of this room? Letting him think I was giving in would give me time for a plan. I hoped.

Locksead didn't look like he believed me any more than I believed him. However, I had to take what he'd offer. He tipped his head and went back into the dining room. Tag and I settled in for a wonderful meal.

"So you guys have your own master chef?" This meal would rival Amara's best. And yet the person behind it was here living with a gang of thieves and killers.

"Yup." Tag finished his bird leg. That was the fourth one he'd had and I was expecting him to have a late growth spurt right in front of me. He put away more food than ten of Foxy's regulars combined. "Joined up a year or so ago. I think he's running from something down south. But he sure can cook."

I had noticed that Tag didn't mention his name. Again, back to secrecy. Locksead must not care that I knew Carlon's name, probably hoping I might report him to the authorities when I got free and take care of the problem for him.

Tag went back to eating, and I looked around the example of the elves' former glory. Alric would love to see this. There were still so many bright colors, and most of the designs looked dusty, not damaged. It said a lot about his ancestors' skill that whatever caused the building to fall completely underground, the room was still intact

"So why are you here?" My question caught Tag off guard and he almost spit out a mouthful of ale, but he recovered.

"That's not something you ask when you run with a gang. It's one of the rules." He was trying to sound older than he was which ended up making the opposite seem true.

I tilted my head. "Want me to guess?" I didn't wait for him to answer, but I made sure no one in the next room had come into our side, and they were all too far away and too noisy to hear us. "You are from the south, subtle cues in your speech tells me that. You were once a houseboy to one of the matriarchs of one of the larger cities. Most likely you got blamed for something you didn't do, or you got bored." I smiled at the widening of his eyes. "Or a bit of both."

He didn't look like he wanted to answer me, but that made it more clear that I'd hit it close to the mark. All of the people here probably lied about where they were from and what life they had before joining. It'd be interesting to find out how fictitious Tag's story had been. If his co-members weren't familiar with houseboys and the southern matriarchs, they never would have guessed. However, once I'd realized it, he gave himself away in almost everything he did.

I was about to promise him that I wouldn't give away his secrets when a stabbing pain hit my head with enough force to blur my vision.

CHAPTER TWENTY-SIX

Tag grabbed me before I could fall off the bench. "Are you okay?"

I thought I saw concern and fear in his eyes but my eyes were still swimming so everything looked blurry. I tilted my head and wiped my eyes. It still hurt to look at anything, so I closed them. An explosion of bright colors and jabbering sounds filled my head. I flung open my eyes to find myself on the ground with Tag peering closely at me. "I've got to get the doc, I don't care what Locksead says."

I grabbed his arm. The pain was fading as suddenly as it came, and as long as I didn't close my eyes for too long, the colors and sounds stayed away. "No, I'm fine." A thought hit me. "But I need some medicine. If I don't take it regularly, I can have fits." My brain was trying to work through the pain to come up with a plausible medicine I'd use in that case, but nothing floated to the surface.

"I can get it for you." His earnestness and genuine concern for me almost made me take it back.

"It's an herbal blend. My friend Covey makes it for me, but I don't know what's in it." Maybe this wasn't the best plan. I wouldn't mind if Locksead or Carlon ended up going against Covey—I knew she'd win. But I didn't want Tag to get hurt.

A pounding at the door in the entrance room cut off our discussion. Tag looked up in shock and Locksead ran out from where they were all eating. He pointed at me. "Stay there." Then at Tag, "Come with me."

Judging by the equally freaked-out look on his face, and the fact that the people in the dining room were all louder and sounding more distressed, someone pounding was not a common occurrence.

I decided to interpret his terse "Stay there" to refer to the room in general and crept forward until I could see into the entrance room. He wasn't kidding about that door being locked. At least five locks and assorted chains had to be undone, and then he pulled out a short sword, slid behind the door, and opened it.

Tag was left to stand in the middle of the room. I almost called out, but he seemed to be watching Locksead's every move and if this was part of their plan, I didn't want to mess something up and risk injuring Tag. I was already thinking of ways to get him free of living with these hoodlums.

The door pushed open and a tall thin man, with his face wrapped in fabric, stepped through. Black hair could be seen and I briefly wondered if Alric had come back and found a way to save me.

"Gravlin, you know you're not to leave your post." Locksead shut and bolted the door and Tag shook himself and moved toward them.

"They're coming. Horrible monsters, they found us and took out Smyd and Doster. They were behind me in the tunnels."

Locksead's blade was at the other man's throat in an instant. "You led them here?"

Even Tag pulled out a knife I hadn't seen on him before and took a step back.

"I never done! They were going right toward it already, we tried leading them off, but they got the other two."

Locksead looked at the formidable door and all the locks, then patted it and motioned for Gravlin and Tag to come with him. I quickly stepped back to my table.

"Come on, princess." Locksead held out his hand for me to rise. "I don't think it's coincidence that we've had our cover blown, right after you join us."

I rose up and found my eyes covered by a rough cloth and my hands bound. "We won't use the bag this time, per the boss. But we can't let you see anyone else, nor where we are." It was Carlon. He'd probably been behind me the entire time I'd been watching the other room.

My hands were bound with a rope that had a long enough lead to allow them to hand me off. I was terrified that Locksead would hand me off to Carlon.

"It's okay, I have you. I'll keep you safe." Tag said. Unlike Locksead, I believed Tag would do what he said.

Judging from the rumble of feet, panicked voices, and slamming of doors, crates, and who knew what else, this had never happened to this group before. And, it sounded like no one was near Tag or I.

"Don't you need to get your stuff? How are we going to get out if these attackers are coming in from the only door?" I turned a bit toward the pull of the rope, but it was weird speaking to someone without knowing where they were.

"Locksead will put my stuff in his wagon; I don't have one of my own." The tension in his voice made him sound younger. "That's not our only entrance. We have one for the wagons, but it's rough going. I don't think anyone has ever found one of Locksead's hideouts. If I were Gravlin, I'd take off as soon as we clear this place."

There was a chance, small as it was, that the monsters they'd seen had been Covey and Harlan. I thought about the weird pain, colors, and buzzing that had hit my head right before the scout had pounded on the door. Could that have been the faeries? I leaned against the table and tried to call out to them.

For a second I thought I would be okay, then the fire ants turned up the volume on the dance contest they were having in my head and I slumped down to the bench. Tag caught me when I almost missed.

"You really need that medicine, don't you? I'm sorry we can't stay and get some from your healer friend, but maybe in Kenithworth we can find another herbalist. Have you been there? I have. I liked it, but we only stayed a few days. Then Locksead brought us down here. Now we have a job back up there but it's too early."

The sounds of slamming and preparation were slowing down and a huge grating sound filled the cavern.

"Get her over here. She'll ride with us." Locksead was somewhere to the far right and high up. Most likely on his wagon.

"Um, don't you guys need horses?"

My question was answered as what sounded like a herd of hooved animals clattered into the cavernous room. Tag led the way, holding my arm instead of pulling on the rope, then helped me up a pair of steps.

"You two stay inside and hang on. I don't know if we're going to make it." As Locksead spoke, I heard a pounding at the front door. I couldn't imagine that those tunnels would allow something as big as a battering ram down them, but from the sounds, someone had made one fit.

CHAPTER TWENTY-SEVEN

The wagon we were in started moving, but not quickly or well. I had to figure the leader of this group got the best of them and if his was this bad, it didn't bode well for the rest of his gang. Tag had been leaning against me in such a way as to keep me from flying about too much but it was hard to keep upright with my hands tied.

"Look, you guys have me, there's no one for me to see until we stop except for you, can't we take the cloth and rope off?"

He was silent for a few moments, then he pulled the rope free of my hands.

"Thanks." Even though it had only been a few minutes, I rubbed my wrists and shuddered. Rope on my wrists did that, gave me flashbacks of my dead former patron, Thaddeus. Having the person you worked for turn into an evil syclarion bent on world domination tended to do that.

After a moment's hesitation, the cloth over my eyes was removed. Obviously, I could have done it myself, but I really hoped that if I built a rapport with Tag, it would help me down the line.

The outsides of the carriages had all looked shabby. The inside was worse. "So how long have you guys had these?" The interior was filled with thick heavy brocades; once upon a time it had probably looked bright and garish. Like probably a hundred years ago. Now it looked tired, sad, and like a dust explosion ready to happen.

I grabbed my nose as that thought brought an overwhelming urge to sneeze.

"Locksead got them right before we came down here. Before we just used to travel on foot or by horse if we could steal some." He pulled back a tattered and heavy-looking purple drape and looked outside. The glass windows must have been replacements, they were in far better shape than the rest of the wagon. Dark shapes passed us, but with hardly any light, I couldn't tell what they were. His lean face was drawn when he turned back to me. "Beccia was going to be our big pay day. Now we're on the run again."

He looked so sad I almost felt bad that I might possibly be the cause of them being discovered. Then I shook myself. It was Locksead who decided to grab me. Carlon had the tile and could have taken off as silently as he came. I felt bad for Tag but not for the rest of the criminal horde.

The carriage was moving unevenly; most likely Locksead was trying to work his way around giant tree roots. I had no idea where we were, but we were clearly still in the elven ruins, which meant massive gapen trees.

I heard yelling, and the carriage picked up speed. Tag looked out again, but it was fear in his eyes now, not sadness. "I only see two carriages behind us now." He sucked in a breath. "One. Some sort of flying creatures attacked the third one; Carlon's a good fighter though, so maybe he can survive. It's us and Jackal and whoever is in his carriage; no one else is behind us."

My mouth went dry. "What kind of flying creatures? Long, snake-like things? About four or five feet long and all black?" The girls had said that fewer of the sceanra anam remained, but they'd also implied there had been a lot more originally than we believed.

Tag's look told me it wasn't them, and he was a bit concerned that I thought it might be. "Naw. Big hawk things, with lion heads. Probably about as tall as Jackal." At my blank look he nodded. "The big guy who carried you in, the one driving the carriage behind us." He looked back out the window and shook his head. "I saw two of them that hit that carriage."

Only Tag and I were in this carriage, with Locksead up front driving. If the one behind us was about the same size, only five or six out of twenty or thirty hadn't been captured or possibly killed. By what sounded like a pair of gryphons.

All of my thoughts slammed out of my head, along with any breath in my lungs, as the carriage took a hard hit that sent Tag and I flying off our seats.

The branches of the trees we raced through were becoming more aggressive in trying to stop us which meant Locksead was heading deeper into the woods. "Why doesn't he go for the road? This carriage will get stuck in here." I was counting the seconds until the axles broke or a wheel fell off and we were at the mercy of whatever creatures were after us.

"He's aiming for a ruin we found months ago. Wasn't big enough for all of us. But it would be fine now." His voice caught and I realized that while, yes, they were all thieves, these people were Tag's family. In addition, a bunch of gryphons had just snatched or eaten most of them. I was studiously ignoring the fact that gryphons didn't exist.

I hadn't been aware of it until it stopped, but Locksead and the driver behind us had both been yelling to their horses. We were still moving, the carriage swaying from side to side, but both drivers were silent. Tag started to look out the window, saw me watching, and held it closed. "I'm sorry, but we can't take the chance, you know?"

I nodded. I'd be lying if I said I hadn't hoped to get a glimpse of where we were, but I wouldn't want Tag to get in trouble.

"So Beccia's guards use those lion birds to chase thieves?" His eyes were round and I thought that maybe for the first time since he'd joined Locksead's gang he was re-thinking things.

I almost laughed at the idea of our criminally lazy city guards having trained creatures of myth on call. "Gryphons. Creatures like you described are called gryphons. They only exist in myth, along with dragons, hippogriffs, and manticores. And no, our guards wouldn't even bother to come into the ruins looking for you, let alone have the kind of magic users involved that could make it seem like a pair of gryphons were attacking people." It was so silent outside as we made our way through goddess knew where in the ruins that I dropped my voice without thinking.

"Someone else with a lot of magic to burn is after you guys. And no, it's not because of me." I'd seen him open his mouth to comment but I shook my head. Alric might be able to pull that off. But he was missing.

A sinking feeling hit my stomach. Whoever and whatever those rakasa were, they had power. Judging by the fact they seemed to be using explosives and pre-set spells to augment their digging, they alone didn't have enough to glamour someone into a creature of myth.

But a certain homicidal and totally crazy elf they dragged out of a cave might.

The wagon started slowing down, then stopped completely.

"He's walking us in. I've only been here once; it's going to be a tight fit with the wagons."

I braced myself to keep from sliding as the wagon suddenly went into a steep incline. We were obviously almost there, wherever there was. "Tag, have you seen any elves aside from Orenda, or any short, dangerous-looking guys who like to stamp things with a dragon symbol?"

He had been looking out the window, but dropped the tattered curtain at my question. "Not sure about another elf. If there was, they were covered. Locksead met with a few folks yesterday, but they all had hoods and cloaks. But they were tall. He didn't have what they were looking for, so they stalked off. Not seen any short folks except for those damn brownies. We've run into them a few times since we got here. They were hiding deeper in the forest but started heading toward town last week. Annoying little buggers but I wouldn't say dangerous." He leaned forward, curiosity overwhelming fear. "What do the dangerous little guys look like?"

I wished I could tell him some wonderfully scary story. From the look on his face, he was one of those kids who loved sitting around a fire late at night scaring his friends. But all I had was the truth. "I have no idea. I assume they look scary from their history. But the elf would be noticeable without a hood: black hair, silver eyes, and full-blooded-insane elf."

The door rattled. "Come on, untie her and get out. I need you both to help push us in." Locksead solved the little untied problem. Which neither Tag nor I had even though of.

We both rustled about, then Tag opened the door for me. Locksead wasn't kidding; the wagon only made it part way inside what looked like a large, steep cave. Without waiting to be told again, Tag and I went to the back and pushed. Jackal and his wagon right behind us dashed any thoughts I had of running away.

We got both of the wagons, the horses, and the six of us inside, then Locksead darted out and came back pulling a huge shrub collection behind him.

Tag grabbed a pair of glows from the wagon and led us past the wagon. He handed me one then lifted his up higher as we entered the biggest part of the cave.

It wasn't a cave, but a smaller, more ornate and less robbed, version of the ballroom we'd been in. Just how many intact and buried buildings were out here in the wild ruins? "How do you guys keep finding these?" I kept the glow up high as I drifted to a gilded wall. The marks looked similar to the sarcophagus, and for a moment I thought perhaps we'd found an Ancient room, but closer inspection pointed out they were similar, but not the same. The relief was built-up paint, not hammered metal.

It was as if someone had seen the sarcophagus but didn't have access to it anymore and made this from memory. The basic feel of the designs on the sarcophagus were there, but the details were off. Parts that I recognized were connected to pieces I knew didn't belong. This entire wall was covered in it, but the rest of the walls looked bare.

Locksead must have felt they were secure in this new hiding place. He went from hunted man to enterprising thief in mere seconds as he waved at the walls. "All right, digger. Earn your keep. This stuff worth anything if we get it off the walls?"

He no longer seemed worried about me seeing the rest of his gangs' faces. Since there were only three others, I guess he figured they could take their chances with me.

"No." I kept looking at the wall, but I'd been able to tell that right off. "This is fascinating, and pure elven royalty. However, you couldn't get it off intact. The gold paint is starting to flake off. This room had probably been sealed whenever it collapsed. Now that air is getting to it, it will completely flake off within a few more weeks."

"I figured." Locksead grunted and turned to a hulking blond brute who had to be Jackal. "Did you get a good look at the attackers?"

The man was easily as tall as Foxy, but as far as I could tell was pure human. Although given his size and bulk, I'd wager there was a very human-looking giant not too far back in his family tree. Thick blond hair hit past his shoulders in a tight ponytail and the more I heard him, I could tell his accent was from the north.

"Just the ones that grabbed Carlon. They were lion-birds, like them stories. One flew up and grabbed the reins, the other smothered Carlon so he couldn't fight back. He didn't even get a chance to scream."

Locksead started pacing. "I don't know if we can pull this off with this few. First we lose our bait, Orenda, now most of my crew. Damn it, this was Carlon's plan. He needed to be here."

I'd gathered the two men didn't get along, but there was more than just a plan going awry in his voice. At some point he and Carlon had been friends.

"What were you after?" I tried to grab the words the moment they jumped out of my mouth. I'd learned one thing dealing with criminals, the less you knew about their evil plans, the safer you were.

Unfortunately, my constant curiosity didn't see it that way.

Locksead scowled then gave a shrug. "Might as well tell you. It was a long shot that a trained group like us could do it, now we can't. So no harm in telling you. There's a big Ancient find up past Kenithworth. Problem is, it's on protected land. We can't go in without sanctioned diggers. I have a dig site pulled, but I was planning on sending in folks pretending to be an established digger couple. I don't have time to create new false papers." His eyes showed him recalculating his plans even as we spoke. "But if you help us pull this off, you'll get a cut."

He looked way too sure I would say yes. My face must have gone into overdrive when he mentioned Ancients. That and they were going north—the general direction the changeling had indicated Alric had been taken.

"I can't just pick up and leave. There are people who will be looking for me." I narrowed my eyes. "Dangerous people. The ones who defeated the syclarions when they invaded our town."

One thing about Locksead, he was the ruler of this group. He didn't even look to the others for agreement, and none of them looked like they'd expected it. "You can tell your friends you're leaving for a trip and get whatever you need. You're not our prisoner." His attempt at a smile was scarier than his scowl. "You'd be one of us, for the time being anyway."

I kept facing him, but gave a quick glance to Tag. The boy's eyes were huge and he gave one short nod. It wasn't as if I'd really be a thief after all. I'd be working a dig site with a specific goal. I was a digger. We dug. Damn, I was really working on talking myself into this.

Part of me couldn't believe I was even considering taking it. They'd kidnapped me. Held me against my will. However, the temptation of a pure Ancient find, and hopefully finding where Alric was, was too much.

I found myself nodding.

Locksead grabbed my hand and shook it vigorously. Soon, the remains of his nefarious gang surrounded me as they pounded me on the back.

"Welcome to our world."

CHAPTER TWENTY-EIGHT

If his temptation of the possibly Ancient find wasn't enough—I still thought of it as only possible to keep my hopes from being dashed—those maps might have been enough for me to join him. Actually, in a way, he'd hired me. Qianru had shut down her dig until she got back next month, and there was nothing to say I couldn't work with another patron.

Locksead was in no way a patron, but even if he had been a legitimate patron, the Antiquities Museum, and all the supporting lists for patrons and diggers, was in a deep hole right now. Because of the size of the ruins in Beccia, the Antiquities Museum there handled all the digs in this half of the Kingdom. With it gone, who was to say if he was a patron or not? I recognized Covey's voice in my head, chastising me for lying to myself to justify doing what I wanted to do but knew I shouldn't. I did what I did in person and ignored her voice.

Then I realized I *was* hearing her. She was on the other side of the shrub collection Locksead had pulled as cover, and she was pissed.

"I know you're in there, and I know you kidnapped Taryn. Let her go now and I will keep the gryphons contained."

"Aye! Let her go! These beasts are hungry!" That was Harlan, trying his best to sound fierce. A farce that would fall apart the moment Locksead saw him.

"This take too long!" That would be Garbage Blossom, and an annoyed one at that. A second after her yell, she, followed closely by Leaf, Crusty and a handful of other colorful and overall-clad faeries, burst through the shrub as if it wasn't even there. Their war sticks whirling at high speed decimated it.

"You die now." Garbage pointed her war stick and she and all of the faeries formed a tight circle around Locksead. None of them had their war feathers on, so they must have gathered in a hurry. I'd expected him to laugh it off but by the look on his face and the way he held perfectly still, he clearly had heard of the faeries and their war sticks. I recognized most of the ones with mine; they were Garbage's best students. A slightly maniacal black and white one named Penqow and a purple one with crooked light pink wings I think I'd heard called Dingle Bottom were right behind Garbage and looked nearly as bloodthirsty as their leader. But none of them looked calm.

Covey broke up the tableau by stomping through the remains of the shrub. "I told you girls to wait. We needed to make sure no others were hiding." She had a sword out, a new look for her but I knew she could use it, and she calmly held it up to Locksead's throat. "We will be freeing our friend now."

She and the faeries had been so focused on Locksead and his people they hadn't seen me standing off to the side.

I coughed to get their attention. "I think I'm going with him." I turned to see Harlan and Orenda bringing up the rear. Maybe the elf had been the one creating the illusion of the gryphons; I hadn't counted her for a heavy magic user, but I could be wrong. "You all might want to as well." I quickly spun back to Locksead. "Girls. Let him go. Extra faeries too." Once they begrudgingly lowered their war sticks and broke their circle, I moved a bit closer to him.

"You need more people; these are good people. And my faeries will match anyone in a fight." I was already committed, might as well drag the rest of my bunch along as well.

"Wait a minute," Covey came next to me. "They kidnapped you, right? Out in the forest? Our little elf friend told Harlan and me about this gang."

Orenda was standing back. Harlan had moved forward, but she hadn't budged and was carefully not standing inside the cave mouth. She also wouldn't look at Locksead.

"You led them to us? They killed your friends. They killed your lover. Carlon was taken as we tried to escape." Locksead's eyes were more hurt than angry. Carlon may have wooed her away from him but Locksead still had a thing for her.

"I didn't lead them here. They found you on their own." She pointed up to the faeries hovering a foot or two in the air above us. "Rather, their *friends* did."

There was a look of wonder and interest on her face now. I'd liked it better when she was afraid of them.

"I'm not saying they should join us, but they didn't kill anyone." That was Carlon stepping out from behind Orenda. She jumped about a foot in the air at his voice then tried to hug him. He shoved her aside and came into the cavern.

He was bulkier than I'd guessed originally. It was more noticeable now because he was soaking wet. He had medium brown hair, badly cut, and ratty at the ends. His face would have been okay, except for the two jagged scars. One just to the far side of his right eye, close enough he'd been lucky he hadn't lost it. The other cut toward his mouth on his left side giving the corner of his mouth a permanent sneer.

But Orenda looked at him as if he was the most gorgeous thing in the world.

Carlon continued to ignore the love-struck elf. "They captured them. They almost got me, one of their shapeshifters, the things who had been pretending to be gryphons, chased me into the stream some ways back. But I got away. Some big guy with tusks and a bunch of gnomes dragged the rest into the city. We need to get moving with this plan. Now. I'm not losing my cut." He seemed to notice the small group for the first time. "Is this all who is left?"

Locksead shook his head. "I knew they couldn't have had gryphons. Yes, this is it." He hooked a finger at Orenda. "So she didn't help at all from what you saw? Answer truth, with your brain not your loins."

Orenda blushed but she was still making goo-goo eyes at the nasty man.

"She didn't. I'm done with her, that's why I left before." He spun toward the stricken elf. "I told you, we're through."

I was watching them both closely, or I probably wouldn't have seen what happened. Orenda's face fell, and she looked ready to start screaming, crying, or most likely both. Then I saw Carlon's right fingers flicker. Like someone casting a small spell.

Orenda's eyes rolled back into her head and she fainted. Luckily, Harlan was close enough to grab her.

Interesting. Tag had said they had no serious magic users with them, yet here we had Carlon shutting up a discarded lover with a spell. I looked to see if Covey had noticed, but she was watching Locksead as if she was deciding where to start chomping parts off.

"Let's try to stay calm here." I stepped between Locksead, Covey, and Carlon. "Yes, they did kidnap me.

That one," I turned to Carlon, "stole a tile I'd found at the epicenter of the most recent shake-up. He, along with these two, then kidnapped me." I pointed to Jackal, who was trying to hide, and Locksead. "However, they were going to offer me a deal for a job, and it involves a find." I turned to Covey. "An Ancient find up in Kenithworth. I was going to say yes."

There were a few moments of silence, only marred by Harlan crooning, "There, there," to an unconscious, but oddly smiling, Orenda.

Garbage dropped down to hover right in front of my face. "So we no get to kill? She say we can hurt people." Her lower lip stuck out and she waved around her war stick as if she were an annoyed cat and it was her tail.

"None of them should come with us. I know enough about relics; we don't need some digger girl and her flying bats." Carlon was getting on my last nerve. He'd annoyed me just hearing about his antics from Tag. Right now, I wanted to find a cliff to drop him off of.

"I get him at least?" Garbage zoomed right up to Carlon and waved her stick in his face. He moved to swing at her but she dodged.

"Look, even if Orenda still wants to come along, Locksead said you need more people. You need me." I took a step toward Carlon and stuck a finger in his chest. "Not that they can't defend themselves, because they can, but if you ever touch one of the faeries, I will destroy you."

The bastard winked at me.

He'd just dumped his former lover in front of me, and now he was trying to get together. "Eww." I hadn't meant to say it out loud, but judging by the muffled snorts behind me I was glad I had. I could see Tag just out of the corner of my eye with both hands over his mouth trying not to laugh. Carlon looked like he wished he'd dropped me in that pit when he found me.

Good to know we felt the same about each other.

"I decide who goes on this mission." Locksead stepped forward, cutting off all of the snickers. "You're right, we do need more people. Since the rest of my team is spending time with your prison system, at least for now, I need extra people to make this work. I'll cut you in for the same amount I would have with others. However, you will have to work, this isn't a free ride. I'll leave you wherever we are the moment I think one of you is slacking off, or trying to betray us."

"We shouldn't take them. They'll slow us down. We don't have the extra wagons anymore," Carlon said.

"Would one more help?" Covey asked with a sigh. "Most of them didn't survive being attacked; you should have taken better care of them. But we hid one and the horse from the guards a little ways back from here."

"I found it." The voice came from behind us. I knew that voice. Just wasn't used to it sounding weasely and defeated. I was used to it sounding weasely and arrogant. Grimwold stepped into view. "Well, to be truthful, I was hiding in it. I moved it here, but the horse wouldn't come any closer."

He moved forward then realized who he was talking to. His face paled as it flashed from Harlan, to Covey, to me.

"Wold, I thought you got snagged in the first wagon?" Jackal came forward and pounded Grimwold on the back which almost sent him flying across the room. Would I never be free of this idiot?

"How long as he been with you?" I kept an eye on him, but he mostly cowered and tried to hide behind Jackal.

"He came here a day ago. Only magic user we have on hand, so we let him join up." Jackal slapped him again. "He had some presents for Locksead. Ain't seen no magic yet though."

I wasn't sure if they were buddies or Grimwold was now Jackal's favorite toy. Last I'd seen Grimwold he was trying to bargain with a criminal to get to Kenithworth. I wondered whom he had robbed to buy passage with this gang, because he clearly didn't have any money before.

I was going to ask them if they knew who he was, but judging by Tag's reactions to me asking about his previous life this was a don't-ask, don't-tell gang. If they knew he used to work for Largen, the former master crime lord of Beccia, it probably would only increase his standing with them.

I simply nodded slowly. At this point Grimwold was more afraid of me than anything else. Whatever gift he'd given Locksead for the ride out of town was stolen and he figured I could identify it.

"Look, we're all here and this is what we do the job with." Locksead had been standing back watching, and clearly decided he'd run with what he had. "The ladies get the wagon in the back. Rest of you sleep where you want."

Carlon's face had been getting darker as the people he clearly didn't want involved, joined his gang. And from what it sounded like, the plan was at least half his. "I'll take first watch. I'll wake Jackal in four hours." He didn't even wait for a response, but stalked off into the night.

Good. Maybe if he was annoyed enough he'd leave.

I watched Orenda as he strode by her, but she didn't even blink. Whatever he'd done to her in bed previously, she was now ready to move on. With the help of whatever spell he'd flung at her at any rate.

Harlan escorted Orenda over to the far wagon, and Covey and I followed. Well, partially. Covey turned to Locksead. "If we're going anywhere, we need our own supplies. I'm going back into town and getting things for

Taryn, Orenda, Harlan, and myself. Don't try to leave without me."

Locksead was tall, but Covey was even taller. His featherlike hair ruffled a bit as if trying to make up the difference, but he finally nodded. He even smiled. "I grew up around trellians. I know better than to piss one off."

Covey nodded to him, then me, and went off into the night.

CHAPTER TWENTY-NINE

Unfortunately, the next day dawned with Carlon still around. Covey had come back a few hours before dawn, dropped all of our stuff in the wagon, then woke me up so I could explain what in the hell I was doing.

If Orenda heard us, she gave no sign, and her uneven snoring told me she was probably wiped out and actually sleeping. After she'd recovered from her collapse, she seemed like a different woman. Not sure better or worse, but definitely different.

Covey and I had bantered back and forth for a bit about the wisdom of what I was thinking in joining up with them. However, after I reminded her that we needed to find Alric, and this was a free trip to the last place we thought he was headed, she didn't argue anymore. She briefly filled me in on what had happened though.

When I hadn't come back, she and Harlan had started searching for me and found one of the changelings who had seen the entire thing from hiding in a tree. He wouldn't say who had dragged him into the ground before, or why they released him, but was willing to help Covey find me as long as she didn't ask questions about who originally hired them.

Once she'd found out from Orenda more about Locksead's gang and where they likely took me, Covey convinced the changelings to disguise themselves as gryphons and help capture the relic thieves and leave them for the guards.

I was the first of us three to wake up, thanks to Carlon stomping about in front of the wagons. The man had probably only gotten a few hours' sleep, but clearly he was determined to get us all on the road before the sun. Locksead might be the leader, but I had a feeling that Carlon was the evil mastermind.

Maybe perpetual lack of sleep was what made him so disagreeable.

I toyed with rolling over on my tiny bed and trying to sleep some more, but then Locksead started shouting orders to get people out of their beds. More importantly, I could smell breakfast.

I rousted the other two and we left the wagon. I didn't see any sight of the faeries and tried to call them without thinking. I froze and waited for the backlash, but my head refrained from exploding.

And I was swarmed by a dozen faeries.

"We here. Is good now." Garbage was practically cheerful.

I narrowed my eyes and studied all of the faeries. They seemed happy but not speed crazy. Still. "Did someone give you tea?"

"No. Better." Crusty did one of her crazed spirals then spun around the front wheel of the wagon. The doll carriage Tag had shown me sat there, clearly explored by the faeries. It would be a bit of a squeeze, but all twelve of them should fit.

Tag stuck his head from around the front of the wagon. "I already had it in the wagon when we fled. I kinda heard about your faeries when I was in town, and thought after all this you could give it to them."

Crusty Bucket looped over to him and sat on his head. Some folks might take exception to that, but Tag looked like she'd showered him in gold.

"Grab some food, and then load up." Locksead had been conferring with Carlon and Jackal, then turned to all of us. "We've got a group looking for us. They're moving slow, but they've got some weird animal with them. We can't see it, but we can hear it. We leave now."

I turned to Covey. "Would Foxy keep looking for us?" I couldn't imagine any animal he'd have on hand that would freak out a hardened thief like Locksead, but who knew.

She shook her head as she gathered things to go back into our wagon. The girls' carriage was the first thing inside. "No. I talked to him when I gathered our stuff. He'll send someone around regularly to check on our places. I also left a note for the dean at the university, telling him I was extending my sabbatical. No one should be looking for us."

Harlan escorted Orenda to our wagon, and from the look in his eyes, he was looking for another wife. The fact that I was still seeing that look on Locksead's face when he looked at her wasn't a good sign.

"Now, even in these rickety conveyances, we should get to Kenithworth within two weeks. If you need to take a rest at any time, simply tell Tag to pull over." Harlan clapped a paw on Tag's shoulder with enough force to almost bowl the boy over. "Our boy and I will take care of you."

The wince on Tag's face was probably more from being put between Orenda, Harlan, and Locksead's triangle than the actual blow. But he simply smiled and got into the driver's seat.

Harlan beamed at Covey and I, then drifted over to his assigned wagon.

"Let's move people!" Locksead was in the lead wagon and didn't wait for anyone to respond before moving out.

Covey was the last in and she took the bench opposite Orenda.

"So how did you fall in with these brigands anyway?"

I was surprised Covey wouldn't have asked her that when it first came out I'd been kidnapped. Most likely Covey's focus at that time was finding me. Unfortunately for Orenda, that focus would now be on her and she was trapped in a moving wagon with a persistent professor.

"Like I said previously, something was taken from my people. My clan is xenophobic, and they wouldn't go into the world to get it. So I did." She drifted off a bit as she looked out the window, but a cough from Covey brought her back. "While I was tracking it down here, I ran across Locksead and Carlon. Locksead can be charming and he said he had a plan to get some rare elven artifacts, but they needed a woman accomplice." She shrugged. "My trail had gone cold, and I didn't have much in the way of money, I had no idea how expensive things were out here, so I joined them."

"And then you left?"

Orenda blushed heavily at that. "I thought I had found a life mate. I was wrong, he left me. I decided to go back to looking for my artifact on my own." She frowned. "But the leads I had vanished. I don't think it's this far south."

All questions about more details about the emerald dragon were met with silence. She might have helped them find me, but she didn't trust us.

The wagon hit something large and far less mobile than it was and we all almost fell off our seats. Tag was doing a decent job of driving, but the ruins were too heavily tree filled to be good for anything with wheels. The faeries had all started out inside the wagon but were already working on pushing the window open to get out.

"Wait. Before you leave," I held the window that Dingle Bottom and Penqow were pushing against, "where is Bunky?" I hadn't been too worried when the girls first showed up without him. He often went to go hang out with the wild faeries and Queen Mungoosey. However, I had no idea how long this trip would take and I didn't want him missing us.

"That who we get," Garbage said as if obviously I should have known that. "He following followers. We get him back."

Following the followers? Damn, trying to get what he was seeing via the faeries would not be easy. I braced myself as the wagon started gaining speed—and bumps.

"Get him, see what you can of who is behind us, and then find us quickly." I felt better now that I knew my magic was as good as it ever was, so I should be able to call them, but I was still worried about being separated too long.

The faeries all crammed out of the window all at once, not waiting for me to open it further.

Orenda was watching them and a small smile crept across her face.

"Not as scary as your myths say, are they?"

She shook her head. "It seems as if many of our stories were wrong. Speaking of stories, back in the forest you had mentioned an elf friend?"

I wasn't thrilled about talking about Alric with her. However, the more I could get her to talk, the greater the chance she might start talking about something of interest. Like her people or this damn emerald dragon. Too many people were looking for it, and we still weren't certain if it was related to the other two artifacts.

"Well, not sure what all to say. His name is Alric. He's an elf and his clan is at least a week's ride to the west. But he's only been in town less than a year." That made me stop; had it really been less than a year? On one hand, it seemed like he'd been in my life forever, but on the other, a recent annoyance. I guess it depended on whether he was pissing me off or charming me.

Orenda leaned forward. "That's an auspicious name, if his people kept to the old ways like my people did. What is his family name?"

I looked to Covey and shrugged. Great, here this man was becoming a possible contender for the big love of my life, and I never asked him for his last name? "I have to say—"

"It's Glasene. Alric de Glasene. Merchant family from what he told us," Covey said with a smile of complete honesty. Her lying was artistic.

Orenda had deflated a bit at the name. And probably at the merchant classification. Most likely, she was far higher up the food chain in her clan.

Voices outside were yelling now and the wagon bounced badly, tossing us to the floor. Tag kept yelling at the horses, but clearly we were still in the ruins and they did not have many speed options.

"We stand and fight!" That was Locksead and the wagon came to an abrupt stop at his words.

CHAPTER THIRTY

I looked around the wagon for anything I could use to fight with. Covey didn't need weapons although she pulled out her newly acquired sword. Later I'd have to ask her where she got it.

Orenda rolled over to her back and pulled free her bow and quiver, then a pair of short swords. She handed one to me. "Can you use this?"

I took it with a nod. I wasn't great. Like my magic, the sword lessons had been slow going. Alric insisted that practice would get me there and at some point, there would be a snap, and I'd get it. I had my doubts about that; swords never seemed to feel balanced right to me. However, I knew enough for the weapon in my hand to be an asset not a hindrance. Probably.

The wagon started moving again, but this time slowly and in a circle. We must have found a meadow to take a stand in.

The faeries hadn't come back yet, but if they were following whoever was behind us, they should be here soon. Covey swung open the door and the bright light of early morning hit us all in the face. After being in a dark forest and even darker ruins the last day, it was a bit of a shock. Not to mention dangerous. I almost broke my neck falling down the steps after Covey.

I caught myself and held my borrowed sword out from my body just in case the damn thing went rogue on me.

The four wagons formed in almost a square, with the horses hidden off in the woods. I took up a position behind one of the driver's seats and looked out into the forest behind us.

The forest was silent at first. Then a growing rustling sound came from the direction we'd come from. I wasn't sure how Locksead feared they were already upon us, based on the length of time it was taking for them to get to us.

"This is taking forever," I said under my breath to Covey. Not that I wanted to try to defend myself against some army of strange creatures that had freaked out a bunch of hardened criminals, but I hated waiting.

She gave me an odd look. "It's only been a few minutes. Probably less than three." She looked down at my left hand. "And you might want to relax your hand a bit. Your knuckles look like they're frozen in place."

I glanced down. Yup, five little white rocks had replaced my knuckles. I switched hands and shook out my left fist. One of the things Alric had been diligent about was teaching me to fight with either hand. As he pointed out you had to figure that in any fight you could be injured. And injured but still able to fight was better than dead.

The rustling noises got stronger, and larger branches started moving. Had those damn crazy brownies tried to make another golem? And this time made it work? I still was having a problem seeing those little lawn ornaments as anything beyond an annoyance. Of course, that would have been different if that first golem had stayed together long enough to hurt anything besides my sense of smell.

The noise got much louder and everyone hunkered down behind their cover. Even Harlan had a weapon, more of a heavy-looking long pole really, but he had claimed to be wicked good with a quarterstaff in his young and wild days. I hoped he was right and his furry bulk wouldn't take more hits than the enemy.

A low crooning filled the air, almost dirge-like, and the branches of the trees at that end of the meadow moved as if an invisible wind rustled them.

Then the creatures came into the clearing.

I took a breath and tried to keep from laughing. It was another golem, but this one had been made in haste, and the parts kept slipping about. One moment it was bipedal and walking on both legs, the next moment it had slipped a leg around and hobbled on a leg and an arm, then started shuffling on all fours. They must have had access to a large supply of cabbages because this time not only was its head one, but it seemed they were the dominant plant. They were however, far fresher than the parts used on the previous golem. Which made the creature less smelly, but also seemed to be contributing to its lack of cohesion.

The others tensed up, but I waved at them and stood up—the golem didn't have projectiles unless it started flinging body parts, and the brownies at its feet only had their tiny swords. "It's okay. I got this—"

My heroic offer was cut off by Carlon bursting from his hiding hole outside of our wagon circle, and laying waste to the golem. The creature fought back but it was hard when parts kept switching position and Carlon's long sword hacked them off.

The brownies started defending it, only to find themselves dive bombed by a pack of faeries. My pack of faeries, who, judging by their excessive antics of annoyance to the brownies, had become quite bored while waiting. A reassuring buzz came through the trees, which was followed by Bunky. He dived for a few brownies, but didn't seem to really see the need so he came over to me.

Orenda let loose an arrow at Bunky, but Covey smacked her bow a second before the release and the arrow missed Bunky but came very close to Carlon. Maybe if we tried harder we could hit him next time.

"He's with us." I grabbed her bow when it looked like she would go for another arrow. Bunky might be a construct but his kind could still be damaged or destroyed.

"What is that flying thing?" Locksead yelled as he ran out to join Carlon in hacking the golem and the brownies equally. Had to give the brownies' credit, their creature stayed together better this time. And even though there were at least two dozen of the tiny beings, they were grossly out matched but they kept charging the two men. It was amazing how far they could fly when kicked, especially considering how thick the trees were.

"He's my friend." I wasn't going to go shouting about Bunky in the middle of the forest. However, if Locksead wanted me on this caper he got the faeries and Bunky as well.

Bunky hunkered down behind me, landing on part of the wagon. He seemed to spend most of his time in the air, but who knew how long he had been flying around the last day or so.

The rest of the gang had come out from behind their wagons, but Carlon and Locksead didn't look like they'd need help so everyone just watched.

The golem eventually collapsed, as the half-assed magic driving it was no longer able to keep it intact. Carlon took one final heavy swing and was rewarded with a shower of plant life as it finally fell apart. He was lucky this one hadn't been decaying like the one I faced.

The brownies looked ready to stand and fight even without their plant monster, but when both Carlon and Locksead charged them, they all ran back into the woods.

Locksead grinned at Carlon, and the two ran after them.

"Even if we're no longer being chased, don't we need to get moving?" I looked around as the faeries came back to the wagons. No one else seemed concerned that their leader was off chasing mostly defenseless brownies. I wasn't worried about the brownies, they were tougher than their size indicated. However, it seemed like a waste of time.

Cook shrugged and he and Jackal went to start moving the wagons out of formation so they could hook them back to the horses. Then an earth-shattering scream ripped through the air, followed by Locksead being thrown into the clearing. He didn't get up. He bent awkwardly on his sword arm, so even if he had survived he wouldn't be fighting any time soon.

Cook and Jackal jumped back into the ring of wagons, pulling the two they'd moved back into place. Orenda and the two other archers had their weapons aimed at the trail behind us, and those of us with swords were trying to appear at the ready. I ignored Tag's shaking and he said nothing about mine.

Covey looked at the forest and growled.

I motioned for Bunky to stay down but waved the faeries to me. "I need you to fly through there fast and high. Don't attack anything. Just see what is in there."

Garbage fingered her war stick. I knew she had no intention of obeying me.

"I'm serious. No sticks. Recon only."

She finally nodded and led her faeries into the branches. In that time, Carlon had started to come running out of the woods. A slithering rope grabbed his feet and dropped him. He twisted to get free, but the rope pulled him back into the woods too fast.

Covey again growled, this time at the people around her. "Your leaders are out there and you do nothing?"

The looks that met her glare were clear. This group had little solidarity, if any.

"So be it." Covey bounded over the wagon at its highest point and charged into the woods.

"Damn it." Covey's sense of honor, even though I was pretty sure she disliked Carlon as much as I did, was going to get us killed. However, I couldn't let her go out there alone. I looked to Harlan and we climbed out from the wagon grouping and followed.

"What are you idiots doing?" Jackal yelled, echoing the looks on the faces around him.

"Our friend went in there, to rescue your companion." Harlan's snarl was impressive but I could see the paw holding his staff was shaking. "We stand with her."

Orenda looked at the others, then she and Tag followed us. More screams and yells filled the air around us, but none of them sounded like Carlon, or Covey, for that matter.

I couldn't see what the four of us could do against something or somethings that had taken down Locksead, who still hadn't moved, and Carlon. But Covey was in there and we had to do something.

We were entering the forest when a dark shape flung itself at us. At me actually. I screamed and shoved it off, not even thinking for a moment about the short sword in my hand.

It was Carlon. He was dazed and leaking blood from a few places, but he shoved himself off of me and ran back the way he'd been thrown.

He might be a jackass, but he clearly didn't know when to stop fighting.

Orenda and I took point, her because of her bow, although it would be of limited use if we got much further into the trees, and me because that was how my life seemed to go. Besides, someone had to protect Tag and Harlan.

We cautiously walked a few more feet and saw that at least two of the brownies hadn't made their escape. Their bodies had been shattered, and then tossed aside. Almost more disturbing were the emblems of a green dragon they'd all sewn onto their red caps. Our suspicion of the brownies following the rakasa appeared to be supported. Then who killed these? What else was out here?

Another couple of steps and I saw what I assumed was one of our enemy who hadn't made it either. Locksead's sword was pinned to a gapen tree. It went through a creature I hoped was one of a kind.

It didn't wear clothing that I could tell, but there was a chance the dirty gray covering was clothing of some kind and not skin. It was pinned by the sword so its head was eye level with mine, but its skinny, clawed feet hung a good two feet from the ground. The huge eyes were white, but I didn't think they started that way. One hand, ending in two-inch-long claw fingernails, clutched the sword running it through. But the worst was the mouth. If the sceanra anam had bred with a dwarf and been spelled for nothing but killing, you might have this mouth. Large enough to fit the head of a full-grown human inside, it seemed to be nothing but rows of sharp, triangle-shaped, and serrated teeth. I looked away when it was clear where some of the brownies had ended up.

"What is it?" Tag had come up closer than the others, but seemed more curious than terrified. I would have to work on him about the benefits of being terrified.

A sound behind us cut my answer of not having a clue off before I could say it. Orenda was leaning over a bush and throwing up.

When she stopped, she wiped her mouth off and turned back to the wagons. Her movements were robotic and all I heard was the word "no" repeatedly.

"Orenda? What is it?" Harlan tried to stop her but she pushed past him.

"Gklinn."

"What? Look, you guys, either come with us or not. But we're getting Covey back." The woods were quiet right now, but I didn't think that was a good thing.

"Demon, she said Gklinn, which means demon. That's a rakasa."

At Harlan's identification, Orenda threw up again, although little remained in her stomach. Then she continued stumbling back to camp. She didn't even look back at us once, and moved like a sleepwalker.

I admitted I wanted to join her in both situations. However, my best friend was out there.

I did wonder why, if the brownies were followers of the rakasa, the rakasa were killing them. Maybe the rakasa really didn't like fans.

Another high-pitched scream filled the air. "Anyone who is with me, come on."

I was pleased to hear both Harlan and Tag follow behind me.

The silence of the forest vanished into a wall of sound as the faeries started yelling war cries—so much for not fighting—and I heard Covey yelling a few choice swear words from her ancestors.

Then we found them. Carlon and Covey faced the creatures across from us and the faeries held a position in the air a few feet above them. There were only four of the little monsters, what I now assumed were the feared rakasa, but they held back. Fighting when anyone got too close, but mostly just to keep everyone away from the thing behind them.

I couldn't see it as it was covered in leaves. For a moment, I thought maybe they had taken control of another one of the brownies' golems. Then I saw one of the rakasa throw a brownie at the pile of leaves. Something within the pile gave a high and tortured scream, and then a clawed hand, far larger than the hands of the rakasa, darted out and grabbed the brownie. The chewing and crunching sounds made me think about joining Orenda in the throwing up thing.

Covey waited until the rakasa looked at whatever creature they had with them, then darted forward with her sword and in a single swing decapitated the closest rakasa.

The remaining three charged forward, and worse, the thing in the leaves came out.

It was broken and naked, its skin covered in welts and bruises. Pointed ears stuck out through the matted hair and I was glad Orenda had fled. Whatever it was now, this creature had once been an elf.

Its legs were twisted so it crawled on all fours. Then it looked at me. I knew the eyes that stared out at me. Now filled with pain and total madness.

CHAPTER THIRTY-ONE

Glorinal's silver eyes faced me. Rather, one did. The other eye was huge and completely black. His ravaged face was uneven now, as if a spell or disease had made one side of it larger than the other. A pox of some kind stole away his cruel beauty into deep pockmarks and welts. His head was mostly bald, and his frame skeletal. Along with terror, I also felt a stabbing of sorrow. Then the images of the sixty-three people he and Jovan had murdered filled my mind.

If anyone deserved to suffer, it was he.

There was no recognition in those mismatched eyes, nor anything even seemingly sane.

We were at a stalemate; one that I didn't think would last for long. I had no idea what Glorinal had become but clearly the rakasa hadn't rescued him just to kill another elf. Although if they hated elven kind as much as was rumored, this would be a fitting use for one in their book. And if this was what they did to them before killing them, I could see why Alric was so terrified of them and why Orenda fled.

I hoped that wherever Alric was it was nowhere near here.

One of the rakasa stepped forward. This one was taller than the others and had a crude crown of branches and animal skins on its head. "You give us, we keep *him* here. Not attack you. You go."

The voice was dry and rusty, as if it hadn't been used in a few hundred years and the owner had been exposed to the elements. But I understood him.

"Give you what?" As annoying as she was, there was no way in hell I was giving up Orenda or anyone else.

Carlon charged forward at that moment, trying to get in the same swing Covey had. He might be a good fighter, but he looked completely unnerved as he ran forward.

Two of the rakasa blocked his attack, and Glorinal leapt up to grab him and pull him down.

Glorinal didn't do anything else. Just sat there with his hands, or what was left of them, on Carlon's chest to keep him down. Carlon's face contorted in fear, but every time he tried to move, Glorinal pushed down harder and clenched his hand. Glorinal turned and whined to the rakasa leader like a dog asking for permission to devour a treat.

"Dragon. We get our dragon back, you live." The voice was getting a bit less rusty, and I started wondering if I had been right. Maybe it hadn't spoken in a few hundred years.

I looked to Covey and the others. Tag and Harlan hadn't run yet but both looked terrified out of their minds. Covey looked like she was waiting for the word to attack. She was muttering something, but while I could see her lips moving, I couldn't hear her. Her gaze was fixed on Glorinal and Carlon.

"We don't have any dragons. Why are you chasing us?"

The rakasa looked at me, and then sniffed in the direction of the wagons. He turned back to Glorinal.

"You sent us this way? Why?" The rakasa asked the thing that used to be Glorinal.

Glorinal kept looking at Carlon.

The rakasa motioned to the other two of his kind. "Get the slave."

Glorinal was pulled off of Carlon and dragged to the leader. Carlon scrambled away but didn't leave the area, he just found his sword and waited.

"Why this way? Why did we follow them? It is too soon for exposure." The rakasa slapped Glorinal with enough force to have taken off his head had Glorinal been his former self. As it was his head snapped back and he cowered.

"Drag-on. Have." His voice was painful to hear, and again I had to keep shoving the memory of the innocent people he murdered into my mind.

"You lie. Not time for this." The lead rakasa looked at the five of us. Then motioned for the other two to drag Glorinal with them and vanished into the woods.

All of us stood there for a few moments. I didn't know about the others, but I couldn't get my limbs to move. Literally. At first, I thought it was fear, and then I realized that creature had put a spell on us.

Or someone had. Someone who didn't want us following them.

The moment passed and we could move. And were surrounded by a flood of faeries, both wild and those from town. I'd wondered where the girls had gone after their initial fly over, but was counting on them staying out of trouble for once.

And they had.

"We here. Where they go?" Garbage had not only gone for reinforcements; she'd gone to get her war feathers on. Or plucked a new batch off some poor bird.

"They went that way." I held up a hand. "But don't follow them."

Crusty looped around the area the rakasa and Glorinal had gone, then came back to me with a confused look. "They no there. Never there."

The other faeries all flew over the spot as well, a few of the wild ones even going down the trail, but all came back with the same confused looks.

"Not there. Where you put?" Garbage had the same tone and look she had when she'd chastised me for destroying a sceanra anam to save my life.

"They went that way." Harlan had finally recovered enough to speak, but he still didn't look good. He was a lover not a fighter and it spoke volumes to how much he cared about Covey and me that he hadn't run off at the first sign of the rakasa.

My three faeries buzzed close to him, then came back.

"They vanish!" Garbage said with conviction. Apparently, they didn't believe my telling of the story. However, if Uncle Harlan said it, he of the treats and belly rubs, it was considered true. Nice to have a reminder of where I stood with them.

"This is all great, but we need to get moving." Carlon didn't completely snarl, but it was close, as he stomped past us and went back to the wagons.

I noticed none of the faeries got anywhere near him. The ones that had been hovering where he marched through rose high in the air before he got close then flew closer to us.

The wild faeries formed a giant circle, then sang a high-pitched note, and flew out of sight. I was standing near Garbage, so I saw the flash of sadness on her face as they left. Then she shook it off, and held a brief meeting with the town faeries. I couldn't understand what they were saying, but they soon left as well, leaving my three and the extra nine that were apparently with us for the duration of this trip. No way would I try to learn all their names. Dingle Bottom and Penqow were the easiest names of the bunch.

By the time we got back to the wagons, Locksead had been retrieved and placed in his wagon. He hadn't regained consciousness yet, but Orenda nodded when I peeked in. His arm was in a sling with sticks, and he was covered in scratches. But it looked like he'd survived.

Which left Carlon stomping around trying to get everyone ready to ride. Locksead wasn't a softy, not by any stretch, but he was compared to Carlon. I wondered again what Orenda had seen in him. Although, he'd used that tiny magic trick when she came back. He could have spelled her from the beginning and then was actually breaking it.

Love spells weren't that hard to learn. Alric wouldn't teach them to me, but he explained them in theory. While they weren't difficult to learn, they were draining for the spell caster. I narrowed my eyes and watched Carlon barking orders. The physical cost would have been heavy. So why would he cast a spell on her, then tire of her after a few weeks? I'd have to keep an eye on Carlon whether I wanted to or not.

The faeries and I went back to our wagon, where an agitated Bunky waited. He'd taken my command to wait there seriously, but wasn't happy about it.

"Sorry, Bunky." I stuck my hand in my cloak and skritched him through it. I needed to see if Covey had brought me any gloves. "But it was better you stayed here."

He gave his rumbling buzz, and then flew up a few inches to eye level with a definite accusation in those black eyes.

"We needed you to stay here and protect everyone else." I motioned to the rest of Locksead's gang that had stayed behind. In truth, I wouldn't have tried to protect them. They couldn't even be bothered to try to get their leader until they were sure the risk was gone. However, my words changed the tone in Bunky's buzz. He clearly was taking his role as guardian of the faeries and me to heart, but it was good to know I could transfer that care if need be.

I opened the door to the wagon and he waited until the faeries flew in. Crusty Bucket as usual was bringing up the rear. She was also flying more sideways than usual and I had to catch her before she flew into the side of the wagon.

I flipped her over to make sure she hadn't been hurt somehow. As far as I knew none of the faeries had been around the rakasa, but who knew what they did before we went out there. "Crusty? Sweetie? Are you okay?"

She shook herself off, staggered about my hand a bit, then flopped down with folded legs. "Stinky. Is very stinky." She waved her hand in front of her nose as if to clear the smell from it.

"What's stinky, sweetie?" We put her down next to the others gathered around their little carriage. Stinky I could deal with; nasty things trying to kill us I had a problem with.

"He stinky. Bad man." She must have cleared her head enough because then she ran off to join the others as they all stuffed themselves in the carriage. A lot of giggling, snorting, and singing. Then silence.

I stuck my head inside. All twelve were sound asleep in a giant mass of overall clad legs and wings.

I was not one to argue with providence. The faeries had already shown to be easily bored when traveling in the wagon, so if they wanted to sleep during it I was all-good with that.

The door swung open and Covey, followed by a very irate Orenda, came inside.

"What's wrong?"

Orenda glared at the closed door. "That man, Carlon. I need to stay with Locksead. I think he's going to recover, but he still hasn't woken up. That idiot is having Cook ride with him because obviously a cook knows how to fix injuries." She flung herself on her seat. "I spent time learning the healing craft as a child; I bet Cook has never even tied a bandage."

There was no haughty elven princess there, only a pissed-off nurse. My opinion of her went up a few notches.

"I thought he was your soul mate?" Covey had leaned back and closed her eyes as soon as she took her seat, but she obviously was listening.

"I was wrong." Orenda's tone possessed enough venom to fuel an army of poisoners for a year. "Horribly, horribly wrong." The shudder she gave reinforced it if there had been any doubt whatsoever.

"Good. That man is a jackass." Covey cracked open an eye and gave the elf a smile.

"I could have killed that...thing...if he hadn't charged forward right when he did."

Covey let that annoyance stew for a bit, then turned to me as the wagon started moving.

"Your ex-boyfriend hasn't improved. But it couldn't happen to a better person." Her eyes narrowed. "I still need to kill him. Although if he's aware at all of what he now is, that would almost be payment enough."

Orenda watched both of us with growing confusion. She'd taken off before Glorinal had arrived. I was actually grateful for that for her sake.

I gave a sigh. It would be better not to tell her about him, but I had a horrible feeling in my gut that this wasn't the last time we'd be seeing him or his keepers. The way they left was both odd and disturbing; clearly Glorinal had given the rakasa some bad information as to what we had with us. But it still seemed like a sudden departure.

"Who are you talking about?" Orenda asked.

Some of the stuff in my head must have shown in my face. Orenda looked like she felt she needed to know, not that she wanted to know.

It took longer than I would have thought to explain the entire Glorinal saga, or at least the crucial aspects. But that was mostly because I kept trying to skim and Covey was relishing all the details. Until it got to the part where he and Jovan had taken Harlan and Covey prisoner. Neither of them had talked much at all about what happened. Coming from Covey that reticence wasn't too unexpected. However, that level of silence for Harlan scared me.

Covey skimmed it now, and I let her.

Orenda looked shocked and concerned. But most of her questions were aimed at the fact that not only had there been other elves around, that both were major magic users—she mentioned her people had only the weaker magics left now—and that Jovan was from before the Breaking. It seemed that her clan had been even worse off than Alric's in terms of older survivors and had been founded by a group of teens and children.

Of course, she seemed to be in complete denial about the rakasa. Even though she had seen them, and judging by her reaction, she had known what they must be from horror stories still passed down by her people, she was blocking them out.

"But how did he survive? Is there any way we can free him? We could question him," She turned to Covey with an understanding nod. "Make him stand proper trial for his actions, including killing one of the Old Ones."

She was back to focusing on Glorinal. Had she seen what he was now, she wouldn't be asking about rescuing him. The nicest thing anyone could do would be to kill him.

Covey answered before I could. "There is nothing left. He was a vile, vicious killer, and he got what he deserved, but there is nothing left, even of that. He is now a monster in the truest sense of the word."

Orenda opened her mouth to try to defend him; he was an elf after all. But Covey closed her eyes, folded her arms, and went to sleep.

"Why don't you tell me what you know about where we're going?" I figured we'd talked enough about Glorinal for one lifetime.

Orenda glanced to Covey, but turned away when she gave a convincing snore. The plan she outlined was simple, but I wondered if that was because Locksead hadn't told her much.

The dig site was a new one, located outside of Kenithworth. Because they didn't have the flood of diggers found in Beccia, and the whole ruins thing was new to them, there weren't the tight restrictions on getting assigned a dig site. You did need to have at least one qualified person on the crew, and they favored groups over individuals. The original plan had been for Orenda and Carlon to pose as a renowned digger couple who was actually currently working down near the Spheres. They looked like the couple well enough, and it was known the woman was a half-elf.

Now that they had Covey, Harlan, and me however, Locksead found himself with an abundance of real cred. He had briefly suggested that Carlon and Orenda still keep up their ruse, but Orenda had shut that down immediately.

The plan was for us to go in as a group of digger explorers, find the best relics, then take off before the gatekeepers realized what we had found. I was hoping to find clues as to where whoever took Alric had gone, but I'd be lying to myself if I didn't admit growing curiosity about the possibility of an untainted Ancient dig site.

As of yet, no respectable diggers knew of the uniqueness of this location. Locksead wouldn't tell where exactly the dig site was nor how he found out about it.

"So how is he doing?" Like the rest of them, who already knew the plan, I now had a vested interest in Locksead's recovery. He was keeping everything vague so everyone needed him alive. Unfortunately, Carlon appeared to be a major part of this, so we couldn't dump him off somewhere.

The scowl Orenda had been wearing earlier came back at my question. "I believe he will be okay, but he still was unconscious. His right arm is shattered. Unless we find a healer, he won't be using it for a while. I can't tell if something attacked him, or the damage is just from being thrown. And now that Carlon has kicked me out, I won't be able to tell what is wrong internally when he wakes up."

She folded her arms and did a great imitation of Covey dozing. I settled back and let my thoughts bounce around my head as we continued down the road. I'd never been to Kenithworth but Harlan had estimated that it would probably take two weeks to get there.

With nothing else to focus on, my mind went back to Alric. I just was having trouble thinking the rakasa would have gone through the trouble to find and hire a pair of changelings to cover his kidnapping. The changeling probably lied about little men hiring him.

Which meant someone else took him. Hopefully, once we got to the city, I could send the faeries on his trail.

CHAPTER THIRTY-TWO

Harlan had been off by a week in our travel estimate. It had taken closer to three weeks and we were still a day out of the city. We'd developed a routine for setting camp, each of the wagons had, and I was out setting the wheel blocks and admiring the view as soon as Tag stopped our horse. We were on a cliff overlooking a valley divided into farms of various colors of green. The city itself was behind that, and even from this distance, it was huge.

My hometown had been little more than a fishing village. And while Beccia had grown significantly in the fifteen years since I had moved there, it was less than ten percent of the sprawling city before me.

My back was toward the rest of the camp, and I was trying to decide if I had time for a closer look at the valley below us before dinner, when Locksead's voice shattered my thoughts.

"Tell your friend to leave Orenda alone. He's married."

Locksead had recovered, but Grimwold's magic hadn't been enough to help heal his arm, so it was still in the sling. A few days after we'd gone on the road, Carlon had created some kind of paste that solidified into a hard cast.

The cast was annoying, and Locksead still couldn't do much with that hand, but it did get him back to his usual self. Unfortunately, it also got him back to focusing on Orenda.

And so was Harlan.

"He's married, but chatalings traditionally have multiple wives, and I think his current ones are done with him." I finished shoving the block under the last wheel and turned back. "I am not going to get involved in anyone's love life, least of all yours."

He looked ready to launch yet another argument against Harlan and Orenda, but Covey appeared from the side of the wagon. "Time to get some drills in before dinner." She glanced at Locksead as if she'd just seen him. "Cook is looking for you."

I smiled as he left. I had grown tired of the weird little love triangle over the last three weeks. Especially since Orenda seemed to be totally oblivious to the drama.

The smile dropped as Covey held out a short sword and dagger. I completely agreed that I needed to be better able to defend myself, but I'd been counting on my magic training to do just that. Covey wouldn't listen and brought up way too many arguments on why relying on magic—even once mine became stronger and more consistent—was a bad idea. A blade could still hurt a magic user if they couldn't get a spell out in time to block it. Actually, all I had to do was look at Grimwold and the point was driven home. What if my magic never got higher than his? Without Alric or another magic user I trusted with my secret, my training was at a standstill.

With a sigh, I took both weapons from Covey and squared myself for another painful and annoying round of training.

I could get the basics of sword and dagger fighting down. However, the subtle nuances that would make me a serious fighter I just couldn't seem to grasp. Covey and

I had been doing some weapons and hand-to-hand training since the whole glass gargoyle incident. But she was now like a woman obsessed.

"No, you dropped your left arm again, right after you swung. You left that side unprotected and I could have run you through." Covey had a blunted practice blade today, so she whapped my side as she spoke in emphasis. She alternated between a real blade and a practice one. So far, she was pulling any strikes with the real blade, so the practice sword was far more painful.

"It just doesn't come naturally." I set down both blades and flexed my fingers. "Maybe I need a longer sword." The one she had me training with was a short curved blade, as favored by the sword dancers of the Akalsat region. It was light, which was good, but it just didn't feel right, as if I was always swinging too short. I had no idea where she'd come up with all the weapons, and she didn't feel like telling me. Most likely she lifted them from the university in one of her odd, "I'll bring them back and it's for the greater good" justifications.

Covey bent down and traded the practice blade for the large sword. "You need to start with a lighter blade, and then go for reach. The bigger ones are heavy. Come on, we still have time for a little more before dinner."

No sooner were the words out of her mouth, than Cook rang his dinner bell. I'd never been so happy to go eat in my life.

I rounded the corner of the wagon to get in line for food—Cook's on-the-road food wasn't half-bad, but he was stingy with the amounts—but ran right into a mass of faery wings.

They were yelling about something. Of course, the more faeries got excited, the higher their voices got. Judging by the high-level squealing I heard, they were very worked up.

I thought about dodging around them, but if I did that, someone would just send me back to deal with them.

"What is wrong?" That launched a barrage of chittering flung my way. "Wait, one of you, Crusty, you tell me what's wrong." As the leader, more or less, of their tribe, Garbage looked affronted that I hadn't asked her. But Crusty was holding back from the argument. Most likely simply because she hadn't noticed it. She was flying in tiny loops, humming to herself.

"Bunky stuck. But he make us promise not to follow." That was possibly the most coherent sentence I'd ever heard from her.

"We want to follow," Garbage said and the rest of the faeries nodded. "But can't."

I looked at all of their tiny, frustrated faces. Bunky had been keeping them in line on this trip, but if he wasn't here, I didn't see how he could enforce it. They never obeyed me if I wasn't around.

"Why can't you?" I held up my hands and all three of my faeries landed on them. The remaining ones hovered nearby.

Garbage looked embarrassed. "He say no." All eleven other faeries nodded their heads in stern agreement.

"Since when has that stopped you?" I was still lost.

"He put spell on us."

I almost dropped the girls at that one. Bunky *was* a spell; he was a construct created by some ancient and insanely powerful mage for who knew what reason. Alric had assured me that constructs couldn't be magic users.

"Why did Bunky put a spell on you?"

Leaf piped in first on this one. "He did for you. You say we listen to him. Him make it happen."

I looked to the other faeries, but they just nodded. Garbage scowled, folded her arms in annoyance, and then nodded.

Bunky was able to cast a spell because I told him to? I tried to think of any transference magic that Alric might have touched on. However, if he had, it had been just that—touched on. And not something I'd kept in my head.

I looked longingly where folks were lining up for dinner, then shook my head. Bunky was lost and in this situation because I wanted him to keep the faeries in line. I had to go find him.

"Fine, I'll go find him. Just point the general direction that he went." Eleven tiny arms pointed down a trail a bit behind our camp. Crusty just reverted to spinning in a circle. "Garbage, tell Covey where I went, and ask her to grab me something to eat."

Bunky was probably still close by, but obviously he'd been gone long enough for the girls to get worried. The trail they pointed out was one possibly used by wagons bringing things for sale to the city below. It was nice and wide and looked harmless. Just how I liked them.

I kicked myself as it started to get steeper. I should have asked the girls why Bunky had gone down here. That thought grew larger as another trailhead appeared to the right. One that, unlike this one, was narrow, dark, and twisty. And had a piece of fabric stuck to it. Fabric not unlike the scraps Glorinal had been wearing.

Crap. Part of me said to go back and get Covey, the other part worried about the setting sun and finding Bunky before full dark.

I went forward.

The trail became even more twisted as it dipped further into the trees. I found another scrap, but both looked like they'd been there a while.

A buzzing and thumping shook me out of my dark thoughts and led me toward a tree stump.

I was glad I'd kept going when I did. Peering down into the stump, I could barely see Bunky. Had night fallen, I might have heard him, but seeing an all-black construct in a blackened tree trunk would have been impossible.

He was caught up in some webbing that at first I thought was some sort of natural plant life. But I realized it was a net when I pulled up a section of it. The edges of the stump were treated with some sort of sap. Whatever Bunky had been out here looking for, he'd triggered a hunter's trap meant for a prey animal.

I slipped on a pair of thin gloves Covey found for me, and went to work on freeing him. It took a few minutes, but I was able to pull him out of the trap. His buzzing had grown stronger as we got closer to freedom, until he was practically singing as I lifted him out and pulled the netting free of his body and wings.

"Now, you fly back to camp immediately; show the girls you're okay. And we will have a talk about this later." Our conversation was mostly me talking and him buzzing, but I usually was able to get my point across.

I was heading back to the wider trail, and feeling good about saving Bunky, when a dark shape dropped onto the path in front of me.

CHAPTER THIRTY-THREE

I took a step backwards. The shape took two steps forward. Whoever it was had successfully blocked the way I came down the trail. I had no idea where the trail behind me went, but it had looked only darker and twistier the further you went in. I regretted not grabbing that sword I'd been using. I still had my knife, but that wouldn't be much use against a trained fighter. Hopefully, it was just some lost old man out for a stroll

The shape moved out of the shadows. It was a man, and a trained fighter. Worse of all, it was Carlon.

Carlon had been hounding me in the last three weeks on the road, especially if he thought no one was looking. I'd managed to never let him get me alone.

This was the first time he'd gotten me far from the others, and alone. He must have seen me leave and followed me. "I need to talk to you."

I backed up. I still had no idea how much of a magic user he was, but I didn't want anyone, let alone him, knowing I was one as well. "I have nothing to say to you."

Some voices could be heard on the main trail and Carlon covered the distance between us in a single stride and pulled me close with far too much familiarity. He looked over his shoulder toward the trail and shook his head. "Sorry about this, but they can't suspect anything."

I recognized Tag and Jackal arguing about what trees burned best coming down the path and heading our way. Right before Carlon kissed me.

I pushed back as hard as I could, but Carlon was strong and he resumed his kiss. He broke away for a split second, just before my knee connected with his groin. "I need them to see this. It's me...." His voice came out in a squeak as he tumbled to the ground.

Tag and Jackal came up at that moment, took in the scenario, and laughed. "Told ya she was smarter than you," Jackal said. Tag made sure Carlon couldn't see him, then gave me a thumbs up. They both continued down the trail looking for firewood.

Carlon writhed on the ground. I'd gotten a good knee in. "Alric."

He'd said something else, but I couldn't hear him. His eyes were watering as he curled around his middle. He looked like he was fighting not to throw up.

"What did you say?" Had he been behind whoever took Alric? I pulled out my knife. If he knew where Alric was, I was getting answers.

"It's me, Alric." For a brief second, the ugly façade vanished, except for the hair, and Alric's annoying—and contorted in pain—face appeared.

My heart jumped. Why was he here? Had he escaped from whoever took him then taken Carlon's place to try to rescue me? Then a darker thought crept in. "Wait a minute, have you been Carlon the whole time?" I put a lot of weight behind those words as everything slipped into place. I'd been worried about him, terrified that someone was torturing him somewhere, and he'd been right beside me for three weeks? I felt even worse when a second thought hit me—he and I had been building a relationship while he made Orenda scream with pleasure every night? If I thought I could have reached them, I would have kicked him in the balls again.

"Yes, but I can explain." He'd put the glamour back up so I was facing Carlon again.

"Go. To. Hell." I couldn't reach his balls but I kicked him anyway.

I got back to the camp without crying but it was only because I was too mad to cry. I made it to the wagon I was sharing with Covey and Orenda. I saw Orenda at the other end of camp talking to Harlan over the remains of their dinner. If I was lucky, Covey was off somewhere as well.

Unfortunately, she was inside the wagon and flung open the door just as I was reaching for the handle. She took one look at my face, and tightly curled fists, and pulled me inside.

"What happened?"

"Carlon is Alric." All the emotion hit me at once. "I've been looking for him, spending time worrying about him, and he's been off playing with his elf girlfriend the entire time." Again, I hadn't meant to say that out loud, but it was that or start crying. When we got back to Beccia after this job, I was joining those nuns Covey had stayed with.

"Now there might be a good reason." Covey trying to be gentle with me wasn't a good sign.

"All the time he took off from us? He was with these thieves. He was with Orenda."

Covey looked confused. "How do you know? I mean he dumped her, but she doesn't seem like a jilted lover to me."

"I heard all about it before you guys showed up. He made her scream with pleasure every night according to the others. As for her getting over him, he used some sort of spell on her. That's why she collapsed the first night we joined them."

Covey's eyes went into flat predator mode. "He slept with her? Repeatedly? While he was supposedly doing research or with his people?"

To be fair, she was a friend, my best friend, but it was the lying that she was the most upset about. That and the fact she thought he'd been with his clan when he took off after the glass gargoyle and the obsidian chimera when instead he'd been hanging out with relic thieves. The fact that he'd just broken my heart was something that would hit her later.

"Yes."

"Are you going to be okay?" Covey got to her feet. I knew she needed to go attack something; her face was what the field mouse sees right before a hawk made him his dinner. Nevertheless, if I said I needed her, she'd stay.

"I will be." I just needed to be alone right now. First Marcos was actually the Jinn brothers in a spell, and then Glorinal was actually a murdering sociopath out to rule the world. Now Alric, the man I thought I was falling in love with, showed his true colors. His current look might be mostly spell, but it obviously reflected who and what he really was.

"I will take care of this." With a curt nod, Covey left the wagon.

I wanted to cry. I needed to cry. But I just couldn't do it. Therefore, I just started pacing and let my mind bash itself around.

A soft knock came at the door. I ignored it and kept pacing.

A moment later, the knock came again, this time joined by a bunch of smaller ones.

"We come in now!" Garbage was not the pillar of subtlety.

I swung open the door. It was easier to let them in than have them get louder and louder. I was heartbroken and furious at Alric, but I didn't want to give away who he was until I was a hundred percent sure he'd betrayed us. Me.

My three faeries flew in along with Tag. The rest of the henchfaeries stayed outside protecting the door although Penqow and Dingle Bottom were tussling over a specific spot in the air.

"Did he hurt you?" Tag's eyes were huge as he scanned my face and arms for injuries.

I forced a smile. "No, but he'll never try that again."

"Oooo! We get to kill him now?" Tag must have filled Garbage in on what had happened. He and the girls were becoming close.

"No, Covey went to go take care of it, just in case he didn't get the hint." I looked at my three faeries. None of them had picked up on Alric. Even under a magic disguise, they should have noticed something.

"Girls? Have you noticed anything unusual about Carlon?"

Crusty frowned. "He no like us, always stinky. On purpose."

That was a new one. I never noticed any odd odors around him, but then I tried to stay away from him. However, little bothered the faeries' sense of smell.

"Smelled like what? He's a jerk but I've never smelled anything on him," Tag said. "Sometimes Wold gets a bit ripe, but Carlon isn't like that."

"Like Elerdowln." Leaf said and the other two nodded encouragingly.

The name sounded vaguely familiar, but racking my brain, I got nothing. Covey or Harlan would probably know, but he was with Orenda and Covey was hopefully taking a certain elven high lord down a few dozen pegs.

"Wanna try a more common name?"

Tag was nodding though. "I know what that is, my former mistress was a plant lover. It's sewerweed. But it doesn't smell like anything unless the leaves are boiled."

I'd noticed that since I had already told him I guessed he'd been in a household to the south, Tag would let slip a few things from his past. Only around the girls and me.

"It does too!" Garbage said. "It is nasty smelling all time. He smell like it."

"Has he always smelled like that?" I might not know what sewerweed was or its effect on the faeries, but I'd bet my last two coins that Alric did.

Crusty entertained herself by darting in and out of the ratty curtains, but paused in mid-air at my question. "Not first night."

"Yup, next morning all stinky," Garbage added and Leaf nodded. He had kept to himself that night and the next morning been up before all of us, "scouting". Damn bastard. He knew the girls would see past him if they got close enough.

"So this stuff affects all faeries?" If Alric knew to use it, others might as well. I'd have to ask Covey if she knew of a way around it. I counted on the girls to find people, if it got around that this weed could block that, I'd lose the advantage of having them.

"Yes, no faeries like." Garbage crossed her arms. She wasn't sure what I was getting at but I could see her defensive lower lip starting to stick out. She knew something had been missed on her watch.

"Except Penqow and Dingle Bottom." Leaf said thoughtfully.

"Yes, they go boom." Crusty was sad. I would have been more worried if the two faeries in question weren't outside my door still fighting over airspace. But boom was such a catchall phrase with them who knew what it meant in this case.

"What kind of boom?"

"Fall in sewer. It go boom. They don't have good smells now."

Ah. And since both of them were Garbage's lieutenants in training, they wouldn't have thought to go near Alric unless she did.

"Garbage, you trust those two? Penqow and Dingle Bottom?" I knew little about them except Penqow seemed to be almost as good at running into walls as Crusty, and Dingle Bottom was often seen just spinning in circles giggling to herself.

Garbage gave it serious thought. Which meant a full two seconds before answering. "Yes."

"Then can you have those two follow Carlon? Report back to me anything odd or interesting about where he goes and what he does?" I would have rather had my three follow him, but since they couldn't get close to him because of the sewerweed, I'd have to hope these two could do the job.

"I do." Garbage started toward the door, and then turned around. "We no get to kill him?"

I smiled and it was a real smile. "Not yet."

All three faeries nodded and Tag opened the door for them to fly out.

He looked like he wanted to ask more questions, but then Locksead bellowed for us to meet near his wagon.

Covey joined us as we followed the others to the wagon. The extra faeries stayed by my wagon door, but Penqow and Dingle Bottom took off after a few words from Garbage.

Covey's eyes narrowed. "Carlon has been hiding. I never got a chance to talk to him."

I almost felt bad; had he not made it back to camp yet? Then I shook my head. What was I thinking? The one thing Alric could do better than any other was survive.

The look in Covey's eyes made me almost feel better about the betrayal. Alric would get payback sooner rather than later. I dropped my voice and slowed our walking. Harlan and Orenda were right in front of us. "We do need to find out what he's doing. But we can't let Harlan know who he is yet." The problem with Harlan was that aside from his many disguises, he was just too sincere to hold a lie well. He couldn't know Carlon was Alric until we were ready to expose him. I did wonder if even with whatever spell Alric put on Orenda, she'd change her mind once she found out her former lover was an elven high lord. I shoved that thought back into the same dark corner all of my Alric thoughts now lived and finished walking toward Locksead.

"This is our last night before we go down to Kenithworth, so I need to make sure everyone is ready." Locksead waved his injured arm at the group. "Since I clearly can't go down as a digger with this arm, I am putting Jackal in charge. You will listen to him as you would me." He looked around as he noticed a missing person.

"Where in the hell is Carlon?"

Jackal stepped forward with a smirk, it was clear no one in this gang held any fondness for Alric's alter ego. "He might be a bit late, had an accident down the trail and needed some time to compose himself."

Locksead shook his head. "When he comes back you, he, and I will meet. The rest of you, just stick to your scripts and we'll be riding out of here in a week very rich."

CHAPTER THIRTY-FOUR

Since Locksead was still not going to give any of us specifics, the meeting, such as it was, broke up early. Covey stayed, talking to Locksead. The two had built up a friendship of sorts based on his growing up around her people. As she explained it, few people understood the nuances of her people's culture and it was refreshing to be around someone who could appreciate it.

Orenda and Harlan had slipped away behind the wagon he rode in. They were never too far away from everyone else, but they definitely had something going on between them.

The faeries were off with Tag and Bunky at the far end of the camp, playing some game only they understood. I'd noticed that whenever he was around them, and playing, he looked much younger. Probably what his real age was.

I reached for the handle of our wagon, when I felt a hand on my shoulder. "Don't scream and don't kick me." It was Alric. When I wasn't having half a dozen negative emotions flooding my brain, I could hear how close his real voice was to Carlon's. Really just a few levels down for Carlon, he mostly made the difference noticeable by the words he used. And the attitude. Carlon was a complete ass. And I was thinking that Alric wasn't too far away from that either. Interesting, but not enough to keep me from spinning around and stomping on his foot.

"You bastard. I was worried about you, and you were out here with that female elf."

I kept my voice down. I'd thought that I wanted Covey to take him down a few pegs, and I still did. But I also wanted answers.

"I can—"

"If the next word out of your mouth is explain, I will kick you so hard the entire camp will feel it." I looked around the group sitting by the fire. No one seemed to have noticed us yet. It'd be best if we kept it that way. I flung open the door. "After you." When Alric tried to motion for me to go first I gave him my best Covey-copied snarl.

He got inside quickly and I followed and locked the door. As soon as it locked, Alric dropped the glamour and even went so far as to pull off the wig. It must have been expensive even though it looked like crap, based on how real it appeared. He looked paler than usual, but it could just be the difference between Alric and Carlon. I'd been looking at Carlon for the last three weeks.

"Let me...." He watched my face, and then shook his head. "No, you go first. Get it all out."

"You son of a bitch. We thought you had been kidnapped, or killed. What were you doing here? What had you been doing with her?" I wouldn't cry. The wetness by my eyes was just dust that must have been kicked up when I stomped on his foot.

"Maybe I should go first." He sat down on one of the sofa cots, mine to be exact, and ran his fingers through his hair. It was such a familiar move it almost broke my heart.

"I have been working with Locksead and his gang off and on for a few years for leads on relics for my people. Carlon is a bastard so no one cares if he drops in for a job or two and then takes off. I make sure they only get relics that aren't of historical significance, or ones we already have too many of like those sarcophagus pieces."

Damn him, he was appealing to the tiny part of me that wanted to believe in him. I shook my head more at myself than at him. "Then what about Orenda? Is seducing an elf from another clan a new game?"

He reached forward and took my hand. Only then did I realize that I'd been digging my nails into my arm. I was starting to rethink just letting Covey at him, then talking to him when he was beaten and bruised.

"I was keeping a presumed innocent away from Locksead and the others. Some of the ones Covey got locked up were brutal." His face was grim and I was glad I'd not met most of the gang. "She was so wide-eyed and innocent I couldn't just let them at her."

I jerked my hand out of his. "So your bed was better since you're an elf? That's rich."

He laughed and shook his head. "I never slept with her. I cast a love spell on her when Locksead first brought her into the group, then knocked her out each night with a sleeping draught and used a spell to mimic her voice."

I wasn't sure about that, but my gut told me he was telling the truth. My heart wasn't ready to believe him though, and my brain had a lot more questions. "Fine. But then why did you leave us? I...we all thought someone had taken you. You left without saying a damn word. Then we've spent three weeks on the trail together and you couldn't tell me who you were?"

He rubbed his forehead. "I'll admit I didn't handle any of this well. And I had been trying to tell you who I was. You're damn difficult to get alone if you put your mind to it." He smiled, though, then let it drop when I didn't smile back. "As for taking off, someone was trying to kill me. The attack on my cave was set with one purpose, to take out that entire area along with me in it. I confirmed that when I went back to look for the girls. I even saw someone who looked like me heading for Covey's house when I started to come back to tell you good-bye. However, a changeling could only mean I wouldn't be around much longer in someone's plan. They captured the faeries and Bunky, and held them so well Garbage couldn't even feel them. I don't know anyone strong enough to break that bond with those faeries."

He looked up and there was real fear in his eyes. "There is someone after me with a lot of magic. I thought it might have been Glorinal since one of my sources mentioned seeing elves in the far ruins. However, there's no way anyone would take what he's become for an elf. I couldn't let whoever was after me hurt them. Or you. So I donned my Carlon disguise and went back to Locksead." He watched me for a minute, then shook his head. "Beyond my being on the run, I think this site may have one of the Ancient relics, one of the pieces of the weapon. I would have had *us* come up here looking for it, but I had to change that plan. I'd just convinced Locksead we needed to leave immediately for Kenithworth when those damn brownies and their golem came after us in the ruins. And we found you."

My heart wanted to believe him. And some part of me did mostly because this twisted explanation completely fit the Alric I knew. I met his eyes for a few moments, and then shook my head. "I'd like to believe all of it. But your life is just too damn complicated. Moreover, you lie far too easily. I won't tell them who you are, but I think we should work on staying away from each other on the rest of this trip." I had to close my eyes as I said the last part, keeping my tears in check was almost impossible.

Alric nodded and there was genuine sorrow on his face. "I understand. However, after this, I'll make it up to you. I promise."

I rose and unlocked the wagon door then briefly stuck my head out to make sure no one was watching. It was clear. I turned back to Alric. "No. After this, I still want you to stay away. If our interests overlap, since we seemed doomed to find all the pieces of that damn Ancient weapon of mass destruction, we maintain a professional relationship." I looked out into the night. It was too hard to look at him.

I heard the cot creak as he rose, and felt him come up behind me.

"I am sorry." His breath was warm against my ear and he sounded so heartbroken, I almost turned to face him.

But I couldn't. Every time I thought I knew who he was, something else popped up. "So am I." I shut the door as quickly as I could, then fell into my cot and cried.

⚬⚬

I finally fell asleep, at least I assumed as much since my next thoughts were that I should have pulled the curtains closed better and that it was way too early to be that sunny. I heard the soft snores of both Covey and Orenda, so clearly they had made it in at some point. I had a full two minutes of calm thoughts before my interaction with Alric came slamming back into my mind. In an avoidance of thinking about the emotional loss, I realized that I'd also lost my magic teacher. The intimacy of learning magic was far too much for me to interact with him that way now. However, unless I was willing to expose my secret to another high-level magic user, I was wouldn't be able to continue training.

I let that float around my head a bit. I'd lived my entire life not having magic; in fact, I'd been a magic sink. I could survive without using it now. A tiny voice in my head pointed out how good it felt the few times I'd been able to complete a spell without the fire ants in my head and how hard it would be to give that up. Then I thought of how messed up Alric was even with his magic.

I could live without using magic. Especially if Covey succeeded in turning me into a fighter.

"Are you okay?" Covey's cot was nearest to mine, and she pitched her voice low. I hadn't even known she was awake.

"I will be. I'll explain later."

Covey grunted in agreement, and then rolled over.

I tried to fall back asleep, but that damn curtain kept letting the sun in. And I just didn't feel like getting up to fix it.

The point was moot as Cook's bell rang to get everyone up for breakfast.

I quickly dressed, checked on the faeries, who were still asleep, and left the wagon. Tag and I were the first ones up. He drove our wagon, but after the first night or two of being stuck in the wagon with three women, he moved to sleep in Harlan's wagon. Both Covey and I had pointed out that we could drive the wagon, but Locksead wanted someone he trusted driving. We were good enough to be together on this one caper, but not to be trusted with one of his wagons.

"So, are you sure you don't want me to take care of Carlon for you?" Tag asked as he dropped in alongside me. He kept his voice down low, but his face was fierce.

The idea of him taking on Alric was charming. And terrifying. I had been afraid of what Carlon could do, but Alric was far more dangerous. No one in this group seemed to have a clue he was a magic user, let alone the level of magic user he was. Had someone like Carlon had that kind of power I'd flee. As it was, while part of me knew Alric would never hurt a kid, the other part pointed out I really didn't know Alric at all. He'd let Grimwold try to heal Locksead when he could have fixed the shattered arm with little more than a word. If he felt his disguise was in danger of becoming compromised, who knew how far he'd go to protect it.

"I think he knows to stay away from me." I reached over and gave Tag's shoulders a squeeze. "But thank you. It's good to know you're there for me."

His smile showed his youth and I wondered again what had caused him to flee to the north and join a bunch of reprobates. Especially if Alric had been right and the nicer ones remained. I almost thought that I should ask Alric if he knew Tag's story, then reminded myself I needed to start distancing myself from him. It would be difficult once this was over, but the sooner I stopped relying on him the better.

CHAPTER THIRTY-FIVE

I hadn't ended up eating last night, so Cook's food should have tasted awesome. However, aside from an overwhelming realization that I should eat, I wasn't enjoying it. Locksead, Cook, Jackal, and the others came out slowly. Alric was the last one out and sat far from Covey, Tag, and I. The faeries and Bunky had gone off hunting almost immediately after eating. I'd warned them that we'd be moving down into town today, so they'd need to find us. I think Garbage heard me. She just waved at me distractedly, grabbed her war stick, and led her troop and Bunky to the west. I had briefly tried to clarify with Bunky just how he put a spell on the faeries, but since our communication only went one direction, I still didn't know how he did it. I left it with an admonishment to refrain from spelling the girls in the future and a promise to talk more when they got back.

Hopefully they'd stay out of trouble. At least no more than usual.

Tag let out a sigh as they vanished from sight. "How did you get them to stay with you?" There was a lot of wistfulness in those words.

"I was cursed with them by a crazy hedge witch years ago. She saved my life and in payment made me take the three faeries as my wards. We thought they were the only ones around until a few months ago when the wild ones started showing up." I gave him a smile. "I'm kind of used to them now."

"Those weren't wild though, were they? They dress like your three."

In my head, I added "and they act like my three, drink like my three, and gamble like my three." Instead, I just smiled. "They *were* wild. My three have managed to corrupt whole flights of formerly wild faeries."

Tag nodded and I could practically see him planning to get some faeries of his own. Not a great idea, but since I was the only one I knew of with her own flock of the little miscreants, I couldn't speak to how well his plans would turn out.

Harlan came to join us, and his scowl was something of epic proportions. "I heard tell that varlet Carlon laid hands on you?"

I glanced to Tag, but he was watching the preparations taking place. Three of the four wagons would be carrying on to the dig site on the outskirts of the town. Locksead and Cook would be staying in the fourth one in a group of trees a few hours from the entrance gate to the town. Locksead's arm had been having more problems. In addition, he'd tripped two nights ago, and along with more injury to his arm, he wasn't walking well.

The three wagons going in needed some final touchups to make them look like they belonged to a group of serious diggers. A lot of it involved heavy applications of dust and dirt to the outside. Apparently, the road dust we'd added on our trip wasn't sufficient in Locksead's eyes.

"Tag, could you make sure they don't get any of that in our wagon? Jackal looks like he's having a little too much fun." I shook my head at Harlan when he started to keep up his questions. Tag didn't seem to have heard him the first time; I wanted to keep it that way.

"What?" He looked back where Jackal was attacking our wagon. "Oh, sure. I'll help him do it right." He nodded to Harlan, and then jogged over to our wagon.

Leaving me with a big problem. Harlan was horrible at keeping secrets, yet, if I didn't tell him, he would keep hounding the Carlon issue, and possibly the man himself, until something gave way. I personally didn't give a rat's ass whether Alric's cover was blown. However, professionally, his position within this known group of relic thieves in general, and this caper in particular, was important. We knew there were at least four more pieces of this Ancient weapon. If one of them was at this dig, like Alric believed, and we could get it and keep it, that still left us with three more to find. We might need Carlon in the future.

I studied Harlan's face, trying to use it to help me decide what to tell him. There was entirely too much stubborn determination there. I had hoped that Orenda would be enough of a distraction to keep him off the Carlon issue. Actually, considering how ill-used Orenda had appeared to have been at Carlon's hands, it may have just exaggerated his concern.

Alric would just have to live with one more person knowing his most recent secret.

"Don't yell, or raise your voice, or do anything to attract attention. It's crucial no one else besides you, me, and Covey know this." I glared at him when he looked ready to argue. "I'm serious, Harlan. The faeries don't even know." I waited until he gave me a begrudging nod before continuing. "Carlon is Alric." I held up one hand when he took a deep breath to explode. "I'm not going into all of it now, but that is him, and no, he did not do what they think he did to Orenda. Nothing happened. He was trying to protect her from the others in this gang, including Locksead. He needs to keep his cover and we can't let anyone else know."

Harlan got up off the bench and started pacing. A good sign. It meant he was thinking instead of reacting. But the way his tail was twitching about made me fear he was thinking of ways to boil Alric in oil. Regardless of whether he took advantage of Orenda or not.

"So he...and then he...." He stomped a few more paces, then spun. "How did you find out and why didn't the girls notice?" He looked triumphant as if he'd found a way out of a situation he didn't want to deal with. There was probably more than a little feeling of betrayal going on. He'd prided himself on becoming Alric's confidant of sorts. Or so he thought.

"He used sewerweed. The girls had a different term for it, but they said he smelled of it so badly, it blocked all the other scents and made them steer clear of him."

"Damn it. I told him about that effect on the faeries a few weeks ago. How dare he use my knowledge to hide from me?" Now he had something justifiable to focus on, his tail was in full lashing form. Betrayal of an emotional kind was harder to address, but betrayal of a knowledge kind was ripe for justifiable annoyance.

He stomped about for a good five minutes, muttering new and inventive swear words under his breath. Then he turned to me with a horrified look. "But what of you? Has that foul bastard broken your heart?" It had taken a while for that thought to run through his head, but his face was full of sorrow now.

I opened my mouth to lie, when a sceanra anam burst into our clearing. The faeries were nowhere in sight, and this one had the look of a hunter not the prey as it circled the group. If the old elves' tales were true, these creatures preferred the evil and guilty. This thing probably thought it hit a smorgasbord.

I stepped in front of Harlan. For my own safety and peace of mind, the last thing I wanted was for anyone in this gang of thieves knowing I was a magic user.

However, I didn't trust that Alric would break his cover and save us.

"Everyone, stay still. Don't try to—"

Jackal ignored my warning and threw a knife at the flying snake. He missed, and the sceanra anam flew right for Jackal. I got ready to pull in a spell, but Alric and Grimwold stepped forward near me.

"Trust me, I've seen a magic user of your caliber take one of these out before. Just concentrate." Alric was holding Grimwold's shaking hand up as he whispered a spell in his ear. I knew Grimwold couldn't blow his nose with a spell, and I knew how much energy it took to blow up a sceanra anam.

However, a moment after the spell left Grimwold's lips, the sceanra anam exploded. Alric patted Grimwold on the back, but he was also leaning on him for support.

Sneaky bastard. He found a way to get around his Carlon persona not having magic. Although, that might be something I could use as well if I needed. I reached out to say something to Alric, and then shook my head at Carlon. Alric was too confusing and too complicated. I knew he'd do anything for his people, but I had begun to think we were his people as well. It made it easier to stay mad at him if I carefully ignored the fact he left all of us to keep us safe.

Locksead let everyone congratulate Grimwold on his skill for a few moments, while I noticed Alric slowly limping away to his wagon. He shouldn't be that drained. I knew frying the thing as he had cost him, in part because he was also trying to funnel it through Grimwold. It would probably have left me passed out on the ground. But Alric was too strong of a magic user for that to have affected him like that.

"That's enough," Locksead said. "It's going to take a few hours for these wagons just to make it to the city, even longer to the dig site I secured for us." That was

MARIE ANDREAS

new; he hadn't told us we had a spot, just that he would tell us what spot to get when we got there. When had he done it? I watched him as he barked a few more commands to the people near him. He probably had it set up before he even got down to Beccia. He was someone who left nothing to chance. I took in his waving his splinted arm about in emphasis. Well, nothing outside of a bunch of tiny monsters who flung him out of a forest.

I quickly grabbed Harlan's arm before he could go to his wagon. "Remember what I told you: no one can know." I caught his automatic glance to where Orenda was loading the last of our stuff back into our wagon. "Especially her." I grabbed his face and turned it to me. "How do you think she'll react if she realizes he's an elf?" My point was brutal but clear. I needed Harlan to have his own motivation for not letting Orenda, or anyone else, know who Carlon really was.

His face darkened. "Point taken. But when this is over he and I are having a long conversation." He lashed his tail a few times for emphasis and then stomped off to his wagon.

Locksead was barking orders again. I glanced over, as they didn't seem to be directed at me but at the wagon drivers. Whenever he yelled, or got aggravated, or well, anytime he was annoyed, his hair ruffled up like a white-plumed show bird. I kept the giggle to myself at that observation.

"Tag's wagon goes first, then Carlon, then you." Locksead's voice was loud enough for the entire camp to hear but was aimed solidly at an also irate Jackal.

Jackal's voice was too low to pick out the words clearly. Unusual, but I noticed over the last three weeks he did that when he was really mad. However, why would he care what order the wagons went?

Then I looked to Alric. Carlon. Whoever he was. He leaned against his wagon with a nasty smirk on his face.

Great, so as part of his persona he was in a pissing match with Jackal?

"Those two wagons have our real diggers. There may be questions when you people go in; I need Taryn, Covey, and Harlan to answer them. You and your boys are grunt labor; you'd be in the back."

Jackal snarled a few more too low to hear words, then shot Alric's back a vicious glare, and stomped over to his wagon.

Alric might need to watch it with Jackal. Something seemed unhinged about him. More so than the rest of this merry crew. He came across as big and stupid, but I had a feeling there was a lot more brain in there than we thought.

I shook my head and started to get in the wagon. Had I not only been on one foot, and that one foot on the flimsy wagon steps, I probably wouldn't have felt the rumble.

CHAPTER THIRTY-SIX

It wasn't a big rumble, not compared to the ones back in Beccia. However, I couldn't be blamed for thinking of those, and their earth-caving outcomes, when I squeaked and jumped off the wagon stair.

I looked around quickly to see if anything collapsed, or even if anyone had seen me. No one seemed to have noticed the shake, or my reaction. Considering that I was pretty sure the shaking was connected to the rakasa somehow, this did not make me happy. I hadn't noticed any shaking in the last three weeks, but we had been going through a large mountain chain—they could have been following us the entire time.

I shuddered at that cheery thought and continued into the wagon.

Covey and Orenda were already inside and had dressed into more appropriate digger-wear. Or what Locksead had determined was more appropriate. I normally wore simple clothes on a dig, not unlike what I might wear around town.

Locksead had decided that even though both Harlan and I were diggers, we clearly didn't know what the fashionable diggers were wearing. He'd managed to get an entire trunk load of clothing a fashion maven might wear out on an exotic trip through a garden. The boots were fine, but I usually wore them, so I'd convinced

Locksead to let me keep my own. The problem started with the pants. Huge, billowing things that tucked into the boots and poofed out about a foot away from my legs. Then tight, long-sleeved shirts that were fitted with a belt. They were bright and obnoxious until Locksead had Cook stir them around in the dirt for an hour or so. Now they were obnoxious and nasty. And those sleeves were tight enough to cut off all circulation. The topper, literally, was the hat. No digger I knew wore a hat on a dig site. Tight, high little beasts, they had large flaps down the back. They weren't practical, and the ruins in Beccia were so covered with monster trees the idea of a single beam of sun making it through was ridiculous. I'd drawn the line on the gloves, fancy things that looked more at home at a tea than out on a dig. I'd won that battle after explaining how my current patroness forbade gloves since there could be important relics damaged if we couldn't feel them.

The men's clothing wasn't much better. Interestingly, Harlan seemed to enjoy the poufy pants and was determined his hat was going with him after this caper.

I quickly changed into the annoying garb and settled in just as the wagon started to move.

"Did either of you feel the ground shake?"

Orenda shook her head, but I didn't know if she hadn't felt anything, or was just not listening. She looked out the window at the wagon behind us, and judging by her face, something was going on in her thoughts.

Covey nodded. "I did. But it was so subtle I wasn't sure."

Covey and I spent the next fifteen minutes, bouncing along inside the wagon with Tag yelling, "Sorry" every few feet, discussing the quakes.

Orenda was suspiciously quiet and kept glancing out the back window. Finally, she turned to Covey and I. "Have either of you noticed a change in Carlon? I still don't understand what I thought I saw in him." She scowled at the memory, but it softened immediately and she glanced back out the window. "But he seems different today. Less scummy, if that makes sense."

Covey and I shared a horrified look while her back was to us. Had his breaking character to tell me who he was somehow lessened his persona's obnoxiousness? I didn't know what, if anything, remained in terms of a relationship between us. I had told him it was over but my heart wasn't really onboard with the idea. However, I knew I didn't want Orenda falling for Alric for real.

I pulled back another portion of the curtain, as if I was taking her inquiry seriously. Then I dropped the curtain and shook my head. "Not at all. If anything, he's more despicable than before. He even tried to kiss me yesterday."

Orenda's face fell. "He what?"

I thought about being offended about her reaction. It said as much about what she thought of me, and someone trying to kiss me, as it did about Carlon. However, I was willing to let that slide if it helped push him completely out of her thoughts.

"Yup." I leaned forward. "He waited until I was down one of the narrower trails, looking for firewood. Then he kissed me. Without even so much as a by-your-leave."

Orenda was furious, then started softening, and got a dreamy look on her face. "Was it wonderful?"

Crap. I shot another quick glance to Covey who just shrugged. Alric had removed the spell he had on her. I might be pissed at him, but he was too good of a magic user to have screwed that up. And my quick glance out the back had confirmed Carlon was just as vile looking as ever. So what in the hell was happening?

I shook my head and tried to mimic the look I was sure I had on my face back when Marcos had been exposed as the Jinn triplets. Disgust and anger.

"Not at all. He was rude, disgusting, and kisses like a dead frog. I kneed him." The fact was Alric was quite skilled at kissing and a number of other things. Had I known it was him at the time I was sure I would have enjoyed it. As it was, I'd been too freaked out at what I thought Carlon was doing to notice.

"Oh." She briefly turned to look out her window, then pulled the curtains closed and faced Covey and I. "I could help, you know. With the training."

For a second I thought she'd meant magic training, but then saw she was looking down at the swords and daggers.

"Since the magic is fading from my people, we've become good at physical fighting." She bent down, picked up a sheathed dagger and threw it my way. "We can't stand and fight, but if Covey doesn't mind switching seats I can work with you on dagger sparring."

I started to point out that Covey was already training me, but she flashed a toothy smile and switched seats. She would enjoy someone else having to listen to my whining for a bit.

"We teach this to our young ones. Even when they are unsteady on their feet, they can learn."

I shrugged and unsheathed the dagger. It was a bit longer and skinnier than the one I usually used, but it seemed like a mate to one of the swords at her feet. Might as well do something productive on our trip, we had at least a few hours before we got to the city gates. Would have been nice if she had come out of her shell a few weeks ago.

Fifteen minutes later, I was regretting I'd agreed to this. If this was a training foisted on all of the children of Orenda's clan, it was amazing they had anyone stay in the clan long enough to grow to adulthood. She was making my training with Covey seem lax by comparison.

The sparring consisted of a series of fancy dagger moves. Not far ranging, they covered both defensive and offensive positions. She did one run quickly. I had to admit she was impressive. Partially because the space involved was small, but also because she did it with such grace. The sureness of her moves told me that while it looked pretty, had she been facing an opponent with just her dagger, there was a good chance her opponent would lose.

I tried it a few times in slow motion with her correcting me with every move. The steps weren't near as easy as she'd made them look. After the first few minutes, Covey got bored of watching, leaned back, and dozed.

A half hour later and I wanted to throw the dagger and Orenda out the window and take the chance that Harlan could find her on the way back out of here. My wrist hurt, my hand hurt, and I already had a few slight but still annoying scratches.

Orenda was beaming. "You're doing well. Another few hours of continuous repetition and the muscles will do it on their own. We should be working on throwing as well, but I don't want a blade to go out the window. Throwing a dagger is far different than throwing a knife." She tilted her head while she watched me with narrowing eyes. "Yes, I think in between all the digging and what not, we can get quite a bit of training in. I might need to continue it after this job as well." She clapped her hands and a shudder went through me.

I swore I heard Covey let out a snort, but her eyes stayed closed. I'd become a project.

CHAPTER THIRTY-SEVEN

Three hours later, Covey was laughing at me. Her eyes were still closed and she feigned sleep. I knew damn well she was laughing at me. Sleeping people didn't jiggle around like she was.

Orenda was possibly even more determined and tenacious than Covey was. We'd only taken one break on her insane plan to turn me into a dagger maiden. That was only because my right hand had become so numb I'd dropped the dagger five out of six tries. So she switched hands.

She finally relented when we heard the sounds of more traffic as Tag led our trio of wagons down a much larger road. She'd decided that diggers shouldn't be seen practicing with daggers. It would give the impression we were thieves.

I was so glad to have her stop that I almost cried. She was right about the muscle memory thing though. I didn't think I could stop my fingers on either hand from twitching to repeat the moves. Was going to make holding my digger tools very interesting.

A wagon started to pull alongside us and Tag yelled for our horse to slow. I couldn't hear what Tag said, but I heard the other driver. Alric.

"We need to make sure we act like we know what we're doing; you might want to pull that Taryn girl up

on front with you. She can answer any questions they
have about credentials, and she knows what she's
doing."

There was almost admiration in his voice. Nice to
hear from Alric, not so much from Carlon. I wondered
what his game was now. Then I realized it hadn't
changed—get whatever artifacts he needed and get them
back home to his people. I would help him do that just
by being me. Which made me believe even more that
whatever else we would find here, that damn emerald
dragon was here.

Tag said something else I couldn't hear, but I knew
that even though he hated Carlon, he'd listen to him. Our
wagon pulled over to the side. Alric dropped his wagon
back behind us again and pulled over. I was getting out
when Jackal drove by.

"No waiting, you guys, we need to get there faster."
He whipped his horse and kept jogging down the trail.

Alric looked ready to yell something, then shook his
head and got down off the driver's seat. He motioned to
me as he walked in front of his horse. "Let me talk to you
for a second. Locksead had some last minute ideas."

That was pure Alric, not Carlon at all. The voice, the
tone, the stance. Everything. Even Tag noticed
something was up and spun around to look. I waved him
off and went back to Alric.

As long as I'd known him, and clearly for many years
prior to that, Alric had disguised whom he was. He was
good at it. When I first tried to bring him in as a bounty
capture, I'd been dumped in a room of his with clothing
from every walk of life. At the time, I'd figured he was
a deranged collector or mad killer. However, that was his
disguise collection.

So why was he dropping it so badly now? He was still
holding his glamour, but barely. Because I knew what I

was looking for I could almost see Alric's features peeking out from behind Carlon's.

"What is going on? Why are you stopping us?" I kept my voice low. We were standing directly behind the window of my wagon. I walked around him, forcing him to turn to face me so anyone looking out the window would see my face but his back. I peered closer. Even the Carlon persona wasn't looking good. "Alric, what the hell is wrong?"

He shook his head, looking around briefly to make sure no one had come out of his wagon, or ours. "Glorinal, or what was left of him, did something to me during that fight. I can't breathe right and I'm losing magic. It's taking everything to keep the glamour up; killing that sceanra anam almost undid me."

That wasn't good. I'd hoped whatever they'd turned Glorinal into had been robbed of all magic. I looked at his chest. He was wearing the same dusty brown clothes Carlon always wore, but they seemed to fit tight across his chest. "Did he stab you?" The fabric was pulling oddly. I reached out to check, and then remembered whom I was dealing with. I waved at the odd area.

"No, I checked before." Then a look crossed his face and for a moment, it was pure Alric looking back at me. His eyes went wide as he must have felt his glamour drop, then he shook his head and Carlon reappeared. He pulled aside a few layers of clothes. All of them had been the same drab brown so I hadn't realized he had so many on; that was what helped Carlon look so much bulkier than Alric. The final layer looked stuck as he got to it. Then he pulled it back, wincing as it stuck to his skin.

Across his chest were three claw marks. Not deep but oozing green ichor and blood. Moreover, they looked fresh. Far too fresh for a three-week old wound.

Alric coughed and it looked like the marks went deeper.

Somehow, that thing that was Glorinal had marked him, but the injuries took weeks to show. "It's a mark of the rakasa. They must have their spells and abilities running through Glorinal." He studied the marks for a bit, then shook his head and wrapped himself back up.

"What are you doing? You're fading fast, and I may be so pissed at you right now that I can't even verbalize it, but I'd rather you didn't die."

The laugh that came out was Carlon, not Alric. He was fighting back against the mark, but for how long? "I'd rather I didn't die either, but we can't deal with this right now. Jackal was right; we do need to claim our dig site. Locksead took longer to get the wagons here than he should have. I think we're being followed and the sooner we can get this done, the better." He held up a hand to stop what I was about to say. "No. Right now we need to get in there, get our piece out, and anything else you find valuable. And get out of that town. I wanted to talk to you to make sure you were in agreement with the plan." He handed me a small scroll. "Read it, but keep it with you at all times."

With that, he turned on his heel and marched back to his wagon.

I couldn't help but react by wanting to run forward when he almost stumbled, but I held off. I slid the scroll into my shirt. I needed to find a chance to look at it when Orenda wasn't around. I also needed to ask Covey and Harlan if they knew what those wounds on his chest meant. Images of what Glorinal currently looked like flashed through my head, but superimposed over Alric's face. I might kind of hate him right now, but there was no way I was going to let that happen.

I waited until Alric was back on his wagon, and looking very much like an annoyed Carlon, and then walked back to my wagon.

Tag stuck his head around. "Is everything okay? Why'd Carlon sound so weird?"

"He's fine." I rolled my eyes and tried to keep my real concern for Alric from showing. "He thinks he has a cold and wanted to know if I knew any quick cures. Let me get the rest of my equipment so I look more official." I shook my head and climbed back on board the wagon. I didn't need anything else; I wanted to let Covey know Alric was having problems.

I ducked inside to face two pairs of questioning eyes. Covey's looked more irritated than questioning, and she was staring right where I'd put the scroll. Even though she hadn't been able to see exactly what happened, she'd clearly seen something change hands.

"Why did Carlon want to talk to you?" Orenda was clearly not trying to sound jealous, but she wasn't succeeding. What if Alric's previous spell had been to break a real attachment on her part, not to break a love spell? He'd left the group to get away from her supposedly; he would have broken any spell he'd cast at that point, especially once he was sure she could hold her own against the more unscrupulous members of the gang. Therefore, that spell I saw could have been something else.

Damn, she was somehow responding to him since his glamour was fading.

"He was concerned I'd screw something up." I shook my head and grabbed the stupid digger hat. It was next to Covey. "He was injured when he was attacked. Not doing well. Magic fading." I'd dropped my voice to extremely low levels, letting the words out on my breath.

Covey nodded. She'd understood. Even though she was possibly even madder at Alric than I was right now, her face showed her concern.

I patted the scroll in my pocket and nodded to her, then went back outside.

Tag had moved over to give me room next to him on the driver's bench, but we were still close. "So he's okay?"

That was weird. Tag definitely didn't like Carlon, yet he had real concern in his voice. Crap. What if not only was Alric's glamour failing, but also he was unintentionally projecting some sort of magical distress? I needed to talk to Covey and Harlan, alone. Maybe by the time we got to the dig site I could separate them out from the others. Of course, even if he was projecting I had no idea how to stop it. Nor how to slow down whatever was happening to him.

"He will be, might have some broken ribs or something from that attack by those monsters a few weeks ago. He kept ignoring it but now it's getting to him." I glanced back but Alric was contemplating the rear end of his horse. "I'd stay clear of him as much as possible at the dig. He's in a lot of pain and will probably be more difficult than usual."

Keeping everyone who didn't know who he was away from Alric was about the best I could do at this point.

Tag looked like he wanted to ask more questions but held off as we rode closer to town. It was a good thing I'd come up when I did. Jackal was at a gate arguing with some very irate city guards. Some very irate syclarion city guards.

CHAPTER THIRTY-EIGHT

Jackal and the other two men riding with him were out of the wagon yelling at the guards. The syclarions held their ground. And their nasty looking pikes.

"I told you, we've got diggers and an assigned dig site. I don't care who's behind the government now, we have approval." Jackal turned back to look at us as we pulled up. "See there? That's the famous digger from Beccia, Taryn." He paused as he clearly was trying to recall my last name, but then shrugged. "You should be honored that she and her group are coming to dig here."

The guard to the left tilted his head to see better. Both guards wore full armor that encased them in metal from head to toe. Their helmets covered the top half of their faces. Although they were clearly made for the long draconian face of the syclarions, they also had a cross piece over the nose that was popular a few years ago. It might protect against a blow to the face, but it made anyone wearing it look cross-eyed and clearly impaired visibility. "She don't look like much." His gravelly voice sent shivers up my spine. I'd say that my distrust of them was due to the whole trying to take over the world trick Thaddeus had pulled with the glass gargoyle a few months ago, except they had freaked me out before then.

I took a deep breath and got down off the wagon. I didn't care about Jackal, Locksead, or the rest. However, like it or not my friends were now tied into this mess, and if another part of that weapon that destroyed the Ancients lurked up here, we had to find it. Before the rakasa did. I hadn't heard that the syclarions were a ruling power up here, but I never paid attention to politics in Beccia, let alone anywhere else in the kingdom.

"I'm Taryn St. Giles, licensed digger from Beccia under Patroness Qianru Del La Floerin. I'm leading this expedition to your ruins. My foreman should have prepared everything." I was doing my best to channel the haughtiest diggers I knew right now. It wasn't easy to look down my nose at two fully armored, seven-foot-high syclarions, but I gave it my best shot.

I heard someone get out of Alric's wagon and stomp up behind me. The voice was pure Harlan.

"I say, what is the slow down? We have too much work to do already and not enough time." Harlan didn't even have to work hard to get that snottier-than-thou tone into his voice.

"And you would be?" the second syclarion asked. Jackal went back to his wagon, waving the other two with him. Had we approached in the order we were supposed to, this probably wouldn't have been a problem. However, by Jackal being an ass, we now had the guards annoyed.

Harlan pulled himself up. "I am Harlan of Beccia. I can assure you, I am well renowned in digger circles. As my associate has stated, we have been given passage." He looked around as if noticing the spiky gate for the first time. "I was unaware that Kenithworth was under martial rule."

The first guard started shaking and it took a few moments to realize he was laughing. "This ain't martial rule. We've had some odd creatures attacking the good citizens, so we're making sure to watch everyone who comes in." He turned to the second guard and they conferred in low voices.

I didn't hear what he started to say as I was then bowled over when a fleet of faeries, followed by Bunky, tore out of the wagon. "We hunt!" Garbage yelled as she raised her stick in the air. They pulled up short when they saw the syclarion guards. Garbage held up her hand for the rest to stay behind her, and she flew closer.

"You no belong here." Her voice was a mix of confusion and annoyance. And, if I heard it right, a tiny bit of fear.

"What the hells is that thing?" The second guard, not the one Garbage was talking to, waved his hand to send her off. However, the first one nodded. I wished I could see their faces better. Another disadvantage of that damn armor.

"Nay, little one, we are here to protect the good people of this city. It is rare to see your people around here. Perhaps after we have finished saving it, your kind can join us."

Not only had there been fear in Garbage's voice, there was an odd underlying fear and greed in the guard's voice. The hair on the back of my neck stood up at the weird tableau, and everything seemed to slow down.

I watched as Garbage hovered in place in the air, gripping and re-gripping her war stick, and the guard doing similar motions with his pike.

Then they both backed down from whatever standoff they were having, and Garbage led the faeries and Bunky away.

"You travel with dangerous companions, Taryn of Beccia." The guard looked ready to say more but instead shook his head and stepped back into his position. A messenger came running to the city gates and handed a note to the first guard. It was short and not so sweet. At least I assumed that by the way he grimaced and crumpled it in his hands.

"There's been a change of your plans." He shoved the crumpled note at the second guard. "The mayor has asked you to come see him. All of you." He glanced to where the faeries and Bunky had flown off and I knew part of his annoyance was that some of us weren't here anymore.

"How did he know we were coming?" Alric, in full Carlon-mode, stomped forward to ask. He had one hand placed carefully across where I'd seen the wound, but he was standing tall. "We don't have time for this. We can meet with the mayor after we get settled."

The guard shrugged. "Taryn of Beccia is better known than the diggers you were originally bringing. All digs get approved by the mayor, and since you had a change of diggers from what was on the original application to dig, he was notified." He went over to unlock the city gate. "I'm afraid there's no option on meeting him now though. Either you go through this gate, or you turn around and go home. The messenger will lead you there if you decide to be sensible about it."

Jackal clicked his horse to move his wagon forward. "We gotta do what they say, Carlon. Don't be a bigger ass than usual." He didn't even look at the guard as he rode through.

That was interesting, since Jackal had been the one fighting with the guards to start with. I wasn't sure how or when they notified their mayor, but I'd bet it was while Jackal was being an ass. He was only being agreeable now to piss off Carlon.

Covey had gotten out of the wagon and now looked ready to argue, but a look from Alric as he crossed back to his wagon stopped her. Besides, arguing wouldn't help us if we wanted to get to that site and the potential for a true Ancient find.

Alric got his wagon moving and without a word, followed Jackal through the gates. Covey was back in the wagon, and Orenda hadn't come out, so that left Tag and I. He looked to me for guidance. He was Locksead's man, but I knew if I said to take us back he would without question. After this was over, I would have to find a way to get this boy free of Locksead.

"We follow. I haven't been trapped in that damn wagon for three weeks to go back empty handed." I said.

Tag gave me a nod and grabbed the reins.

Orenda and Covey had been talking when I climbed back into the wagon but dropped it when I came in. I didn't need to ride outside at this point.

"Say it. Whatever it is, say it."

The look on Orenda's face told me she was the one with a problem, although Covey looked concerned as well.

"Are we sure this is a good idea? Those guards look very serious. I've never seen their species before, but I find I don't like them." Orenda did one of her dagger routines with her left hand. I wasn't even sure she knew she was doing it.

"Syclarions," Covey said with even more venom than I felt toward them. "If your people don't know who they are, count yourselves lucky."

Orenda's face grew more concerned as she watched both of us, but especially at Covey's reaction. I wouldn't get into Covey turning feral because of the syclarions. If Covey wanted her to know, she'd tell her.

"A rogue group of syclarions tried to destroy Beccia with an artifact a few months ago," I said quickly. "We fought them off." That was all she needed to know right now. If she stuck around, Harlan could give her the details. "As for this being a good idea, there's no way to tell."

Covey was still muttering under her breath about syclarions, but then looked up. "We need to be careful. I hadn't thought much of it at the time, some academics get lost in their work for months, but I have lost contact with a fellow researcher at Kenithworth University. I haven't heard from him in over six months and we usually exchanged missives every week or so. It may be nothing, but combined with armed syclarion guards, I think we should be cautious."

I'd agree with her about academics getting lost in their work. There would be times I wouldn't see more than a distracted glimpse of Covey for weeks at a time. Nevertheless, the armed guards bothered me as well. Not to mention the reaction and comment about the faeries. Aside from a few misguided souls, like the elves, and hereditary enemies, like the brownies, the only people who would think the faeries were dangerous were those who had been at the battle of Beccia. Or who were connected to those who were. The syclarion ambassador had assured the Beccian politicians, and even the kingdom's politicians, that Thaddeus and his group had acted alone. I was really questioning that at this point.

Orenda nodded, but the worried look didn't leave her face. Instead, she pulled back the curtain nearest to her. I did the same with the one on my side. Might as well see the sights. I'd never been to Kenithworth, but I knew a little about it. It was the closest large city to Beccia and the only major city on this side of the kingdom of Lindor. The west end of the kingdom, where we were, was considered the outskirts. Kenithworth was our one claim as a region to having a big city with big-city style,

Which wasn't much in evidence right now.

The day was bright and sunny, but the buildings around us still managed to look gray and cold. The style of the buildings we passed was exotic and glamorous, at least to a small-town girl like me. Yet, for all of their grace, they carried a weight of despair. I leaned over to look out the other side, but they were just as bad there.

Even more so. That side was full of shops and vendors, but many appeared closed or extremely understocked.

"How long ago did you say you lost track of your friend?" I asked Covey.

She'd been lost in her own thoughts but shook them off at my question. "Right before the issue with Alric and that glass gargoyle. The last time I heard from him was about a week before Alric stole the scroll."

Orenda and I had leaned away from the windows but both curtains were still open. Covey frowned and leaned first into one, then the other. Her frown deepened.

"This isn't right. Kenithworth is a bustling city. I was here last year for a conference at their university. It didn't look like this at all." She turned and pulled open the curtain at the back of the wagon as well, then quickly dropped it.

"There are a dozen armored syclarions marching behind us. The people in the shops are cowing and bowing as they go by. I don't think this is a simple meeting with the mayor."

Orenda peeked out the back curtain as well. "But if this is their city, wouldn't there be a lot of them? Some people in my clan fear our legions as well, but it is good they are there to protect us."

Covey took the curtain out of Orenda's hand, and closed it again. "This isn't their city. Lindor isn't their kingdom. And no populace should fear those legitimately in place to protect them." She looked around the wagon and pulled out a few of her smaller weapons. After she stashed them on her person, she nodded to both of us. "I know a lot of our belongings are out of reach, but I'd advise you both to arm yourselves."

CHAPTER THIRTY-NINE

Orenda and I had armed ourselves as best we could. However, I didn't think walking in to meet a mayor, especially a potentially hostile one, bristling with weapons was a good idea. That meant we were limited to what small and sneaky items Covey and Orenda had brought along.

Covey was very excited when Orenda pulled out a garrote with two delicately carved wooden ends. She was even more excited when Orenda pulled out another one and handed it to her.

"Just what do they teach your people back in your homeland?" No one outside of assassins or odd folks like Covey would use a garrote.

"We are all trained from birth to protect ourselves. We're taught the people in the world outside are vicious and barbaric and we must be vigilant against them to hold off the end of days." Orenda was still digging for more small weapons, so she missed the look Covey and I shared.

"You do realize that we're from the world outside, right? So is everyone you've met out here." I didn't laugh at her comments, but they did seem a bit automatic.

Orenda's head popped up out of her bag. "Oh, I'm sure they didn't mean people like you. At first, I thought they did, but I believe I was wrong. They mean the other people." Satisfied that was resolved; she went back to looking for weapons we could hide on our persons.

I couldn't fight her on that, and her lack of logic was sound in her head.

The wagon started slowing down. From the outside it appeared that we'd come to the much nicer part of town, but while the buildings were even more ornate than the ones at the edge of the city, a feeling of despair loomed over them.

"You were here only a year ago? And it didn't look like this?" I asked Covey as I waved at the window.

She was securing the garrote Orenda had lent her inside her shirt. "Not at all. I can't believe any city, especially a major one like this, could fall apart so quickly." She closed all of the curtains as the wagon slowed. "I'm going to try and get out of here and go to the university to see if I can find out anything. Just go along with whatever I do. I'll be back as soon as possible, and if you don't come out of that meeting, I'll go get help."

I nodded. I seemed to be the one they were focusing on. They'd seen Covey, but her name wasn't on the papers and most thugs didn't know academics. If things did go bad, it would be good to have someone outside to get us back out.

The wagon came to a halt, and Tag popped open the door. "They're asking for you all to come out."

I nodded to the others and led the way.

The people in the other two wagons were also coming out, and we instinctively bunched together. Covey drifted toward the back and I noticed she was in a brief, yet earnest, conversation with Grimwold.

My attention was drawn as the sound of our armored escort filled the street. They must have slowed down as we did but had dropped behind us. They halted quite a bit behind the wagons.

A small group coming down the flight of stairs echoed their movements. Not all were syclarions, but they were all tall and armed. They dropped down the stairs with each one staying on a step. The doors again opened behind them and this time stayed open as a man came out of them. This person wore no armor and at first I thought it might be the mayor. He was tall and thin with strands of rich brown hair creatively drifting out of a very elaborate hat. Long flaps down the sides and back were made of the most delicately cut felt I'd ever seen. And I seriously doubted that shade of teal could be found anywhere in nature. Large orange and green feathers were artistically, if horrifically, arranged on top.

Kenithworth might be going through something dark and scary, but they were keeping up their cutting–edge fashion. Whether that was a good idea or not was open for debate.

He looked down at us, nodded to the guards, then motioned. "The mayor will see you now. Please do try not to touch anything."

We'd started moving forward when Grimwold made a break for it. I had no idea what he and Covey had been talking about, but he was completely freaked when he burst through us and ran down the road. Covey waited until most of the guards started after him, then ducked down the alley behind us and took off with no one the wiser. The guards probably faced a losing race. Syclarions weren't known for their speed and Grimwold ran like his ass was on fire.

The pompous jerk at the top of the stairs watched the guards jog off with a disgusted look, and wrinkled his nose as he looked around the crowd of us. "In fact, we only need the diggers, a person named Carlon, and one named Jackal. The rest of you may stay out here."

Harlan joined me, and Alric and Jackal followed. The everyone else went back to their wagons to wait.

It was a bit unnerving climbing the stairs with armed guards standing there. With their armor all you could really see were their mouths. While I'd been right, and they weren't all syclarions—there seemed to be a fair number of humans and troll-human breeds—at least judging from what I could see below the helmets.

A large golden ball hovered over the double doorway. It hadn't been visible from the street, but I felt a magical pull from it now. It looked like a spell bubble. Like what Covey had in her kitchen, but about five times the size. They were designed to break spells on anyone coming into a room or building.

I gave a quick glance back to Alric. I knew he could hold his own against minor spell breakers, but he was injured whether he was showing it or not, and this wasn't a minor spell ball. He gave a brief nod and took a few long breaths. He also moved closer to me.

Had he really been Carlon I would have pushed him down the stairs. His body was so close I could feel heat coming off of him. However, exposing Alric here and now was a very bad thing. If those syclarions knew who the faeries were and what they did in the battle of Beccia against fellow syclarions, they sure as hell would know whom Alric was. Moreover, what he did to their people.

I felt the back of his hand press against the palm of mine as we walked through the doorway. I kept my hand still to maintain the touch, yet keep it hidden. Not only did I not want the mayor's people seeing it, I knew Jackal would draw unwanted attention if he did.

An odd tingle started at the top of my head and quickly worked its way down. After a pause when it hit our hands, it continued. Alric leaned into me a bit more as it went through him, but his glamour held.

"Can't you even walk straight? You've been drinking again?" Jackal was behind us but his annoying remarks meant he hadn't noticed us touching.

Alric pulled back a step away from me. "I have to drink to deal with morons like you." The two silently snarled at each other, but I thought I saw a slight grin flash on Jackal's face and an echo on Alric's. They were clearly not the enemies they pretended to be, or rather Carlon and Jackal weren't. I wasn't sure how I felt about that. Jackal gave me the creeps.

The guards behind us pushed us through the foyer and into a large office. The outside of the buildings and people might be sad and faded looking, but that was not the case here. The room was easily twice the size of The Shimmering Dewdrop, with a ceiling that the long-lost elves would have admired. Ornate paintings had been crafted to fill the ceiling above us, mostly of people who I assumed were the prior mayors. Most were human, with a few other races scattered in. All looked like extremely successful, and grossly overdressed, merchants. Which made sense—Kenithworth was primarily a merchant town. At least it had been.

The mayor's desk took up almost the entire back wall. He sat high above the rest of us, his desk and surrounding furnishings all displayed on a raised platform at least two feet off the ground. The entire collection was carved out of a single gapen tree, and judging by the rings still showing in the wood, it had been a giant.

The mayor himself was made to look even smaller in comparison. It was difficult to see much of his features—his hat was even larger and more ridiculous looking than his assistant's—but he looked to be some sort of gnome half-breed. I didn't know gnomes could be civil enough to breed with other races. He bowed and waved us all into the room. His assistant and two of the guards stepped forward with us, and the rest of the guards stayed outside and shut the door behind us. "Please, sit, my esteemed guests. I am so honored by your presence."

I didn't point out that we hadn't had an option on coming, but silently took one of the fancy, overstuffed, velvet chairs. The cost of one of these behemoths could fund a team of diggers for at least a year, probably two.

"I'm sure you are wondering why I have called you here. We have been having some recent difficulties with odd creatures attacking the city as well as very peculiar things going on at our dig sites. I will be forthright with you; people are vanishing out in the wilds around the city. I am extremely honored that the famous archeologist from Beccia and her equally talented companion, Harlan, is here at our small site, but you must take extreme caution."

Both Harlan and I sat a bit straighter. It was so common for us to call ourselves diggers that when someone used our proper name it made us giddy.

"I am afraid I will have to insist on sending guards with you, for your own protection, you realize." He beamed at his own good will and concern for us.

There went the real reason. Whether people were vanishing at the area or not, he wanted to have eyes on what we were going after. Not good.

"The location that you have secured was attacked a few days ago. No one was working it, clearly, since you had not yet arrived. However, there were a few minor explosions there."

He turned toward Alric and Jackal. "You were listed as the primary aids to your boss, one Locksead, whom I believe is not in attendance?"

Jackal nodded. "Aye, we're the foremen for the site. Locksead is hurt and couldn't make it." He scowled at the guards. "But we are perfectly able to guard our own."

Alric stayed silent. However, he folded his arms and gave a fierce Carlon scowl. He also looked a bit paler than before. The injury must not be mixing too well with the energy he needed to avoid that huge spell breaker ball outside.

"I do not mean to cast doubt upon your skills." The mayor gave a toothy grin to both Alric and Jackal. "Two such men must truly be fearsome in a fight. However, you do understand that we cannot take a risk with Beccia's celebrities. We would be bereft if anything should happen to anyone in this party."

Jackal took a breath to continue arguing, but Alric turned to him and shook his head. Considering I had a feeling that it was mostly because of Jackal's hardheaded nature that we had been forced to detour into this town, instead of on our way to set up camp at the site, I agreed with Alric. The mayor was clearly some kind of despot and wouldn't let anything in his mini-kingdom happen without knowing about it. We played by his rules, or we went home.

Alric stepped forward with a nod. "Agreed. Thank you for the extra protection. We'd like to set up camp before the sun falls, may we leave now?" The voice was Carlon, but the words were completely Alric. Hopefully it wouldn't make Jackal question anything.

The small mayor nodded regally and waved one hand for the guards. "Of course, we wouldn't want anything to happen if you got there in the dark. However, be very wary of the pits. We do not know what the ruffians were up to, but we felt it better to leave them undisturbed for the archeologists to assess."

The guards on the other side of the door pushed it open and we started heading out.

"Taryn, could you please stay? Just for a moment." The mayor's voice caught me as I was almost out the door. Again, my choices were nonexistent.

I waved Harlan to keep going and plastered a smile on my face. "Of course." I kept the smile locked in and went back to my chair. To my surprise, the mayor stepped down from his platform desk and took up the seat next to mine.

"Thank you ever so for waiting." He looked up and waited until the doors were shut again.

I forced down the chill that went up my back.

"I have a proposal for you; one which I and my backers believe only you can assist us on." He was still trying to sound polite and considerate, but I could hear how forced it was now. "There are a number of prophecies that speak of a time that we believe is coming upon us. They all have different names and details, but they all speak of a time of fixing. Of changes that will forever alter this world for better or worse."

I kept my face calm. I knew the faeries had prophesies, ones big enough that by breaking them to help save my life and the city of Beccia, they had caused a rift in the faery population. I hadn't heard of others, but prophesies were really more Covey and Alric's area, not mine.

"Very interesting. However, I don't know how that pertains to me. I'm a simple digger, nothing more."

He leaned forward and his grin grew more predatory. "I doubt you are a simple anything. However, you may be correct; this may not pertain to you. A massive weapon of destruction, one so far back in time its exact function has been long lost, is slowly coming to the surface of our world. You have found two pieces." He held up his hand as I started to shake my head. "I know you do not have them. I will not ask you where they are. Not yet anyway. However, since you found two, there's a good chance you are connected to the finder of myth. Many of the prophesies speak of a finder who will call forth the pieces and allow the resurrection of the seventh Sphere. We believe you are she." He held his hands out to encompass the room. "All of this and far more could be yours if you work with my people." He leaned forward as if to say something else, and then instead patted my knee. "No need to worry about it now. Just think on it." He quickly rose to his feet and paused until I did so as well. I wasn't sure what had changed but something was making him very anxious to get me out of the office. He rang a small bell and the door flew open immediately, held by one of the guards.

"Thank you again, we will be in contact." The mayor followed us out into the hall, shook my hand distractedly, and then popped back into his office. Had I not moved fast enough the door would have smacked me.

"Your companions are outside." The voice sounded like the first guard who had been at the gate. That was interesting. Either they'd only been at the gate for us, or they switched guards regularly.

I quickly got outside. Once they saw me come out, the few stragglers still outside their wagons got inside. Each driver's seat now also had a non-armor wearing, but still armed, guard with our drivers. Two were syclarions; the one with Tag was human. Six more guards on horseback waited to ride out behind us.

I was the last one getting to the wagons when Covey came running up.

"Thank you for waiting for me." She pitched her voice loud enough for anyone who wanted to hear to do so. "I was unable to catch Grimwold. I'm afraid he's left us for good."

I nodded and motioned for her to climb in the wagon, and then I followed.

"Harlan said the mayor wanted to talk to you separately. Is everything all right?" Orenda leaned forward and dropped her voice. "Is he one of those vile syclarions? They did nothing but stare at me the entire time you were all inside."

"No, he's some sort of gnome-breed. As to what he wanted, I'm not sure. He mentioned some prophesies and a finder of some sort who would put a fearsome weapon back together." I gave a quick lowdown of his brief conversation, including the fact I believed there had been something more, but he ended it suddenly.

"Did you find your friend?"

Covey's face, which had drifted into her 'scholar thinking about prophesies' expression, dropped into a deep frown. "No. Worse than that, many of their top minds are also missing. The ones left are docile and stupid and are too afraid to talk about their missing peers." She held out a small square puzzle box. "I found this tucked away under a floor board in his empty office." She flipped it around a few times. "I have no idea what's in it, or if it has any bearing on why he vanished. But I'll figure it out eventually."

She was just putting it in her bag, when Orenda reached out. "Can I see that? It looks familiar."

Covey narrowed her eyes, and then slowly handed it over.

"Yes, this is from my people." Orenda tapped on one scuffed panel that held faint markings. "You see right here is where you'd enter the combination to open it. These are very rare; no one has made them since before the Breaking." She reluctantly handed it back. "Be careful when you do try to open it. Many of them had spells attached that could explode in your face, release toxic air, or at the least, destroy whatever is in there if the code wasn't entered correctly."

Covey took it and finished putting it back in her bag. However, I noticed she did it with more caution now.

All three of us were silently lost in our thoughts as Tag called the horse to move and the wagon continued its journey. Any excitement I'd originally felt about this adventure got stomped into dust. Alric, and whatever Glorinal did to him, took it down a few notches, and the syclarions and the cryptically creepy mayor wiped out the rest. I hadn't said anything, but I had a bad feeling about what they were doing in town. Covey's missing friend and the other vanished intellectuals just made it more solid.

Covey broke the silence with a pointed look at me. "That rib of Carlon's must be getting worse. He doesn't look good." The look in her eyes worried me more than her words. Alric must be in bad shape for that look. I knew even with whatever help he was able to draw from my magic, that spell breaker ball had been hard on him. If something was about to go weird out here, we definitely needed his fighting and his magic. I didn't care that Carlon didn't have magic; if things went sideways, I'd expose Alric myself. Except he wouldn't be much use if he collapsed before something happened.

Since I couldn't say anything really about Alric/Carlon with Orenda here, I just nodded and fiddled with one of the scrolls Covey had brought from Beccia.

Scroll. I patted my vest pocket to confirm the scroll Alric gave me was still there. I needed to look at it, and so did Covey. But I couldn't see a way to exclude Orenda. I had intended to wait until we set up camp at the dig site; since we were traveling in, we'd camp at the site. However, the way things were moving I wasn't sure if we could wait that long.

"I think I found one of your scrolls." I pulled out the one Alric gave me and leaned toward Covey. She knew that I knew she wouldn't misplace a scroll. Hopefully she'd guess where it came from.

She shot a quick look in Orenda's direction, but the elf was lost in thought.

Covey unrolled the scroll. "Ah yes, I must have set it down at our last camp." Her eyes darted back and forth as she tried to scan it quickly. I hadn't done anything more than glance at it, but it was elven, and very old. Not good for a quick read.

Covey's face went pale. She rolled it back up and was about to tuck it inside her cloak, when she shot me a look, then nodded to herself. And held the scroll out to Orenda.

I had grown less annoyed by the elf woman's high and mighty attitude over the last three weeks. And I sort of trusted her. Well, with Harlan's heart anyway. I wasn't sure I trusted her with a scroll. Especially one that made Covey go pale like that. It took a hell of a lot to freak her out, and she was currently extremely concerned and heading toward freaked out.

"Orenda, what do you make of this?" Covey's tone was neutral and she'd schooled her face, but she was watching Orenda like a snake with a mouse when the snake feared the mouse might bite back.

Orenda blinked as she pulled her thoughts free. She looked genuinely grateful to be offered a diversion and took the scroll.

That gratitude only lasted a minute. "What is this?" She held the scroll back to Covey, but Covey shook her head. "Why do you have this? These are the monsters who almost destroyed my people."

I took the scroll from Orenda's hands. I wasn't sure if Covey was hoping she'd tell her more about it, or was simply testing Orenda's alliances.

I wasn't surprised when I couldn't make out much at first. However, a closer look let words like 'world's end', 'destruction', and 'dark death' pop out for me. I had no idea why some elven words seemed to translate themselves for me, when the rest of the language seemed beyond my ability to learn. "It's a manifesto from the Dark, isn't it?"

Neither said anything, but they both nodded slowly.

Great. What in the hell was Alric doing with a scroll from Jovan's band of homicidal maniacs?

CHAPTER FORTY

"I think I might need to check on Carlon when we stop," Covey said as she watched me put the scroll away.

I had no idea why Alric gave me something he knew I couldn't read. Unless he was counting on Covey or Orenda to read it. "That might be a good idea."

Orenda looked ready to step in with a comment, but I beat her to it. "Covey was a trained healer before she became a professor. Broken bones were her specialty." I wasn't lying really. Covey had certainly caused enough broken bones in her lifetime. And I didn't know why Alric's weakening glamour seemed to be affecting Orenda, but I needed to keep those two apart.

I might not be sure he and I belonged together, but I knew I wasn't ready to let some elf girl take him.

It was a short ride to the ruins. Providing we were at the ruins when Tag yelled for the horse to stop. It had been less than an hour since we left the city and we'd been going down an incline the entire time. Covey had peered out the back curtain at least a dozen times, but I wasn't sure if her scowls were because of Alric looking bad or the guards we had trailing behind us. Probably both.

I pushed open the wagon door as soon as we stopped and blinked at the bright late afternoon sun. I might actually be grateful for Locksead's weird hats. Unlike the ruins in Beccia, which were being devoured by huge trees at a rapid rate, these were almost completely bare. Well, relatively so. The trees were far narrower than the ones back home and more spread out. If the gapens in Beccia were the giant mob, the tall, thin pines up here were the aloof academics of the tree world. It was colder up here, so that was maybe why each tree seemed intent on having enough space around it to get all of the sun itself.

"If you want to go climb one, you could while we get set up," Covey said as she came out of the wagon behind me.

"Funny." I walked back past her and got my bags from the top of the wagon. Covey and Orenda had weapons and, in Covey's case, scrolls with them, so they kept most of their belongings in the wagon. I didn't have much of value aside from my dagger and digger kit, both of which stayed on me. The rest of my belongings I had stuffed on top of the wagon along with Tag's small bags.

Usually, Tag would climb up first and toss down my bags with his, but he was locked in a deep discussion about the wagons with our ride-along guard, a tall skinny man, so I climbed up the side. Which gave me a perfect view of the faeries and Bunky as they came tearing into the site at full speed. Jackal's wagon raced in right behind them. He threw the reins for the confused horse at the syclarion guard sitting next to him, then jumped off the driver's seat as he came into the clearing.

The faeries zipped by me, and Garbage started pounding on the wagon door.

"Stop them!" Jackal yelled as he skidded to a halt just as Orenda opened the door and let the faeries in. Bunky stayed outside and buzzed fiercely at the irate man.

"Why are you chasing my faeries?" I folded my arms but kept one hand on my dagger. I didn't think he would be able to hurt them, but his face was bright red and he looked ready to choke something.

"I've been losing ale this entire trip. Carlon kept saying I was drinking it and forgetting." He spat toward Alric's wagon. "But it weren't that at all. They been taking it! They slipped in and took it while I was driving."

I made a show of looking inside the wagon. Yup, twelve little faeries all sitting there nice as could be. I noticed that Garbage, Leaf, and Dingle Bottom all had familiar looking tiny black bags in their hands.

I shot them a stern glare, and then turned back to Jackal. "You're welcome to look for yourself, but they don't have anything."

He shoved Orenda and I out of the way and leaned into the wagon. I could still see the faeries and they were still holding perfectly still and looking as innocent as a bunch of newborn baby deer.

"What's in them bags?"

Orenda and I both looked inside, then back to Jackal. "How small is your ale? Those bags are smaller than the faeries and only meant to hold twigs and small rocks."

Orenda gave him her extremely well practiced 'you are an idiot' stare. She wouldn't know what those bags could do, but on the surface it did look like Jackal's accusation was a bit crazy.

I was watching him so I saw a quick flash of something, I wasn't sure what, and for a moment thought he would demand they empty those bags. Then he turned and silently stomped away. As far as I knew, Alric, Covey, Harlan, and I were the only people outside of faery-kind who knew about those bags. Yet Jackal knew there was something odd about them.

I looked at Alric. He was still looking bad, but with Carlon's appearance, it was hard to tell. Covey had gone over to help him. Why would he have told someone like Jackal about the faeries' bags?

Orenda had gone back to setting up her area, so I went back into the wagon and shut the door.

The girls were all under my cot and were enjoying the five bottles of ale they'd stolen from Jackal. They might have taken more, but they only had five out now. "That wasn't smart, girls. To steal it right in front of him?"

Garbage had been working on a bottle all to herself, her right as leader. At least in her head. "Needed. You no bring." Again the look of accusation of my failing along with a tinge of disappointment. I killed their toys, I misplaced Alric, I didn't think to bring ale for my faeries on a dangerous expedition. I was a failure.

"Need for fight!" That was Crusty's contribution before she slid into the bottle she'd been sharing with a few other faeries.

I wasn't sure if she knew who she was talking about fighting. However, I was all right without knowing. I had enough issues going on without adding faery shenanigans to the mix.

I called Bunky to come inside, and then shut all of them up in the wagon. We normally didn't lock the doors except at night, but I did this time. I needed those crazed maniacs to stay in one place where they couldn't get into more trouble. I also needed Jackal to stay out.

"Taryn? You need to see this." Harlan's voice came from out of sight, but fairly close. I went around the wagons, and the others who were setting up camp, and found him, Covey, and Orenda all standing in front of a pit.

Crap. When the mayor had said there had been damage to the dig site, I didn't think he meant a hole bigger than one of the wagons. I walked over, but I could already see some of the damage. The ground was harder up here, and that, combined with less aggressive trees, meant more of the ruins were above ground. That also meant they'd been more exposed to hundreds, if not thousands, of years of weather. However, judging by the wide radius of shattered stones and bricks, I had to think whatever caused the huge pit also took out the building before me. Or what had once been a building and was now nothing more than a pile of rocks.

"I've never seen anything like this." Harlan stepped back from the edge to let me see.

Whatever had done this had been precise and focused. The hole was deep, but almost perfectly round in shape. I'd seen this before. Swearing under my breath, I dropped to the ground and started wiping off the band of dark dust that was almost out of arm's reach.

I could barely clear off enough dust to see, but it looked like the same odd band of tile that I'd seen in the wild ruins outside of Beccia. What were those tiles made of, that an explosion, magic, natural, blasting powder, whatever was behind it, could move huge chunks of earth and rock, decimate a large building, and yet leave them mostly intact?

"Covey? Can you see if you can pry one of these up?" I rolled back to my feet and brushed myself off. She looked at me oddly until I pointed out the tile I'd cleared off below us. Once you knew what it was, you couldn't miss the dark band that circled the inside of the hole.

"What are those?" She quickly dropped to her feet and leaned over the edge.

"Be careful now." The voice behind us made me jump about a foot. It was the human guard; he had silently come up behind us. His name was Markin and he didn't seem quite as bad as the syclarions.

He didn't move any closer, but clearly wanted to make us take note he was there. I wondered what kind of person joined a group of syclarions. I couldn't come up with any good reasons for it.

"It's a band of some sort in the rock of the pit. Not a relic though," Covey said from her position on the ground. "I need to study it closer to make sure the area is safe for Taryn and Harlan to descend. Orenda and I are their academic advisors." She put just enough snotty professor into her voice to get the point across.

Markin sighed and folded his arms. "I should have known. Academics." He gave it the same twist most people gave to assassins and from the look on his face that was exactly how he viewed them. "Carry on." He stalked back to camp. At least that was good. We might be stuck with these watchers, but hopefully they meant a general watching, not hover-over-everything-we-do watching.

Covey waited until he was gone, then flopped back to the ground and scooted closer to the edge. "Harlan, sit on my legs. I need to lower myself down to pry some of these up."

Harlan sat on her legs while Orenda and I watched. Well, I kept watching for Markin or any of the other guards to come back.

A few very Covey-invented swear words later, and we were all peering down at a pair of tiles. She'd only been able to pry off two before it started getting too dark to see into the pit. All four of us looked at them, but none of us had the slightest idea what the odd script or images meant.

I was pretty sure that Alric still had the one he took from me, but I couldn't figure out how to get it from him without anyone noticing. I settled for telling the others about the ring of them in Beccia, and adding it to our collection of potentially dangerous mysteries.

The next two days were uneventful. The city guards would change out, we'd get up and start working on the pit—an endeavor that took help from most of our people.

Lowering me down wasn't that hard, but Harlan was another situation completely. Then he and I would slowly work our way through the explosion debris to get to the actual ruins. The pit looked to be created by the same actions that had caused the one in our ruins, a fact that really didn't make the others or me happy.

The morning of the third day started just like the other two, until I found the dragon.

CHAPTER FORTY-ONE

We'd finally worked through most of the debris caused by the explosion. I tried not to think about how many relics had been destroyed when whoever or whatever set the explosion off.

There was an area that looked a little lighter than the rest. Still packed solid, so I didn't think the explosion had gotten down that far, but light enough to indicate a magical find. One thing I'd found in my years of digging. Relics with magic seemed to lighten the dirt. Not all magical finds did it, but when I saw dirt like this it was always a magical find. I'd tried showing other diggers, but they never saw it. And telling Covey just brought a few very concerned looks. But I knew it was true for me at least.

Harlan was showing Covey and Orenda some shards of pottery he'd found. Most likely elven, possibly just refuse from the city.

I worked my way around the find, carefully using a small trowel, then my duster. The item was large and smooth. Odd for a relic, but there was definitely something there. After about a half hour I freed it. It wasn't completely round but a large green oval about the size of Bunky. It wasn't a dragon, but it was definitely the largest emerald I'd ever heard of.

I was about to turn and call the others over when I looked at it again. The image of a dragon appeared within the shape of the stone. Glorious and magically, it was as if it was alive. A wave of paranoia and greed flooded over me. This was mine. I could be unimaginably rich and escape from all the madness that had invaded my life. However, if I let anyone know about it, they would take it. The dragon nodded as if it heard my thoughts. I must hide it, keep it safe.

I glanced over my shoulder at my friends, but they no longer seemed like the faces I knew. They would take it from me, and stop me from getting the nice quiet life I wanted. They'd always been against me. Without another thought, I used the rope to climb up. My prize was wrapped up in my jacket and tucked into my clothing in such a way those people behind me shouldn't be able to see it.

After making sure no one above the pit was looking, I ran deeper into the ruins and buried my prize. I could come back for it tonight and leave all these people behind.

I turned and walked back toward camp, and almost immediately felt completely foolish about what I'd just done. That was what we were looking for, it was why we were here. I needed to tell Covey and Harlan. I almost walked back to the pit when the tiny voice in my head told me to wait.

It was right. I could wait until tomorrow to tell them.

∽

Two days later and I still hadn't told them. I just wasn't ready to tell anyone about it yet. I wasn't sleeping well and was staying away from the others more and more. My dreams were filled with a giant green dragon, one that would appear and take me away from all of this once I gave him the emerald. But it also terrified me. I woke up ten or more times a night sweating and clutching my blankets so tightly my hands cramped up.

That day I was digging in the same area, hoping to find something I could show my friends, when Jackal stuck his head over the edge and bellowed at me.

"We have someone from the mayor who says he needs to talk to you. And only you."

I waved him off, but he made as if ready to climb down the rope.

"Look, can't you just deal with it?" I really thought today might be when I told the others about the emerald dragon. The urge not to speak of it was almost gone. As long as I ignored the dreams and didn't get near where I'd hidden the damn thing.

"Not my call. He wants you. Come up so we can get this over with." Jackal waited until I was out of the pit. He then motioned for me to walk back to camp ahead of him.

"I really don't see why you needed to call me in for this, Jackal." I waved my small spade over my head at him as he walked behind me. "I don't need to talk to anyone who comes from town. You can handle it." He knew I was leader in name only. We'd only been here a few days, but the mayor of Kenithworth had sent down visitors each day. Jackal had been fine dealing with all of the others. I had no idea why he had to pull me away from the site this time just to speak to someone.

Covey and Orenda were back at the site still getting their crash course from Harlan on the basics of digging. They both had thought they could observe and kibitz. But their "we're the advisors" stance only worked for the guards from the city—not us. Harlan and I put an end to that. Even with them gone, Tag and the others still should have been in camp though.

The emptiness was surprising.

I was about to turn and ask Jackal what was going on, when Bunky came flying over our wagon and slammed right into the man. Jackal had been a lot closer to me than I'd thought, and must have been watching me instead of Bunky so the flying attack took him by surprise.

He fell back then reached for Bunky. Bunky made a furious noise, almost more roar than buzz and flew higher. I could tell he was going to dive at Jackal again. I was going to yell for both to stop it, when a bit of netting in Jackal's right hand caught my eye. He was trying to capture Bunky.

"Bunky! Fly away! Leave!" I waved my hands at him and backed away from Jackal.

Bunky lowered his voice to his normal buzz, then, still staying far too high for Jackal's net, he flew past me and over the table we all used. He buzzed louder until I came closer.

A pile of what I thought was swamp muck in a cage lying in the middle of the table turned out to be a mass of chocolate-covered, and completely passed out, faeries. My faeries. Even in the muck of the chocolate, it was clear they all had war sticks and bits of war feathers were sticking out of the mess. They were in a large cage most likely used for trapping fur animals.

There was no way that they would have had chocolate if they were mad enough to feather up. I hadn't even known that the newer group of faeries had war feathers yet. Not to mention there had been no chocolate with anyone in camp and no one other than Harlan, Covey, Alric, and myself knew what it did to faeries.

"What did you do to them?" I kept my voice calm, but I reached for my dagger. I also waved Bunky to leave and this time he obeyed.

"What we had to do to keep them out of things. Jackal realized that they figured out what was really going on out here, and made us move up our timeline." Alric came out from behind his wagon looking fully Carlon all the way down to his sneer. He also looked far healthier than he'd been prior to getting here.

I pulled back in shock and tried to step back so that I could keep an eye on both of them. Alric had betrayed the faeries? And me? Again? Clearly, he'd been the one who set up a chocolate trap for the girls. He and Jackal were counting on Bunky coming out of hiding when he saw me.

"What the hell is going on? Is Locksead sabotaging his own heist?" I kept slowly walking backwards, but I didn't want to get too far from the faeries' cage. Alric knew everything about them. If anyone might know how to seriously hurt, or possibly kill, them it would be him.

"Locksead is an idiot," Jackal said as he tossed the net he was holding on the table. "He only thinks about what he can sell. Not what he can rule."

I debated grabbing the cage and seeing how far I could get, but I had a feeling it wasn't very far. Even so, I shifted my weight just enough for Alric to shake his head. "Grab her."

I felt the hands grab my arms before I even knew anyone was behind me. I twisted back to see Markin give me a shrug. He didn't look thrilled about grabbing me, but he also didn't look like he would let go.

"You see, Taryn." Alric came forward slowly and I saw the bastard had been drinking. A green bottle sloshed in his hand. "Some of us are tired of being the lackeys of the movers of the world. Some of us want to be in charge of our own kingdoms under a new and glorious destiny. And you are going to help with that by supplying the weapons we need. Not to mention the other benefits of joining us." He leaned in very close to my face as if to kiss me and the smell of what he'd been drinking hit me. Dragon bane.

He looked me clearly in the eye and his eyes changed briefly from Carlon to Alric. "You were right, Jackal, I think she may need some convincing. Capturing her little flying rats isn't enough."

He made as if to pour some of the dragon bane down my throat, but strategically spilled it on me instead. I was grateful for that. Last two times I'd drank the stuff I started attacking any man around me, starting by ripping off their clothes. I was even more grateful that it appeared Alric hadn't joined the bad guys, but was trying to throw off Jackal's plan. Whatever that plan was I was sure I didn't want to be part of it.

I yelled as he spilled the stuff on me. Squirming a bit to try and break Markin's hold.

"Damn it, Carlon!" Markin swore and removed one hand from my arm as the sticky liquid got on him as well.

The dragon bane was starting to tingle when I pushed back at Markin and swung out with my dagger.

He dropped back faster than I'd expected so I only got a slice in his upper arm instead of a stab to the chest. But it was his dominant arm and thanks to my dagger training with Orenda I'd gotten in a fancy twist as I hit so it did more damage than it would have normally.

Alric stumbled away, supposedly going for the sword he used as Carlon. However, his fake drunk routine brought him right in Markin's path and they both stumbled to the ground. Alric was still playing his role, still keeping the Carlon persona alive, but he was doing his best to interfere with Jackal's plan.

The smell of dragon bane and the familiar burning hit the skin of my face and I leaned over to throw up. Not great in a fight, but I couldn't hold it long enough to throw up on one of my attackers.

I spun around and charged Jackal. He was bigger than me, but stupidly unarmed, aside from a log he'd pulled out of the pile for the fire. He laughed at first, easily blocking my dagger. His laugh died as the dragon bane hit my system and my speed increased. I got in two serious stabs, sadly neither of them fatal, before a blow to my head took me out.

CHAPTER FORTY-TWO

I woke up with dirt in my mouth and no memory of what had happened. I kept my eyes closed as soon as I realized that my hands were tied behind me and I was lying on the ground. The dirt in my mouth was from a rag someone had shoved in there. As the buzzing in my head started to fade, I heard voices and everything came back to me.

"I don't know why you say we need her." Markin sounded far surlier than he had previously. "She's not going along willingly, and she's useless to us if she won't cooperate."

Jackal's grunt was followed by a long swallow of liquid. "I can find a use for her, but she won't like it."

"Knock it off, both of you." That was Alric. Or right now, very much Carlon. "You're not going to rape our chance at having this work. If you break her, we will never get what we need. She can find the artifact and she will lead us to the rest of the weapon." I heard his boots crunching gravel and fought to not flinch as he came closer. "She will cooperate. We have her friends and her faeries. I don't have a problem killing any of them to make this work."

He had to have seen me cringe; I felt the tip of his boot against my side. Nevertheless, he said nothing and walked away. I had to force myself to believe Alric hadn't really betrayed us. However, he made it difficult.

There were so many aspects to him that he never told me about. Too many to figure what the truth was.

"Fine. What the hell is taking the others so long? And where's the rest of the team?" Jackal clearly hadn't been too inconvenienced by my stabs. Unfortunately, whoever hit me from behind broke the spell of the dragon bane, and I doubted I could move that fast now.

"The trellian was too hard to fight, she got away." One of Locksead's men spoke, whose name I hadn't bothered to learn. He grunted and walked closer to me. "But I got the cat." Something heavy was dropped on my legs and I assumed he meant Harlan. Hopefully like me Harlan was of more value alive than dead.

I needed to find out who was behind this before they realized I was conscious. I knew the rakasa were after the emerald dragon, but I had a feeling their plans for it wouldn't be sharing world domination with a bunch of thieves. That left the mayor as the instrument of my current situation. Whether he'd bribed Locksead's men recently, or they were part of a bigger plan I had no idea. Right now, I needed to figure out how to break free, save Harlan and the faeries, and flee. Great. At least Covey was still free. Maybe Orenda was as well.

"Tag! Bring in that damn elf!"

My heart broke at that yell. More for the fact that Tag was working with these bastards than Orenda being grabbed, but there was a little bit about her as well.

"I have her, stop yelling." There was a shuffle of feet. It sounded like Orenda was still conscious and walking in.

"Why ain't she gagged?" Jackal said. "You know she won't shut up."

"I'll have you know, my clan will find me no matter what you do. And they will destroy you." Orenda sounded rattled but not scared. That was a good start. Just from what I'd seen during our trip she was a better fighter than most of the morons in camp.

"I told you what would happen if you kept talking!" Tag yelled then I heard a slap. Orenda was quiet.

"Gag that one, now." A deep voice rumbled from the far end of the camp. "I think the digger girl is awake. Want me to check?"

My heart dropped at that voice. It was the syclarion guard who'd rode in from the city gates with us. Of course he was part of this; he and Jackal had been best friends the last few days. Booted feet told me the rest of the syclarion guard contingent had now joined us.

"You always break them when you check." Another syclarion voice, this one was one of the guards from the gate. "Let one of the other people do it. We need her alive."

I heard voices coming closer and I tried reaching out for anything. Magic. Leftover dragon bane strength. Anything. Nothing. I had nothing to grab. I hadn't done any magic since we started this trip, so I couldn't have over-taxed myself. However, there were no fire ants, no urges to throw up, no connection of anything even remotely magical for me to grab. It was as if I'd reverted to being a magic sink.

Hands flipped me from my side to my back, twisting me awkwardly since my legs were still pinned by an unmoving Harlan. I couldn't fake it anymore, so I opened my eyes. Carlon stared back at me.

"She's up, but she don't look too good." He roughly pulled me to my feet, pushing aside Harlan's breathing but unconscious body as he did so. "We need some tea."

I didn't know who was more shocked at that, me or the gang of thugs surrounding us.

"This ain't a tea party, boy." That was the gate guard, with three of his men behind him. The others had taken positions around the edge of the camp. None of them were in armor, so that was a plus. Not that that mattered when it came to fighting syclarions. They didn't need metal to make them damn hard to kill.

"I know it's not." Alric almost sounded like himself with his snarl. "It's fatal to faeries and if she doesn't start talking I'll pour it all over them." He pulled me around to where a pair of teakettles were left on the remains of the morning fire.

I was facing Alric, so my brief relief didn't show to anyone else. I wasn't sure how hyper faeries would help us, especially since we were extremely outnumbered. However, if it meant getting the girls out of here, I was all for it.

"Please don't do that!" I worked on channeling Harlan's acting buddies. "I'll do what you want, just don't do that." I forgot my hands had been bound, so I automatically reached out for the tea and then realized my hands were untied. Alric had done it as he pulled me up and I hadn't even noticed. My momentum unbalanced both of us for a moment, which still gave us the mostly desired result. A huge pot of cold tea poured all over the passed-out faeries.

I thought it hadn't been enough, as not a single faery moved. Then the pile started moving and Garbage Blossom stood on top and gave a huge shake. I grabbed the second teakettle out of Alric's hand and got as much of it onto and into the faeries as I could. At this point even Jackal had probably figured out tea wouldn't kill them. Garbage was good. She got enough in her to start pulling at the other faeries. All of them started lapping tea off themselves like a bunch of kittens.

We were blocking the faeries' cage from the others, but my throwing the contents of the second teakettle on them hadn't been what should have happened, not to mention I was free.

"Grab her. Can't you idiots do anything right?" The syclarion gate guard was clearly the leader of the group and started barking orders. I ran and dove under the table. Peering out from under it, I saw Tag toss a dagger to Orenda—clearly her hands had been freed as well—and arm himself with one. I flashed him a smile. I would never tell him I'd briefly believed he had betrayed us.

Most of our weapons were still inside our wagon, but I wasn't sure how I would get to them. Alric was even further away from them than I was but was somehow still holding on to his Carlon persona as he drunkenly tried to chase me, then stumbled back to the faeries' cage just as Garbage Blossom forced the door open. I rolled out from under the other side of table.

A dozen very messy and extremely pissed-off faeries flew into his face before the stench of the sewerweed he wore pushed them away. They weren't moving like they would have if they had drunk all of that tea, but it had cleared the chocolate stupor off them.

I waved my hands at them to get their attention. "Get away from here!" They were focusing on attacking the people around them but I saw the guards pulling out crossbows. Right now the faeries couldn't win, but they might be able to later. "Go find Bunky!" I still couldn't feel anything magical, but I thought as hard as I could for them to leave, get help, then save us. I had no idea where they'd find help. Not with the closest city clearly under syclarion control.

Garbage whistled for the others, and they all circled the camp once, and then vanished.

One of the syclarions reached over to grab me, and Alric shot him with a crossbow.

Then all hell broke loose.

Covey charged into the clearing and jumped on the back of a syclarion guard. She had the garrote she'd borrowed from Orenda and found a way to make it work through that thick neck. Then she stabbed him through the heart a few times for good measure and jumped off as he tumbled to the ground.

Tag and Orenda both came out swinging and engaged another syclarion. I had to do something, so reached down for a sword lying near the table, and fought back. No idea where the sword came from, but I wouldn't argue with plain luck.

We were massively outnumbered; all of Jackal's men, except for Alric and Tag, were working with the syclarions. We were being cornered, as if they wanted us all alive. For now.

One of the syclarions got a lucky strike on Alric that could have killed him had he not blocked most of it. Okay, they wanted some of us alive.

I was about to surrender. I'd give them the emerald dragon, make them let the others go, then try to find a way to blow up the relic, the syclarions, and myself.

It was hard to hear over all of the fighting, but I thought I heard faery war cries. A fleet of flying snakes was heading our way. However, they were flying oddly. Then I realized it wasn't a bunch of sceanra anam, but regular snakes, huge ones from the look of them, carried by a bunch of hyperactive faeries. Judging from their speed, I'd venture to say they went into town and found some more tea.

People were still fighting but the war cries and the hisses of the snakes were getting louder. I had a bad feeling about this. "Everyone, move away from the enemy. Now."

The screams came once the faeries dumped their snakes onto all of the syclarions and Jackal's men. Apparently, they were venomous. And equally apparent, even the thick skin of the syclarions wasn't enough to stop these vipers.

My friends all moved a step or two away at my yell; if I didn't know better I'd almost say they moved at the exact moment of my yell. Once the snakes were dropped they moved even further.

It took a few minutes for the snakes to kill whom they could. Then they vanished.

I looked around, but there wasn't a single snake in sight. Nor any faeries.

Jackal and all of his men were down and their stiffness told me the snakes had gotten them.

Only three syclarions were left standing. They might not have gotten a full dose of the venom, but all the rest of the attackers had succumbed.

One started to run off, and Alric tore after him. We couldn't afford to have the mayor know what happened and send more guards.

Orenda squared off against another one. She was pale, but she also looked pissed and still caught up in the fury of the fighting.

The last one was closest to me, I raised my newfound sword, but Covey charged forward and pushed me out of the way to face him.

Within a few minutes, both remaining syclarions had collapsed and weren't ever getting up. Orenda started shaking, and Tag led her off to the steps of our wagon to sit.

I looked around at the carnage before us. There were seven syclarion bodies here. One was missing, the one Alric had chased. I waved to Covey, who was running the syclarions through with a sword in case any were faking it, and jogged in the direction that Alric had been running.

I had to go a little bit away from the camp, but I found a body. It wasn't the syclarion. It was Alric, still holding onto his Carlon facade. I ran to him, but he was convulsing and a green froth was bubbling out of his clenched teeth.

He had a nasty looking sword wound on his left side, but I had a bad feeling that wasn't what had actually taken him down. I ripped open his shirt. His entire chest was a mass of green ooze and blood. The wound from Glorinal was being helped by the injury he took fighting the syclarion. Together, they were killing him.

I wiped away the tears. I knew whatever Glorinal did was magical, but I had no way to know how to heal him. Whatever had blocked my magic vanished when the syclarions died. However, I didn't know what spells to use. The only one who would know the spells was the man dying in my arms. Or maybe not.

"Orenda! Covey!" I knew Orenda had collapsed after the fight. But I needed her. I needed anyone and everyone to save Alric.

"Now! I need you now." Sobs swallowed my voice as Alric's chest started rattling. He was going to die and I couldn't stop it.

"I'm here, what do you...." Orenda arrived first. She stopped running when she saw Alric.

I wiped the tears away again, and turned to her. "You need to heal him. Now. Save him, work whatever healer magic you have. But save him."

She looked at me oddly. Even dying as he was, he was holding on to that damn glamour. Carlon's passing shouldn't be affecting me this much. I didn't care. "I will explain later, just heal him."

Covey and Harlan came running up as well, with Tag limping behind. I felt Covey and Harlan each grab one of my shoulders and squeeze.

Orenda looked at all of us, confusion clear on her face, but she dropped down next to Alric's head. She closed her eyes and held her hands over his chest. After a moment she shook her head. "There's nothing for me to hang onto. I simply don't have enough magic to do what needs to be done."

I moved closer to her and held out my hand. "I have no idea if this will work or simply blow all of us up. But I have magic, use mine and your skills. Save him."

Orenda looked to Covey and Harlan, and at their nods, then took my hand. I was dragged through her healing spell and saw what fought to take Alric's life. The injury on his side was serious, but it was the poison from Glorinal doing the most damage. Orenda repeated spell upon spell, targeting the poison.

I felt the poison fighting back. Orenda wasn't going to be able to handle it. I sent all of my hatred for Glorinal into the ball of poison killing Alric. Then I destroyed it.

CHAPTER FORTY-THREE

I felt the poison vanish from his bloodstream, but I doubted I'd be able to say how I knew for sure. However, the force of the spell releasing it also sent both Orenda and I flying backwards. Since the others had been close behind us, that meant we all ended up in a massive pile of arms and legs. I rolled to my feet first. To find Alric stiffly pushing himself up on one arm and looking at all of us.

"What happened?"

I ran forward and started kissing his face. All the pain and confusion I'd had about him vanished the moment I thought I'd been about to lose him. I didn't care who saw, let them think I'd gone crazy for...Carlon? That wasn't whom I was kissing.

"Who is that and why is he in Carlon's clothes?" Tag had gotten to his feet after me. He was watching Alric, for that was who lay there, with a wary look.

Orenda slowly rose to her feet as well, her face was a mix of confusion, fear, and something else. "I broke the glamour. But I didn't know there was one."

"Actually, we broke it." I gave Alric's battered face one more kiss—this one he had the ability to return—then looked back to Orenda. "Orenda and Tag, meet Alric. No, he's not Carlon. There was no Carlon."

"I thought of him as being real," Alric said as he stiffly stood up. He looked much better now, even though his clothes were covered in the remains of the green slime from his wound, and his face still had a few bruises. But even his sword wound was healed. Apparently, Orenda and I were very good at this shared magic bit. "And right now we need him to get us out of here before that damn mayor sends more syclarion guards. The last one I fought couldn't have lived to make it to the gates, but they'll send more when they don't hear back from anyone. And when they don't get this." He reached back where he'd been lying and pulled out the emerald dragon from one of the faeries' tiny bags. I wasn't going to ask how he made the bag work, at least not in front of everyone. As far as I knew only my flying miscreants could use them.

Part of my mind immediately went into panic mode. He'd found my stone, that was mine, he couldn't have it. But when I looked at Alric, I felt the power it had over me vanish. It was as if I was now aware what that stupid green dragon was doing to me for the first time. I swear I saw the eye wink at me.

Orenda's eyes got larger as she looked from Alric to the stone and back. Alric ignored her and closed his eyes. Then opened them with a start. "I can't fix the glamour. Not for anything." He looked at me and said a few words and I found myself a foot in the air, then gently set down. "My magic is fine, I simply can't glamour."

I winced. "That may have been me. Orenda needed my magic to help heal you, and I may have been a little overzealous."

Alric shook his head. He could disguise himself without glamour, but aside from his bad hair, he was looking far too elven lord-ish right now. Even the elven lord markings on his left cheek were showing, faint under the dirt and bruises, but I could see them. "There's nothing we can do about my appearance here. We need to leave, now." He looked down at the sword I'd been fighting with and took a step back.

I looked down wondering what was wrong. It was far more ornate than anything I'd seen Locksead's men or the syclarions have. However, it was just a sword.

"Where did you get that?" The whole lack of glamour thing was making him pale, but he seemed to have gone another shade lighter as he looked at my sword.

"I picked it up during the fight, it was just there on the ground. I have no idea whose it was, but it must have been one of the syclarions." Even Covey, Harlan, and Orenda were looking at me oddly. Tag wasn't, but he looked as confused as I felt. "What? It's a sword, people. Alric's is fancy. Now that he's not hiding it again anyway." I waved to his and noticed they looked similar. Did he have a spare?

Orenda was shaking her head. "That looks like a spirit sword. They both do. But they can't be real."

"Oh yes they can be." Covey peered over at my sword. "Never noticed about his, but yours definitely is."

I backed up from all of them. "Would someone just tell me what a spirit sword is?"

The ground gave a sudden jolt and I fought to keep my feet. The others bounced a bit, but
    only Tag actually fell.

"It is mine." The voice behind us was raw and gravelly and once belonged to Glorinal.

We all spun to find Glorinal and five rakasa behind us. Glorinal was on a long chain held by the largest rakasa, but with enough slack that I knew he could reach all of us if his master let him.

One of the rakasa took advantage of our distraction by the mutated elf and charged forward. I barely saw him out of the corner of my eye, but the sword and my arm went up with speed and sliced the creature in half as it leapt toward me.

Alric swore as he engaged another one, but it met the same fate. The rakasa and these odd swords were not good companions. Although Alric's action had probably been more skill-based than mine had. I knew I moved the sword, but I didn't recall thinking it. It just happened. Covey and Orenda engaged two of the last rakasa, with Tag running an assist for Orenda. She looked pale and terrified but her people would be proud at how well she fought. Still, it took far too long for either Covey or Orenda to take down the creatures. Alric and I had an advantage with these odd swords, but if more came we'd be hard pressed to keep up.

Glorinal grinned and scuttled forward on all fours. "I will take sword. And bring masters glory." He bowed to the lead rakasa. He'd paid for misleading them before and was back in their good graces.

"This time, we know you have dragon. We feel it." The lead rakasa turned toward Alric, pulling Glorinal's leash with him. The former elf whined a bit and tried to keep his eye on my sword but turned toward Alric.

"You cannot fight all." The lead rakasa raised his clawed hand and twenty more of the creatures came out of a small crack in the ground behind Glorinal.

"Everyone get behind Alric and I. We'll hold as long as we can, but you need to be ready to run." Two more rakasa charged and two more were sliced down. Covey didn't argue but she also didn't look like she was planning on running anywhere.

They were toying with us. As if the lead rakasa was sacrificing his own people for some reason instead of sending them all at once. I was focusing on trying to survive, when the sword in my hand vanished.

"Alric!"

He spun and saw my empty hand. "Call it back. Someone is trying to break the connection. You somehow called it to you. Call it back." He spun back to slice three more rakasa.

I didn't know how I called the thing in the first place so I had no clue as to how to do it this time. I just thought hard about the feel of it in my hand. Suddenly it was there.

And another rakasa lost its head.

Glorinal wasn't fighting but was extremely focused on my sword. I had a bad feeling who had made it vanish.

The rest of the rakasa, aside from the large one holding Glorinal's chain, charged forward. Alric went down on one knee as one went under his defenses and clawed his thigh. But he rose immediately and ran through that one and three more. It took me a few seconds longer, but I managed to do the same. Covey and Orenda were still fighting, but we'd kept Tag and Harlan in the middle of us.

"We can't keep this up," I said to Alric as eight more rakasa came out of the ground and charged us. For a race of beings who had supposedly been destroyed, they'd managed to repopulate themselves very well.

A clash of metal boots running in step came from down the road, but they weren't close enough to see who was coming toward us. Most likely the mayor had figured out something was wrong and sent reinforcements. Armored reinforcements. Our only hope was that the syclarions and the rakasa would take each other out fighting for the honor to kill us.

I was focusing on the next wave of rakasa when Orenda let out a gasp. One echoed by Covey and Harlan. I heard a few very colorful swear words come from Alric. I looked up, but instead of armored syclarions, a group of about twenty, elaborately armored men jogged into view. Rather, elves. At least if the markings on their armor and weapons were any indication. They looked like they had stepped out of one of Covey's history books.

"In the name of the king of the elven empire of the west, stand down." His voice was cultured and elegant but the massive two-handed sword at his side said his fighting wouldn't be.

I wasn't sure if he was talking to us or the rakasa, but the rakasa knew. With a roar they spun around and charged the elven fighters. Glorinal whined, but the rakasa holding his leash was the only one who held back.

The lead knight unsheathed his sword. The men behind him pulled out theirs as well and the area became a massive battlefield. More rakasa came out of the crevice to replace their fallen brethren.

Alric and I stepped back, trying to stay between the battle and our friends. It said a lot that aside from the initial gasp at the sight of the elves, none of them said anything. Alric's face had turned to stone, but he was mostly watching Glorinal. I would have thought he'd be happy at being rescued by his own people but his reaction looked like he would have been happier with the syclarions.

Within minutes, only a dozen rakasa remained, and no new ones had appeared out of the ground. Glorinal pulled on his chain, but whether he wanted to leave or be allowed to attack the elves was unclear.

"You win now." The lead rakasa didn't seem too upset about the huge piles of his people lying on the ground. "We will get our dragon back and we will take you." He spun back to Alric and I. "All."

Within the blink of an eye, Glorinal and the rakasa vanished into the crevice and the ground slammed shut after them.

Adrenaline fled my body and I debated if collapsing in front of a bunch of elven knights was proper etiquette or not. The thought would soon be moot, as my legs were seriously thinking of buckling.

Orenda had no such problems. "Thank you, kind sirs." She said as she walked around Alric and me to the elves. "Our warriors were hard pressed." She did an elaborate curtsy, but the lead elf barely looked at her. In fact he stepped around her and stopped in front of Alric.

The captain took off his helmet. I think everyone still conscious drew in a breath at his beauty. Pale hair, far lighter than even Alric's natural color tumbled out from under the helmet to fall halfway down his back. Unlike Alric, his high lord facial markings were proudly displayed on his left cheek. A high lord in the military.

"Alricianel Lis Treann Flairn Delpina, you are under arrest for grand thievery from a royal outpost. Hand over the artifact and we will not bring in your companions." The lead elf knight looked barely winded after his fight.

Alric didn't flinch but reached in his jacket and pulled out the emerald dragon. Orenda started to object, but stopped before she got any words out once one of the elven knights turned to her.

She might be an elf, and a full-blooded high ranking one at that. But these knights didn't care.

The lead knight waved to one closest to us to take the dragon.

"I was referring to the artifact you stole. The glass gargoyle of binding."

I think all of us choked on that one.

"I brought that to the elders, I haven't been back since. Why the hell would I steal it?" Alric looked more winded than I'd ever seen him after a fight, but he also looked confused at the knight's comments.

"Wait, they lost the glass gargoyle?" That was Harlan. He'd been staying out of things as much as possible, but that affront was too much for him.

"We didn't lose anything. This person," the elf captain pointed to Alric, "used a bag of human gold to bribe one of the few outside merchants we allow to breach our enclave. Alricianel rode with the merchant into the enclave. He then broke into a guarded facility and stole the glass gargoyle. Many witnesses saw him engage in this activity." His voice changed and I could almost see him reading from an official decree. "Under orders of the king and queen, I have been charged to bring you back to answer for your crimes. The addition of this other artifact in your possession might raise the crime of treason. You had the obsidian chimera as well, yet have failed to bring it to our people. You have much to answer for."

Alric had traded the obsidian chimera for the lives of one-third of the people in Beccia. He'd almost lost his life trying to get it back before the mine collapsed.

I knew this elf before me wouldn't care one bit if I told him any of it.

The set look on Alric's face told me he knew that as well. He stepped forward, handing his sword to the nearest guard, and held his hands out for the chain the captain carried. "I will have my day in court. This will be resolved." He looked toward me and nodded. "This is the only way to clear my name."

The elven guard glanced at my sword and me. "What treachery is this? How does she bear a spirit sword?" The disgust in his voice was akin to finding something slimy and gooey on the bottom of one's shoe.

Alric opened his mouth to answer, but I had had enough. "I *called* it. Isn't that how it works?" I showed off some of the fancy moves I'd modified from Orenda's knife teaching. "Per your people, it belongs to the one who calls it." I was making this up, but now that I knew what these swords were, some of Covey's past comments about them came back to me. The concept of them had been an obsession of hers a few years ago. I had no idea how this one came to be lying on the ground near me, but I wasn't telling this bastard that.

He stared at me for a few moments. I spun the sword slower, then, while keeping my eyes on him, sent it back to its calling place. I still wasn't sure how or why it worked, but I was glad it did.

"Take her." He put his helmet back on and waved to the others. "And take one more person for each time she fights back. Or if she calls the sword."

"You can't take her against her will, she's not of our people. She's done nothing wrong." Alric wasn't doing well. Without anyone to lean on he was listing a bit to the left where the rakasa had clawed him. Orenda and I might have saved his life, but his body still hadn't recovered.

"You have your own answering to do." The captain, or whatever he was of the elves, held up the emerald dragon. "You were willing to betray your own kind for her. And how do we know you didn't teach her how to call the sword? You are a spirit sword caller yourself; perhaps you wanted your lover to have one."

"I gave you the dragon, if you know what the glass gargoyle is, you know what that emerald pertains to. Let her go." Alric's teeth clenched shut. I thought it was annoyance, and then I realized the elf before me was a magic user and was doing something to Alric.

"Fight and we will drag your body back home." The captain gave a small smile, then turned and waved his hand toward me. Pressure slammed in behind my eyes. Even without checking, I knew all access to my magic was blocked.

"As for you, I will make a deal." He waved his other hand to the guards behind him. There was a brief rustle and two guards came forward with a cage. Bunky and the faeries were cramped up inside. Whatever the magic dampening he was doing to Alric and me, it was affecting them as well. All were barely moving. "These would have been valuable specimens for our alchemists, however, a non-elven sword caller might prove even more valuable. I will let these go, not speak of them to my people, and not take or harm them or your friends, if you come along with us peacefully. And swear to not try to escape."

I looked at Bunky and the faeries. They were too drained to even raise their heads. I turned to my friends. None of them, even Covey, was in any shape to fight. They had to get out of the area and back to Beccia before the people behind those syclarion guards realized what happened.

And I couldn't let any of them be taken by the elves, not if I had a chance to keep it from happening. I glanced to the captain of the elven knights. I might not know how I called that spirit sword to me, but he did and he wasn't happy about it. There was no way they would have let me go at this point even if I refused to go peacefully. And I couldn't leave Alric to his fate. Saving him made me realize I did love him, and where he went, I went.

I slowly nodded to the elven captain, as fear and curiosity battled in my gut. I'd grown up wanting to know what happened to the elves. Now I would see for myself. I hoped I survived the experience.

The End

Dear Reader,

Thank you for joining Taryn, Alric, and the faeries in the third book of the six book series—The Lost Ancients. We all really appreciate when folks come to play in "our" world, and hope you enjoyed it too.

This series will continue with THE SAPPHIRE MANTICORE, then on to two more books in 2017.

If you're also interested in a little bit of space opera, please check out the first book in The Asarlaí Wars trilogy- WARRIOR WENCH.

I really appreciate each and every one of you so please keep in touch. You can find me at www.marieandreas.com.

And please feel free to email me directly at **Marie@marieandreas.com** as well, I love to hear from readers!

If you enjoyed this book (or any book for that matter ;)) please spread the word! Positive reviews on Amazon, Goodreads, and blogs are like emotional gold to any writer and mean more than you know.

Thank you again, and we all hope to see you back here in THE SAPPHIRE MANTICORE!

ABOUT THE AUTHOR

Marie is a fantasy and science fiction reader with a serious writing addiction. If she wasn't writing about all of the people in her head, she'd be lurking about coffee shops annoying innocent passer-by with her stories. So really, writing is a way of saving the masses. She lives in Southern California and is currently owned by two very faery-minded cats. And yes, sometimes they race.

When not saving the general populace from coffee shop shenanigans, Marie likes to visit the UK and keeps hoping someone will give her a nice summer home in the Forest of Dean.